A PECULIAR COMBINATION

ALSO BY ASHLEY WEAVER

THE AMORY AMES MYSTERIES

Murder at the Brightwell

Death Wears a Mask

A Most Novel Revenge

Intrigue in Capri (ebook short)

The Essence of Malice

An Act of Villainy

A Dangerous Engagement

A Deception at Thornecrest

A PECULIAR COMBINATION

An Electra McDonnell Novel

ASHLEY WEAVER

MINOTAUR
BOOKS
NEW YORK

First published in the United States by Minotaur Books, an imprint of St. Martin's Publishing Group

A PECULIAR COMBINATION. Copyright © 2021 by Ashley Weaver. All rights reserved. Printed in the United States of America. For information, address St. Martin's Publishing Group, 120 Broadway, New York, NY 10271.

Designed by Omar Chapa

www.minotaurbooks.com

Library of Congress Cataloging-in-Publication Data

Names: Weaver, Ashley, author.
Title: A peculiar combination : an Electra McDonnell novel / Ashley Weaver.
Identifiers: LCCN 2020053225 | ISBN 9781250780485 (hardcover) | ISBN 9781250780492 (ebook)
Subjects: GSAFD: War stories.
Classification: LCC PS3623.E3828 P43 2021 | DDC 813/.6—dc23
LC record available at https://lccn.loc.gov/2020053225

Our books may be purchased in bulk for promotional, educational, or business use. Please contact your local bookseller or the Macmillan Corporate and Premium Sales Department at 1-800-221-7945, extension 5442, or by email at MacmillanSpecialMarkets@macmillan.com.

First Edition: 2021

10 9 8 7 6 5 4 3 2 1

For Nancy Vik and Kris Newman,
teachers, mentors, and lifelong friends.

A PECULIAR COMBINATION

CHAPTER ONE

We were going to get caught.

The alarming idea buzzed around inside my head like the menacing drone of an approaching Luftwaffe bomber, even as I tried to banish it. I had never had this sensation in the middle of a job before, and it was disquieting to say the least. It was unlucky to think such things, especially at moments like these. To lose concentration was the first step in making mistakes. And we couldn't afford to make mistakes.

I drew in a deep, steadying breath of the cool night air, freshened by a light rain earlier in the day, and glanced again down the darkened street. There was no one in sight. The whole neighborhood was quiet.

That's the way most streets were now, with the blackouts. Our brave boys of the RAF had valiantly defended the homeland in dogfights high above the Channel for the past month, but Cardiff and Plymouth had already been hit, and there was little doubt in the minds of most Londoners that it was only a matter of time before the bombs started dropping here. And so we covered our windows, blotting out any light that might make us a target from the night sky, and waited.

The cloak of darkness made things a lot easier for people like Uncle Mick and me, those whose pursuits were of the less noble variety. Of course, it also made it more difficult to know which houses were empty and which were full of people trying to go on about their normal lives behind shades that protected them, at least in theory, from the terrors of enemy aircraft.

But there was no question about our target. The house was deserted; I was quite sure of that. Even though our source had told us the occupants were away, we had been watching it for several days now to make certain. There hadn't been any sign of activity, not even of a housekeeper or charwoman.

A sudden whisper of movement behind me made me tense, the premonition of a moment before flashing through my mind. Standing absolutely still, I turned my head slowly toward the sound, my eyes searching the shadows for its source. For a moment there was nothing, just an eerie quiet. Then a cat emerged from a nearby bush and pranced past me without a glance as I let out a breath. I was needlessly on edge; it was time to pull myself together. Refocusing my thoughts, I turned my attention back to the house.

It sat dark and silent, just as it had for the past several nights. I had raised the concern that the occupants might have left the country. A lot of people—at least among those who could afford it—were leaving before the Nazis arrived, and if the residents of this house had gone to greener pastures, they would surely have taken their valuables with them.

Uncle Mick, however, had assured me that this wasn't the case. "My information's sound, Ellie girl. There's goods in the safe."

Uncle Mick's informants were seldom wrong, and so we had gone ahead with our plans. So far, everything was proceeding just as we had hoped. But still I felt that sense of unease, like the drip of cold rain down the back of my neck.

I stared out into the darkness and wondered if it was too late to call it off. Uncle Mick should be around the corner. Perhaps, if I were to go to him before we got started, I could convince him that we should try again tomorrow night.

But no. That was silly. We'd been planning for a week, and I knew time was of the essence. It was possible that the residents of this house would be gone for another night or even a fortnight, but it was just as likely they might return tomorrow and all our work would have been in vain.

Besides, we needed money, the sooner the better. Uncle Mick's business had been slow since the war started. We were as patriotic as the next family, and, knowing it wasn't exactly cricket to rob houses in wartime, we'd held off as long as possible. But now our coffers, such as they were, were low. It was time to put scruples aside. Desperate times and all that.

So we'd ventured out onto streets patrolled by watchful bobbies and sharp-eyed air-raid wardens. Uncle Mick had allowed me in on this riskier job, one he would normally have done with my cousins, Colm and Toby. That's the way it was now, with the men away fighting. Women stepping up to do the jobs we'd been telling them we were capable of all along.

Not that Uncle Mick doubted my capabilities. He had never done that. It was just that his urge to protect me was strong. With the boys gone, however, the time for that was past.

I took another look at the house. It was a sturdy Georgian brick residence with tidy hedges and an iron fence surrounding the property, gates at the front and back. It was just the kind of place I'd hoped to live in one day when I was young and romantic minded. Now it didn't appeal to me. I thought it seemed too formal, too stuffy somehow, with its rooms full of antiques and bric-a-brac.

It wasn't a mansion. We didn't go in for the biggest houses, the kind with live-in household staff. Instead, we slipped in and out with no one the wiser until they opened their safe again and discovered things were missing.

We were very good at what we did, and we had always been successful. That was what made the uneasy feeling I had tonight all the more distracting.

I glanced at my watch, the luminous dial showing me that it was nearly midnight. Uncle Mick would be in place. There was no more time for hesitation.

With one last glance up and down the street, I walked casually along the pavement until I reached the edge of the gate. The iron door was slightly ajar, which meant Uncle Mick was ahead of me. I slipped through it and followed the pathway that ran along the side of the house, shielded by the hedges, to the side entrance.

Ahead of me, barely discernible in the darkness, I saw a shadow at the doorway and heard the faint sounds of a lock beneath metal instruments. Uncle Mick, when in a law-abiding frame of mind, was a locksmith, and he'd never met a lock that didn't bend to his will.

"Ah, there you are, my girl," he said as I approached. "Right on time."

There was a click as the lock yielded to the hand of a master, and the door opened inward.

Uncle Mick stood silently in the doorway for a moment, listening for any sounds within the house. Then he beckoned me forward and we went inside.

"You didn't see anyone?" he asked, as he switched on his torch. That was another benefit of the blackout shades. Normally, we would have to stand inside a house waiting for our eyes to adjust to a darker shade of dark.

"No," I replied. "Though something feels . . . a bit off."

"It's the unnatural dark," he said. "The whole city feels like a tomb."

"Yes," I agreed, though I didn't think that was what was bothering me.

He grinned. "All the better for us, though, eh, Ellie?"

"I suppose so."

I switched on my own torch and followed him as he led the way from the entry through the tidy kitchen and into the dining room. There we paused for a moment, and I shined my torch across the heavy ornamental furniture, the velvet curtains, the paintings that hung on the walls, and the quality rug upon the gleaming wooden floor.

My torchlight lingered on the rug, and then I stopped. There was a footprint against the pattern, a man's shoe by the size of it. Who had tracked mud into the house? It seemed odd that it hadn't been cleaned. Then again, a lot of things weren't the same during the war as they had been before.

I put the thought away. I had more important matters to consider at the moment. My concentration was something I prided myself on. I had always been able to focus on a thing and give it my sole attention. What was it about tonight that had set me so on edge? Perhaps I was just missing Colm and Toby. Nothing had seemed the same since they went off to war.

My light flickered across a sideboard that sat loaded with crystal and china. The resident had taken no precautions against bombing, and I had the sudden image of shards of glass exploding across the room like a rain shower.

Our own china, aside from a few everyday pieces, had been packed away with most of the other fragile items we owned in the coal cellar for safekeeping.

Glancing again at the sideboard, I noticed a pair of candlesticks I was certain were silver, but that was not what we had come for.

Never get distracted by less than your target, Uncle Mick had always told me. So I didn't give the silver a second thought as I followed him silently through the room and into the foyer, where we began to make our way up the staircase.

Uncle Mick had talked to a woman who had once worked in the

house and had gotten a fairly good idea of what the layout was. He was good at that sort of thing, finding sources and gathering information in an offhanded way that didn't arouse suspicion.

At the top of the stairs, we moved unerringly toward a room at the end of the hall.

The light from our torches played over the walls as we went, casting strange shadows against several paintings, none of them noteworthy, hung upon the dark green silk paper.

We reached the end of the hall, and Uncle Mick opened the door to our right and entered the office. This room was decorated in the same style as the rest of the house, good-but-not-exceptional-quality furniture, mediocre art. There was a large desk and one wall was lined with bookshelves.

Uncle Mick scanned the wall behind the desk with his torch. There was a large painting hung there in an expensive gilt frame. It was just the sort of piece that might hide a safe. Cheap wall safes were somewhat typical in people of this class, people with property valuable enough to be locked away but not so grand as to be stored in a bank box.

We had it on good authority that there was jewelry in that safe. We were rather counting on it, in fact. I tried not to get my hopes up, reminding myself that, if we didn't come across what we were after, there was always the dining room silver.

Uncle Mick turned to look at me. "Come see what you think."

Holding my torch up with one hand, I reached out and touched the frame, testing it for any hint of movement. At first I felt nothing, but as I ran my fingers around the edge, I felt a little projection, almost like a knob of some sort. I pressed it, heard a slight click, and the painting swung back from the wall on hinges.

"That's my girl," Uncle Mick said.

I flashed my torchlight over the face of the safe that was set into the wall behind the painting.

I frowned. This wasn't an inexpensive wall safe. It was a Milner, rather more heavy-duty and more of a challenge than the cheaper model I had been expecting.

Uncle Mick was apparently thinking the same thing, for he gave a low whistle. "Looks like they take their valuables seriously."

This was said in a cheery tone. This more difficult lock might take him a bit longer, but Uncle Mick had always relished a challenge.

I stepped to the side, giving him room and holding up the light so he could see, and he moved closer.

Watching Uncle Mick open a safe was like watching an artist paint a picture or a violinist play a complicated piece of music. There is an art to it, and Uncle Mick had flair. What isn't as obvious, however, is that it is also like watching a mathematician solve a complicated equation. I used paper when I worked out combinations, but Uncle Mick did it all in his head. I suppose, if he'd come from a different background with better opportunities, he might have been a great success at any number of lofty professions.

The room was dead silent as he worked. I studied his face in the light of the torch. He was a thin, wiry man, with a shock of black hair gone gray and sharp gray-green eyes. Those eyes were focused, his head tilted toward the dial as he moved it, listening. The minutes passed, all quiet in the room except for the tick of a clock somewhere behind us.

"Ha," he said at last, and the safe handle gave beneath his grasp. I let out a breath I didn't know I had been holding.

He pulled the safe open and reached inside. A smile spread across his face as he turned, took my hand, and placed a flat velvet box into it. A necklace.

He reached inside again and pulled out four more jewelry boxes: two for rings, and two I assumed might be bracelets and earrings. I couldn't resist opening one of the boxes and was met with the brilliant flash of diamonds and rubies.

"Not bad for a night's work," Uncle Mick said with a smile.

"No," I said, smiling myself for the first time that evening. "Not bad at all."

Uncle Mick put each of the items into the bag that was slung across his torso. It was an excellent prize, and it had been exceptionally easy, all told.

Too easy, my mind said, and I tried to push the thought aside, longing to be back out in the safety of the streets, where we could blend into the shadows. The worst we might have to deal with was encountering an air-raid warden, out patrolling for errant lights. We could slip through the mews and out onto another street and disappear into the night.

Uncle Mick closed the safe, and we left the room and went out the way we had come.

Stepping out into the night, I immediately noticed that something felt strange. The air felt different, as though there was some kind of change in the atmosphere. It was like a sixth sense warning of impending danger. I suppose some people would call it superstition. My Irish ancestors might have called it the Sight. Whatever the case, I've learned to trust my instincts, and, in that moment, they were banging the alarms.

I was about to turn to whisper to Uncle Mick when I heard the footsteps. I thought someone might be passing along the front of the house, and I stilled, waiting for them to move out of earshot. But an instant later, I realized, whoever it was, they were coming toward us. And they were coming from both directions.

I turned to Uncle Mick, eyes wide, as I assessed our options.

Ahead of us, parallel to the house, was the hedge and, behind that, the high iron fence. Much too high to climb. And we had relocked the door of the house before closing it behind us, so that route was closed to us, too.

It was Uncle Mick who found his voice first.

"Run, Ellie!" he hissed, giving me a little push forward, but it was too late.

A man materialized out of the darkness beside me. "Not so fast, love," he said, grabbing my arm just as my wits returned and I made to run off.

I struggled, but I knew right away he was much too big for me to fight, so, after a moment of resistance, I stilled. Besides, if Uncle Mick was caught, I wouldn't leave him, even if I could escape this brute's clutches somehow.

The man had pulled my hands behind my back, and I felt the cold metal against my wrists as he latched the handcuffs.

"This way," he said, grasping my arm and roughly pushing me toward the front of the house.

I managed to glance over my shoulder and saw that whoever had come from the other direction had taken Uncle Mick toward the back of the house, away from me.

There were several of them, I realized, now that my eyes had grown accustomed to the darkness. Four or five men in dark clothes. Somehow, they must have been expecting us.

And so we were caught.

CHAPTER TWO

There are a lot of things that go through a girl's mind when she's arrested. First there's the surprise, then fear, then worry, then the tedium of waiting for something—anything—to happen.

I had passed through the first two stages fairly quickly and was on to worry as I rode in the back of the car, its headlights hooded, through the darkened streets.

The city was dark, but, in the moonlight, I could make out landmarks as we went. We crossed the Thames toward Central London, and I saw the spires of the Palace of Westminster and the silhouette of Big Ben, his darkened face quietly but watchfully guarding his domain.

A bit farther and we passed St James's Park, and I thought, unaccountably, of a happy day I'd spent there in my youth, ambling along the shady paths and feeding dry scraps of bread to the birds at Duck Island. Would I ever have the chance to do such carefree things again?

I lost track after that as we made several turns along smaller, less familiar streets. My best guess was that we were in Belgravia, but I could think of no good reason why we should be.

Uncle Mick would have known where we were headed. I was convinced he held a map of the entire city in his head. Surprisingly, however, they had taken him in a different car—a waste of pet-rol rations, I would have thought, but who was I to question police methods?

In any case, I had more important things to worry about. How was I going to get out of this mess? That was first and foremost among my worries. We had been caught fair and square, so I doubted there was much I could do to talk my way out of it. There was always a chance, of course. Uncle Mick had a silver tongue, and he'd talked his way out of more than one sticky situation.

Perhaps we could claim it had been some kind of misunderstand-ing, that we were friends or relations of the owners of the house. But that would only work until they contacted the owners. No, that was no good.

I realized suddenly that I had never given much thought to what would happen if we were arrested. Call it overconfidence, but we had been doing this a long time, and we were very sure of ourselves. Maybe that's where the trouble lay. A haughty spirit before a fall.

At least it had just been Uncle Mick and me who were caught. I was glad the boys weren't here. For one thing, I was fairly certain they wouldn't have come easily, and they might have been hurt in the struggle.

They were tough boys, my cousins, both of them bold and reck-less, though they were also kindhearted and terribly clever. Colm was a mechanic for the RAF. He'd always been good with machines, and airplanes were no exception. I was glad he had found a place where he belonged and where his skills could be put to good use. He had been eager to do his bit for the cause, both my cousins had.

I hadn't wanted to see them go, but Uncle Mick, despite his native Ireland's neutrality in the war, felt the same way the boys did, that this country could only be defended if our young men were willing to step forward and do their part.

We hadn't heard from Toby since Dunkirk. He was officially listed as missing, meaning he had likely been captured or killed. Ever since we had heard, we had gone about with the assumption that he was in a German prison somewhere, that sooner or later we would get a letter from him.

Uncle Mick never let on that he was worried. He said that, when the war was over, Toby would be back with his tales of adventure. He never addressed the possibility that Toby might be dead, never seemed even to consider it, and I thought surely he must be right. The four of us had always been so close—thick as thieves, Uncle Mick liked to say with a chuckle; we'd have felt something different if he was gone.

I hoped he was all right, but the truth of it was that I sometimes thought he would be better off dead than in a German prison. He had the McDonnell fighting spirit and a strong will, but I had heard enough horror stories about the Nazis to know that breaking strong wills was one of their specialties.

No good comes of worry, Nacy Dean, our housekeeper and my surrogate mother of sorts, always said, and so I tried not to fret. I prayed for Toby daily and spoke about him lightly, as though he had just stepped out of the room and would be back before we knew it.

But now was not the time to think about Toby. As hard as it was, I pushed the thoughts of him away. He would want me to focus on making the best of the situation at hand.

I tried again to determine where they were taking us. It was hard to see much with the streets so dark, but I was fairly certain this was Belgravia now, as the rows of white stucco houses rather gave it away.

We pulled up in front of one of the buildings. The outside was sandbagged against bombing, as a lot of places were now, and the windows were, naturally, blacked out, but for all that it still looked rather grand and imposing in the moonlight with its pillared entrance and wrought iron terrace. Definitely not a police station. What was happening here?

The big bloke who had seized me at the scene took my arm again as he alighted from the car and led me up the front steps and into the building. Entering through the front door, we found ourselves in a marble-floored foyer. A winding staircase ahead of us spiraled upward, the steps covered in a green patterned carpet. Behind it a hallway, papered in emerald-green stripes, extended back into the shadowed depths of the house.

What were we doing here, in this lovely house?

There was a slight noise to my right, and I turned to see that it came from a sitting room, or what had been at one point. Now it looked to be an office, where a sleepy-looking young man was standing behind a desk. Apparently, he had jumped up when we'd come in, though he didn't do much but watch us with barely concealed alarm as I was led past the stairway and down the hall.

There was noise behind us as they brought Uncle Mick in, and I turned to look over my shoulder at him. Our eyes met and he winked at me before he was led out of sight, and I felt a little lump in my throat.

I wasn't going to cry, though. We'd been through rough times before, and we'd make it out of this one somehow.

The man, who still held my arm, stopped before a door and opened it, half pushing me inside. I didn't apologize when I stumbled and stepped hard on his foot.

It wasn't a cell, not even in the loosest sense of the word. Though the room was small with boarded-up windows, the flooring was an elaborate parquet and there were white moldings on the pale blue paneled walls and a white stucco fireplace. The lighting was very dim, and the only furniture was a table with two chairs on opposite sides.

Without a word, he unlocked the handcuffs and took them off. Then he turned and left, closing the door behind him with what I supposed was meant to be an ominous thud. He made much ado about locking it from the other side, as though to impress upon me the impossibility of escape. I glanced at the lock; Uncle

Mick or I could have it open in five minutes with the right tools. I thought I could even make a decent go of it with the pins in my hair, but I wasn't about to leave Uncle Mick here alone, even if I could manage to get out.

I knew they would likely leave me to wait awhile, give my nerves a chance to build until I would confess or do whatever it was that they expected me to do. In the interim, I might as well make myself comfortable.

I moved to the chair facing the door and sat down.

They'd left me with my coat, but I still wished I was wearing warmer clothes. My black dress, the one I usually wore for our jobs, was thin cotton and the building was cold. I hugged myself for warmth.

It felt as though I waited an age. When the door finally opened, a grim-faced gentleman in a dark suit came in. Though this certainly wasn't a police station, this fellow had the look of the detective inspector if ever I saw one.

He sat down opposite me without comment. He had a long, straight nose and looked down it at me with his dark, disapproving eyes.

"Which of you opened the safe?" he asked, dispensing with the pleasantries.

"I don't know what you mean," I said in my most innocent of voices.

"How did you get in the house?"

"I wasn't in the house." They couldn't prove that I had been, after all. We were wearing gloves, we hadn't left any traces of our visit, aside from the empty safe, and we'd been outside when they apprehended us. And, most important, they hadn't found the stuff on us. At least, I didn't think they had. If I knew Uncle Mick, he had dropped the bag before he was pinched, thrown it in the hedges or something. They would find it, of course, but we hadn't technically been in possession of it.

"I'm afraid you left evidence behind."

There wasn't evidence, and so I said nothing.

"You went into the house, opened the safe, and stole a great deal of jewelry."

"If you think you know what happened, why are you asking me all these questions?" I realized my tone had lost its pleasantness, but I was getting very tired. I had been here a long time, and I was thirsty and cold. I wanted nothing so much in the world as my old tattered wool jumper and a cup of tea from my blue teacup.

The idea that I might not get either for a very long time, perhaps for years, made my stomach clench. But no. I wasn't going to think about that now. I hadn't been raised to concentrate on what might be.

I determined I would just live in this moment and make the best of it, which definitely meant I wouldn't be confessing. Perhaps if I continued to insist it had been some kind of mistake, they would have to let me go.

"What tools did you use?"

"I don't know what you're talking about."

"How long did the safe take to open?"

"We didn't open a safe."

I was doing my best to annoy him, but I had the impression that he didn't much care about me one way or the other. It was strange. He was giving me a fairly thorough questioning, but I could sense that my answers meant little to him and were somewhat perfunctory. Perhaps he thought he had a sound enough case that it didn't matter.

Nevertheless, I kept avoiding the inspector's questions. Everything he asked, I would answer noncommittally or respond with a question. After half an hour or so of this, he seemed to lose interest in the conversation, rising without another word to me and leaving the room, the lock sliding home.

I wondered what was happening to Uncle Mick. If they were expecting either of us to grass on the other, they were going to be disappointed.

It occurred to me again how very unusual all of this was. We had been caught robbing a house, not attempting to smuggle the Crown Jewels from the Tower of London. Was there something in that safe we hadn't known about?

I glanced at my watch, realizing it was a bit odd they hadn't relieved me of my personal effects upon arrival. Wasn't that usual, to empty pockets and take away mufflers prisoners might use to do themselves in? It was now after three o'clock. Didn't these people want to sleep? Surely they could put me somewhere for the night and finish this tomorrow. It wasn't as though we had killed someone. A few diamonds and rubies weren't worth all this.

I wondered how many years of my life those jewels were worth. To be honest, I had a dread of prison. The place hung like a shadow in the background of our lives, but I had refused to consider it a part of my future.

A lot of people thought the courts went easy on women, but I knew very well that examples were just as often made of them. That their sentences were meant to send a message to other young ladies who might be tempted to be led astray.

These thoughts and more crossed my mind as I sat in the cold room. Once or twice I began to nod off but caught myself. I wanted to stay alert, keep my wits about me.

At last, I heard the sound of the lock again. Then the door opened, and someone entered. I was feeling peevish by this point and didn't look up to see who it was. When he sat down across from me, I was surprised to see he was in military uniform, army by the looks of it. He was much younger than the inspector had been. Not many years past thirty, I'd guess. With the war on, I hadn't expected a young man, let alone a specimen such as this.

He was broad shouldered and well built, the picture of strapping good health, and I wondered why he was here rather than off fighting. Surely the Nazis' impending invasion was more of a concern than a few paltry jewel thieves.

As the inspector fellow had done, he didn't introduce himself and watched me for a long moment without saying a word.

It was all part of the intimidation routine, and I didn't expect to be impressed. But there was something impressive about this gent nonetheless. For one thing, he was terribly good looking. I've never been a silly girl to have my head turned by a pretty face, but he was the sort any girl would give a second look to.

In addition to his soldierly bearing, his features were made up of perfect masculine symmetry: strong jaw, straight nose, excellent cheekbones. He was blond with pale blue eyes, and I couldn't help but think he looked a bit like a Jerry himself.

All this time I was looking at him, he had been studying me as well. I doubted I cut as impressive a figure as he did. I knew well enough that I was pretty, and, though I'd never been one to flaunt my looks, I'd turned a few heads of my own in my time.

I was black-haired and green-eyed, just like Uncle Mick and his sons. In fact, Colm and Toby could easily have been mistaken for my brothers. I was slightly above average height and had curves in all the right places. But I felt right away that none of this was going to help me with this man.

He set a file down on the table between us and flipped it open.

"Electra Niall McDonnell," he said.

It was difficult to hide my surprise. No one called me Electra. Very few people at all even knew it was my given name. I hadn't even put it on my identification card or ration books.

"Born 15 June 1916 at Holloway prison."

I felt myself grow cold, like a bucket of ice water had been dumped over my head. That particular detail was something only Uncle Mick and our housekeeper, Nacy, knew. How had this man come by it?

I tensed, waiting for the next bit of information, the piece of my life that was always there, hovering over me like a ghost I couldn't escape, but he didn't say it.

Instead, he looked up from the papers before him. "You've a remarkably clean criminal record for a woman involved in this sort of work. The safecracking was professionally done; this clearly isn't your first endeavor."

I said nothing. I certainly wasn't going to admit to anything, but he was right about my record. We had never been caught before this. I thought it a pity that we'd had to start now.

"How long had you been casing that house?"

I didn't reply.

"Did you know what type of safe was in the house before you went there?"

It occurred to me that both he and the man who had been here before him were extraordinarily interested in the safe. How did they know about it, after all? I supposed it might be surmised if they had discovered the bag of valuables, but those could just as easily have been left carelessly in a jewelry box or bureau drawer. He had no way of knowing that I'd been in that safe, and I had again the impression that something was not what it seemed.

"You don't expect me to answer these questions, do you?" I asked him. "After all, though your officers neglected to caution me, I know very well that what I say may be taken down and used in evidence."

He looked up, fixing me in his cool gaze.

"We're not the police," he said at last. "I'm afraid this is more serious than that."

CHAPTER THREE

I frowned a bit at this. I might have thought he was bluffing, but I'd known from the start this wasn't a proper police station. If this man was from the army, perhaps the people we had tried to rob were of more importance than we had realized. Uncle Mick was always careful about choosing targets, never anyone who was too important, who might pose too much of a risk, but it did appear that we'd miscalculated somewhere.

Why had this military gent come to have a chat with me in the middle of the night?

Thinking of the time reminded me again how tired and cold I was. "Might I have a cigarette?" I asked.

He said nothing for a moment and then rose and went to the door, pulling it open. He motioned to someone and a moment later returned with a cigarette.

As he handed it to me, I noticed the lighter shading of his wrist beneath his cuff compared with the bronzed skin of his hand. It hadn't been noticeable at first in the bad lighting, but his face was tanned, too. He hadn't gotten that coloring in England. He'd been stationed someplace much warmer and had, for some reason, been pulled in to question a pair of housebreakers from Hendon.

I took the cigarette without thanks. I wasn't really much of a smoker. I had meant to get myself a bit of time to think and, if I was truthful, a bit of time to recover from my surprise at the easy way he had thrown out those private details about me. The casual manner in which he had mentioned my birthplace had rattled me more than I liked to admit.

I put the cigarette between my lips, and he struck a match and leaned to light it for me. I inhaled, the smoke working its way into my lungs. At least it would warm me up a bit.

"The work on that safe was excellent," he said, as though we had had no pause in our conversation. "No marks or any sign you'd even been there."

I couldn't help the feeling of satisfaction that came over me at the acknowledgment of Uncle Mick's skill. I knew how talented he was, but so few other people knew it. That safe was opened with a precision that not many people possess, but one can't exactly go around bragging about such things.

"Was it you or your uncle who opened it?"

How did he know how Uncle Mick and I were related? I doubted my uncle had told him, but he had clearly learned it somewhere.

"I suppose I'd better see a solicitor before I answer any questions," I said, blowing out smoke. I ought to have asked for one before, but Uncle Mick had always said it was best not to get drawn into their games at all if possible. Wait it out first.

Something told me, however, that this man was not likely to be as easily diverted as the irritating inspector had been.

"I've told you: we're not the police. We're not obligated to offer you the same courtesies."

I felt the faintest hint of alarm, but it was quickly pushed away by irritation. He was trying to frighten me. As a young woman raised with two older male cousins, my instinctive reaction to attempted intimidation was stubbornness.

I crossed my arms, the ash from the cigarette dropping to the lovely parquet floor. "Well, I'm not going to say anything else."

"That is, of course, your prerogative. You are, after all, young with a lot of life left before you. Your uncle, however, may not fare as well in prison. Prison can have . . . unfortunate effects on health."

I felt myself go pale and clenched my teeth against this ruthless play on my emotions. I refused to let him see how his words had affected me.

"What is it you want?" I demanded.

He looked up at me, and those cool eyes of his settled on mine for several long seconds. At last, he spoke. "I have a proposition for you."

My brow rose, though I went a bit cold on the inside. I hadn't pegged this man as a lecherous blighter. Surely, with looks like that, he could have his choice of ladies. Of course, there was always the possibility he might be one of those degenerates who preferred his women unwilling.

He must have guessed what I was thinking, for something like disdain flickered momentarily across his face. I wasn't sure if it was my assumption that he was having lascivious thoughts in general or that he might be having them about *me* in particular that disgusted him, but I rather suspected the latter. Though probably insulting, this set my mind at ease about his intentions.

"What sort of proposition?" I asked.

"An exchange of favors," he said. "If you choose to help me, this matter will be forgotten, and you and your uncle will go free."

As much as I hated to admit it, he had my interest now. I waited for him to continue.

"There is, in this city, a gentleman in possession of several papers that we have need of. Those papers are being held in a safe."

I realized then what he was telling me, and everything began to make sense. If I hadn't been awake so long, my nerves all in a jangle from sitting alone in this cold room, I might have worked it out sooner.

He needed a safecracker.

Suddenly, the absurdity of it all hit me. I couldn't help but laugh.

If my sudden show of levity surprised him, he didn't give any sign of it. He just sat and waited. I sobered soon enough, for I realized that he was dead earnest and that my answer to his proposal was what would mean the difference between prison or freedom.

But there were still a few matters that needed clearing up before I made any sort of commitments.

"Who is this 'we' who needs the papers?" I asked, eyeing his uniform. "I wasn't aware the British Army was in the habit of nabbing civilians to do their job for them."

"That's not important at the moment."

"It's important to me," I said, stubbing out the cigarette on the corner of the table for want of an ashtray. "I need to know what sort of people I'm getting in with."

"You mean you're afraid we might be involved in some kind of dishonest work?" There was a dry sort of mockery in his tone, and I realized that I was very quickly growing to hate this man.

"I like to know who I'm sticking my neck out for," I replied coldly.

"This is a matter of national importance. I can tell you no more than that at present." He said this very gravely.

"You're spies, you mean."

He met my gaze. "Something like that."

It wasn't entirely surprising, now that I considered it. After all, we'd been told often enough to be careful of German agents in our midst. "Careless talk costs lives" and all that. Surely there must be some of our own fellows wandering about, working to intercept them.

But, for that matter, how did I know this man wasn't a German spy himself, enlisting the aid of criminals to steal important documents? A house in Belgravia and an army officer's uniform weren't proof of anything.

"Can you offer me any evidence you are who you say you are?" I asked.

"I haven't said who I am," he replied.

I let out an irritated breath. "We can go on like this all night, or you can give me proof that you're working for the government."

He reached into the pocket of his jacket and pulled out a folded document, which he slid across the table to me.

I picked it up and opened it, noting first the Metropolitan Police Service stationery on which it had been written.

To Whom It May Concern:
The bearer of this letter is entitled to take into custody any housebreakers detained in the month of August in the year 1940. Officers of the Metropolitan Police are hereby ordered to stand down.

It was signed by the commissioner himself.

That seemed legitimate enough, I supposed. Whoever this man was, he had enough clout that he carried around in his pocket an order for the police to stay out of his way.

"Satisfied?" he asked.

I wordlessly returned the letter to him, and he tucked it back into his jacket.

"Now that we've cleared that up, what do you say?" he asked.

It was on the tip of my tongue to accept, to take this chance that was offered to us, but something stopped me. I needed to know more. After all, if they were willing to take a chance on criminals, there must surely be some risk involved.

"What sort of documents will we be retrieving?"

"The classified sort," he answered flatly.

"Where is this house?" I tried again.

"I'm afraid I can't tell you that at the moment."

"Is there anything you can tell me?" I demanded.

"Only that, in addition to the benefit you'll derive from this by keeping out of prison, you'll be doing a great service for your country and, perhaps, for the free world as we know it."

He was laying it on a bit thick, but the idea had merit. It was an appealing thought, using our skills to help fight the enemy, even if we were being blackmailed into it.

Still, something held me back. I considered myself an independent woman, but I wished I could see Uncle Mick, that we could confer over what was happening. Of course, that was likely why they had kept us apart.

No doubt Uncle Mick had been given the same pretty speech. I wondered if he had told them they would need to talk to me.

"I'm not sure what to say . . ." I glanced at the insignia on his uniform, guessed at his rank, and then purposefully demoted him. "Lieutenant."

"Major," he said, without a blink. "Major Ramsey."

"Well, Major Ramsey," I said, recrossing my arms, "before I commit to anything, I want to talk to my uncle. Alone."

After another half hour or so of waiting, one of the men who had arrested us—or perhaps abducted was more accurate, now that we knew they weren't police—let Uncle Mick into my room and closed the door behind him.

I was surprised at the weight that lifted off my shoulders at the sight of him. He looked tired, gray stubble bristling his face and shadows beneath his eyes, but he grinned as he slid into the seat across from me, and I saw that whatever tactics they had tried on him had not dimmed his spirit.

"Are you all right?" I asked, placing my hand over his on the table. It was warm beneath my own chilled skin.

"I'm right as rain, Ellie girl. It'll take more than a night of questions to shake your old Uncle Mick."

I knew it was true, but I still didn't like the thought of it.

"Did you speak to that dreadful major?" I asked, hoping the man was listening.

He grinned. "Got under your skin, did he? I figured he might.

Not the most charming of fellows, perhaps, but no doubt he's clever and capable."

"He certainly orchestrated our kidnapping cleverly enough," I answered tartly. I told him about the order from the Commissioner of Police.

Uncle Mick nodded. "I've been thinking about that, about the information we got about the safe. It was planted. Why else would a safe full of valuables be sitting in a big empty house, ripe for the taking? They were trying to catch us all along."

I was certain he was correct. We had been fed information about that house to test our capabilities and so that we might be caught and pressed into service if we succeeded. Contrary to Uncle Mick's assessment of the situation, I didn't think it made the major seem clever and capable. I thought it made him seem devious and despicable.

"Did he tell you what he wants us to do?" I asked.

"Only that there are some papers that need to be retrieved. It sounds simple enough." Amusement flashed in his eyes. "Which makes me believe it won't be simple at all."

At last, we agreed on something.

"I'm not afraid of danger," I said. "It's that man I don't like."

Uncle Mick studied me closely. "Did he behave improperly toward you?"

I flushed. "No. Certainly not. But he acted so . . . superior."

"They don't get to be majors without developing a bit of an authoritative manner."

I sighed. "You think we should do it, then."

"I don't see that there's much choice," Uncle Mick said. "He's got us dead to rights. It's in with them or to prison we go."

"Yes, but . . ."

"Think of Colm and Toby," he said gently. "They'll need someone to come home to."

He was right. Prison had taken enough from our family.

"Besides, Ellie." Now he placed his hand over mine. "It'll do us good to do our part. We'll all have to if we want to win this war. We've our own outlook on the matter of law and order, but this is something different altogether."

I nodded, knowing it was true. In all honesty, I had been feeling rather helpless where the war was concerned. There are only so many gardens a woman can plant and socks she can knit for soldiers before she begins to feel useless as she watches the men march off to battle. This was my turn to do something that could matter, that would make a significant difference.

I drew in a deep breath. "All right. Then we'll do it."

CHAPTER FOUR

Uncle Mick went back to the door and knocked. It was opened by the man who had let him in, and my uncle told him we were ready to speak to the major.

A few minutes later, Major Ramsey came back with two of his large henchmen.

"Escort Mr. McDonnell back to his room," he instructed them.

"No," I said. "There are matters we wish to discuss . . ."

"You and I will discuss them," he said, motioning for the men to continue taking Uncle Mick away.

I stood quickly from my chair, the legs scraping against the bare wooden floor. "No," I protested.

"It's all right, Ellie," Uncle Mick said softly. "I know you'll work things out just fine."

I opened my mouth to object, but my uncle shook his head ever so slightly. In that easy way we'd always had of understanding each other, I knew that he wanted me to cooperate, to arrange things as best I could to our advantage. And so I closed my mouth and watched as he followed the men from the room.

Then I looked back up—scowled, really—at Major Ramsey, who gestured for me to take my seat. Reluctantly, I sat, and he settled back into the chair across from me.

"Well?" he asked.

"It doesn't seem as though you've left us much choice," I replied darkly.

"I hoped you would see it that way."

I was tempted to make a sharp reply, but I wanted to leave this place and I wanted Uncle Mick to get out with me. So I bit my tongue.

"It's late," the major said, seemingly oblivious to my masterly display of self-control. "We'll discuss the details tomorrow."

"Then you'll let us go now?" His words had given me hope. I ought to have known better.

"You may go, yes. Your uncle will remain here until the mission is accomplished."

I felt my blood rise, and my voice rose along with it. "That is out of the question."

"I'm afraid this is not a negotiation." The way he said it made it sound as though his mind was quite made up, and I despised him and his calm, authoritative tone.

"You can't keep him here," I said, unable to stop my voice from shaking with some mixture of fury and fear. I hated losing control.

"It's a simple matter of collateral," he said evenly. "Surely you understand that."

I was trembling now, and trying very hard not to let him see. "I'll write out a confession. You can keep that as collateral."

"Less effective than keeping your uncle, I think." His eyes were on mine, and I knew he was reading every bit of emotion in them. My mind was whirling, and the temper I had worked so hard to control since I was a girl was in danger of erupting.

Meanwhile, the major sat across from me with no expression. He was completely in command of the situation, and I was beginning to come apart at the seams. That would not do at all. I martialed every last bit of my self-control and tamped down my growing panic.

"It was my uncle who opened the safe," I said in the most level tone I could manage. "I don't know how. I only accompanied him as a lookout."

"You'll find, Miss McDonnell, that lying to me will never get you very far. I know you're perfectly capable of doing it. Your uncle has told me as much."

I mentally chided Uncle Mick for giving that away. It was like him, of course, trying to help me in any way he could. But, by rights, he should be the one to do it.

"He's better than me," I said honestly. "Let him help you, and keep me here."

"That's very noble of you, but I doubt your uncle would permit it."

He was right, of course. Uncle Mick would want me to do the job rather than remaining locked up. He would refuse to leave me here.

I looked up at the major and saw that he was waiting patiently for my answer.

"You might have told us that my uncle was to remain here before you took him away," I said bitterly. "We might have discussed it."

"There's nothing to discuss," he said. "Will you do it or not?"

I realized then that separating me from Uncle Mick before revealing he was to remain a prisoner had all been part of the plan. The major had meant to throw me off guard, to make me realize how little choice I had in any of this. The maddening part of it all was that I knew he was going to get his way in the end. He had all the power, after all.

"Very well," I said at last.

He took a slip of paper and a pen from his pocket and scrawled something on the paper before sliding it across the desk toward me. His handwriting was like his personality: bold yet precise.

"Ring this number tomorrow afternoon, and I'll tell you where you might meet me to discuss the details."

"This is rather cloak-and-dagger stuff, isn't it?" I asked sarcastically.

"I'm afraid the enemy's moved beyond cloaks and daggers to swastikas and tanks, Miss McDonnell. We're just trying to keep up."

The car that had brought me to that place—*the dungeon* was how I now thought of it, for, as grand as it was, it was linked in my mind with the detaining and coercing of prisoners and deserved the epithet—dropped me off at my flat shortly before dawn. I had thought of refusing a ride to maintain my privacy, but there was no doubt they already knew my address. They knew everything else about me, after all.

I went through the front gate and passed the house where Uncle Mick lived, taking the path through the kitchen garden on the side, and went to the little building that rested behind the house. It had been a stable once upon a time but had been converted into a comfortable little flat that Uncle Mick had given me for my own.

Hurrying inside, I breathed a sigh of relief as I closed the door behind me and leaned against it. It had been less than twenty-four hours since I had been here last, but somehow it felt like an eternity. Perhaps it was the reality that I might never have returned that made it all seem so precious to me somehow.

I glanced around the familiar surroundings: the worn but comfortable blue sofa with the pillows Nacy had embroidered, the writing desk and chair, the rug with its cheery pattern of blue and yellow flowers. I had a new appreciation for all of it. The windows were covered now, of course, my bookcases moved in front of them to keep glass from coming into the room in the event of a bombing. I'd strung sturdy twine across the shelves to keep my beloved books from toppling to the floor. I'd put away all my glass knickknacks, too, and taken pictures down from the walls. But, even in this altered state, it was home, and I was incredibly relieved to be back.

The sense of relief was short-lived, however. Uncle Mick was still being held at the dungeon and the thought made me sick to my stomach.

I knew that he was safe enough, but that didn't stop me from worrying.

Following my familiar habits, I put on the kettle and pulled my worn jumper over my shoulders. I hadn't been warm since sometime yesterday afternoon.

Having been awake the whole night, I ought to have been exhausted, but my mind was racing and I knew I couldn't sleep if I tried. Not yet. I thought again how cruel it was that the major had kept Uncle Mick. It wasn't as though we could have run. Where would we go, with Europe at war? Besides, our entire lives were here.

And it wasn't as though we were some diabolical criminal enterprise. We were just a family. Albeit, a family who sometimes dabbled in illegal pursuits.

Not for the first time since last night, I wished desperately that I had followed my instincts to leave that house. If we had, we wouldn't be in this mess.

I was tempted to believe that even the police would have been preferable to the hands into which we had fallen. But some part of me had to acknowledge that I would do a great many things in order to stay out of prison.

Having been born in prison, I wasn't eager to return. I didn't want those memories. I had a dark enough legacy as it was.

A sudden sound outside the door startled me, and I stepped away from it just as it burst open.

"Ellie, where have you been?"

It was Nancy Dean, our housekeeper. She had been christened "Nacy" by me as a young child, unable to quite pronounce her name, and the rest of the family had soon taken up the nickname. She came into the room like a gust of wind. She was short and stout, but she moved with grace and surprising speed. Her hair, dove gray for as far back as I could remember, was brushed back from a wide, ruddy face, and her blue eyes were sharp and piercing from trying to keep three rambunctious children—plus Uncle Mick—in line.

Nacy was the closest thing I'd ever had to a mother, the closest thing for Colm and Toby, too, as my aunt, Uncle Mick's wife, Mary, had died when Toby was very young.

It was Nacy who had helped me with the womanly things that Uncle Mick would have stumbled or flushed to his ears over. She had braided my hair and taken me to buy underthings and explained the ways of womanhood to a young, motherless girl. She was gruff and often stern, but there was humor and great kindness in her, and I loved her dearly.

"I'm afraid we've been caught," I said.

She looked at me like I'd lost my wits, but even when she realized I was serious she didn't seem much alarmed.

"I knew it would happen one of these days," she said dourly. "Where's your uncle? In prison, is he?"

Despite her seeming indifference to Uncle Mick's fate, I knew she was worried about him. She'd always had a soft spot for my uncle. I debated on telling her the truth, but I had been led to believe that secrecy was a vital part of our deal with the devil.

"I hope he'll be home tomorrow," I said. "It's all been a misunderstanding."

Her mouth tightened into a thin line. "A misunderstanding, is it? I think the misunderstanding is that you have thought that you're above the law all these years."

I was too tired to argue with her.

"It's going to be all right," I said. "I'll explain it to you later, but right now I need to get some sleep."

"Can I get you anything?" Nacy was of the formidable yet motherly variety of women who scolded and coddled in turn.

"No, I don't think so. I just want to rest and think things over."

She went away, grumbling, without any more questions. I might have felt bad for sending her away, but I knew she would enjoy stewing about the matter. Someday, when this was over, I would discuss the major's proposition with her. She would have strong opinions on the matter, no doubt.

I went back to my kettle and made a pot of very strong tea. I poured a cup and allowed myself two spoons of sugar, flouting the strict allowance I had made for myself now that it was rationed. There was nothing like it for settling the nerves as far as I was concerned, and right now my nerves needed to be settled.

It was Nacy's fault that I had a sweet tooth. Growing up, she had frequently fed us children her delicious biscuits and cups of strong, sugary tea. As we aged into adulthood, Colm and Toby had moved on to stronger beverages, but I had never outgrown my syrupy cuppa.

I took my cup and saucer into the little sitting area and sank onto the faded blue sofa. The flat was small but very comfortable. Uncle Mick had made a present of it for me when I turned eighteen. "A woman needs a place she can call her own, a bit of privacy," he had told me when handing me the key.

It had been a little bit like moving away when I had left the main house, but I had soon settled into the little flat, enjoying the feeling of independence. And it wasn't as though the rest of them were far away. The boys had always come to visit me often, as though my moving to the little flat had simply made it an extension of the house.

Everything was so much quieter without Colm and Toby bursting in and out at all hours. I felt the sharp pang of loneliness. I missed them both dreadfully.

I drained my teacup and leaned back against the cushions, falling almost at once into an exhausted sleep.

CHAPTER FIVE

I awoke several hours later feeling well rested and almost at peace. After a hot bath and some buttered bread, I had the sensation that things were settled and we had only to move forward. Worry about what is, not what was or what might be, Uncle Mick always said. I was going to take his advice.

I was just about to ring Major Ramsey when there was a tap on my front door. It surprised me, for Nacy never knocked, and the Women's Voluntary Services or anyone else collecting donations door-to-door would have gone to the main house.

It crossed my mind that it might be Major Ramsey, but he had told me to contact him, not the other way around.

All of this passed through my mind in the space of time it took to cross the room and open the door.

"Hello, my lovely." I stared at the man before me. He was like an apparition, a specter of some long-ago past, and I felt frozen in place for just a moment.

"Felix!" I breathed. Then, as if propelled by some invisible force, I flung myself into his arms, heedless of what anyone observing might think.

He pulled me against him, and I was met with the familiar scent of sandalwood soap, tobacco, and aftershave as I pressed my face into his shoulder. It was all so comfortingly familiar that I felt tears spring to my eyes.

At last, he disentangled himself from my embrace, grasping my arms and stepping back to look at me.

"You look as wonderful as I've been picturing you all these months. Even better. Oh, don't cry, love. I can't bear it."

"I won't," I said, dashing away the tears. "I'm just so happy to see you, that's all. Why didn't you tell me you were coming back?"

"I wanted it to be a surprise."

"Well, you've certainly achieved that."

His eyes were on my face, looking me over as though it had been years since we had seen each other last. In some ways it felt like it had. "You really do look wonderful, Ellie."

I studied him in turn. He was as debonairly handsome as ever—dark hair, smoothed and parted to one side, the flashing white-teethed smile beneath a thin mustache. But his dark eyes held something different now, and his face was thinner. All of him was thinner, in fact. He wore one of his suits from before the war, not his uniform, and it hung loosely in places.

But now was not the time to stand gaping at him on the doorstep. I half suspected Nacy would be watching us from the windows of the house. If she saw Felix, she would likely come to greet him, and I wanted him to myself for the moment.

I took his arm. "Come in, Felix. I want to hear everything."

He followed me inside, and I saw that there was something a bit stiff in his movements.

"Are you hurt?" I asked suddenly.

"Nothing too bad," he said lightly. I could tell from his tone that he didn't want me to press him further, so I let the matter drop for the moment. For now, I would just enjoy the fact that he was here, alive and well.

He seemed to be feeling the same way, for he looked around the room with a smile. "It hasn't changed much."

"No, I suppose not. You haven't been gone all that long, you know."

"It just seems like an eternity, I suppose."

"Yes," I said solemnly. "I can imagine that it does."

He settled onto the end of the sofa, loosening his tie. The gesture was so familiar that I felt a little pang of happiness.

"How are Colm and Toby?" he asked.

"Colm's stationed in Torquay, fixing RAF planes."

Felix smiled. "All those hours at the Aerodrome came in handy, eh?"

I nodded. From the time he was young, Colm had gone frequently to the Hendon Aerodrome, and not just for the Aerial Derbies and Royal Air Force Displays. He'd spent so much time hanging around that he'd begun to know some of the airplane mechanics. They'd taken a liking to his gregarious and eager-to-learn personality, and by the time he was twelve or thirteen, he'd known the workings of airplanes inside and out. The RAF couldn't ask for a more knowledgeable man.

"They're lucky to have him, and he loves the work. He was home on leave last month and looking well," I said as I took a seat beside Felix. I managed to get the next words out without too much strain in my voice. "We haven't heard from Toby since Dunkirk."

He swore. "Have you written . . ."

"Yes, we've done everything we can. They don't know what happened to him. He . . . it's assumed that he was either captured or . . . killed."

"I'm sorry, Ellie." He reached out to squeeze my hand and then held it tight. There was something so solemn in his normally jovial tone that the tears I had done so well at holding back all these months seemed to spring into my eyes without my even noticing them.

"I don't think he's dead," I said, glad that the words came out sounding as though I meant them. Sometimes I was very sure of it, but sometimes I only pretended to be sure in order to convince myself.

"Yes, don't give up hope. There was a lot of confusion at Dunkirk. It's very possible that you'll hear something any day now."

He sounded as certain as I had, and I appreciated it. Of course, I knew what a good actor Felix had always been, how easily he spun illusions, but, in this moment, it was something we both wanted to believe.

I remembered with a pang of nostalgia the last time the four of us were together. Felix had come to the house one rainy afternoon with Colm and Toby. The boys had shouldered their way in through the door as they always did, as though they were still children and not grown men, trying to get the best of each other when crossing the threshold. They were hatless, both their dark heads wet from the rain, their jackets dripping water onto Nacy's clean floors. She'd scold them later and they'd charm her and all would be forgiven. And then Felix had come in behind them, closing his umbrella with a flourish and wiping his feet on the rug before he stepped into the room.

He was tall, thin, and elegant, so different from my rugged, sturdy cousins. There was a debonair set to him, a smoothness to his movements and expressions. He carried himself with the perpetual grace of an actor making his entrance onstage.

"Hello, Ellie," he said, his eyes settling on me. "You're looking as beautiful as ever."

"You say that to all the girls, and don't think I don't know it," I retorted.

"But I only mean it when I say it to you," he answered with a grin.

Colm watched this exchange, his eyes going from one to the other of us, that set look coming over his face that appeared whenever he thought a man was getting fresh with me.

Felix had flirted with me for years, of course, but that never stopped Colm from scowling at him. Colm had been protective of me since I was a wee thing, like a big brother. Toby cared about me deeply, but his was a quieter, less observant way. Colm had enough bluster for the both of them.

"Is the kettle on?" Toby asked. "I need something to warm me up. I'm soaked to the skin."

"I'll take something that works quicker than tea," Colm said, moving toward the sideboard where Uncle Mick kept a few bottles of liquor. "Want a drink, Felix?"

"No, I think I'll take tea."

"I don't suppose Nacy's got anything we can eat," Toby said.

I laughed, for I knew he meant it in jest. I couldn't remember a day in my life when the cupboards hadn't contained some treat Nacy had baked for us.

"As though you've ever had to go an hour of your life without food, Toby Liam," Nacy said, making her fortuitous entrance into the room with a tray holding the teapot and a plate of fresh scones with cream.

"Nacy, you're like a vision from Heaven," Toby said, reaching for one of the scones.

"Mind your manners," she said. "Sit down like a civilized person."

"I'm a soldier now," he protested. But he pulled his hand back. "I have to learn to eat quick."

"You're not on the battlefield yet, young man." Her voice was gruffer than usual as she tried to hide her emotion. It was hard for her, knowing Colm and Toby were going off to fight. She was as much a mother to them as she was to me. I knew she felt the same sick feeling in the pit of her stomach that I did when I thought about them leaving.

We ate Nacy's treats with great relish and drank our strong tea. Even Colm had a cup after he'd thrown back his glass of whiskey. Then the boys smoked as we sat listening to the radio.

We tried to be merry, but there was a certain heaviness that had fallen over things at the mention of war. The boys were shipping out soon—Felix, too—and it would be a long time before we were all together again. *If* we were all together again . . .

I pushed that memory from my mind and focused on the here and now.

"Would you like some tea?" I asked, taking my hand from Felix's and rising from the sofa. I wanted a few moments to gather my thoughts, to pull myself together. It wasn't at all like me to get weepy and maudlin, but so much had been happening these past few days that this sudden taste of what things had been had caught me off guard.

"I would love some tea. I haven't had a proper cup in days."

I went to the kitchen and put the kettle on the hob, glad for the few moments of comfortable routine to regain my composure. I didn't make conversation with him as I did so, and none was needed. Felix and I had always been comfortable together.

Felix Lacey and I had an unusual relationship. He'd been a neighborhood boy, a friend of my cousins, and we had known each other practically since we were children. We had got on well from the start, enjoyed each other's company, and our relationship had grown into something of its own, outside of his friendship with Colm and Toby.

Felix had always been a rogue, but I knew better than to take him seriously and he knew better than to push things too far with my uncle Mick and my cousins looking out for me. So we'd teased and flirted with each other and he would sometimes jokingly refer to the children we would one day have together, but it was all in good fun. For the past few years, however, it felt as though we had begun to walk a somewhat rocky road between friendship and something more.

There had never been anything formal between us. There had been one night a year or so before when, as he walked me home, we'd shared a few reckless kisses under an irresistibly romantic starlit sky. The next day we pretended it had never happened.

When he left for the war, I kissed him again, standing on a railroad platform surrounded by all the other men in uniform being kissed by other women holding back tears.

Now that he was back, I didn't know quite where things stood. I only knew that I was terribly glad he was home.

A few minutes later I came back into the room with the tea-things on a tray. I even pulled out a tray of chocolate biscuits I had been saving for a special occasion.

His gaze followed me as I moved toward him. "You're a sight for sore eyes, Ellie."

"Thank you, Felix. I feel the same way about you."

"It changes a man's perspective, fighting does. Makes him appreciate the things he had when life was ordinary."

"Yes, I imagine so." I set the tray on the table near the sofa and then looked up at him, caught by the somber tone of his words. There had never been a solemn bone in his body, and I found it was unsettling. I supposed war never left men unscathed, not even men like Felix.

He had lit a cigarette while I was in the kitchen, and he blew out a stream of smoke, watching it rise into the air.

"But let's talk of gayer things," he said, the old Felix suddenly restored. "I want to hear all about what you've been doing with yourself while I've been gone."

I made his tea the same way he had always taken it, with sugar and milk, while I debated on how much I should tell him about the predicament with Major Ramsey. I would trust Felix with my life, but I was certain Major Ramsey would not feel the same way, so I decided to keep it to myself for now.

"I've been helping Uncle Mick with the shop. Business isn't as good as it once was."

"Not so many people worried about opening locks when a bomb might blow them open any day, eh?"

I gave him a grim smile as I handed him his teacup. "Something like that, I suppose."

"And what about the other business?" Felix knew what sort of things we got up to on the wrong side of the law. He'd been involved in a few of our capers over the years.

"That's been slow as well," I said. "But we're getting on all right."

"I'd never bet against your Uncle Mick."

"No," I agreed, retaking my seat beside him, cup and saucer in hand. "How long is your leave?"

"I'm afraid it may be indefinite."

I felt a surge of relief, as though a knot in my chest had eased ever so slightly. "You mean you won't have to go back to the Continent?"

"A part of me is still there, in a manner of speaking." He reached down and pulled the hem of his left trouser leg slightly up.

"Oh!" I gasped, the cup rattling in the saucer. The lower portion of his left leg was gone, replaced with an artificial limb that looked to be made of tin.

"I took a rather destructive round to the shin. There was no salvaging the leg. Or my career in the navy, I'm afraid."

"Oh, Felix." I reached to set my cup on the table with a shaking hand. "I'm so sorry."

All at once, the weight of everything seemed to hit me, and I couldn't stop the tears that suddenly began to fall.

He reached out to cup my face, brushing a tear aside with his thumb. "Don't cry, sweet. It's not as bad as all that."

I covered his hand with mine, relishing the nearness of him, the utter relief that he was sitting here on my sofa, safe. To think how close to death he had been . . .

"Everything's so dreadful," I whispered. "This war, and Toby, and you . . ."

"Ellie, look at me," he said gently.

I raised my eyes to his. They were dark and warm, his gaze that strange mixture of familiar and unfathomable that had always drawn me to him.

"It's going to be all right," he said. "All of it."

As our eyes held, I had a sense of the rightness and harmony that existed between us, the way we seemed to be able to communicate in a manner that went deeper than words. Not even his months of absence had changed that. If anything, I felt it stronger than before.

I knew in that moment that he wanted to kiss me, but instead he took his hand from my face and sat back against the sofa, putting distance between us in more ways than one. "Now, how about some more tea? Tea always makes everything a bit better, doesn't it?"

I sniffed, wiping away the remnants of my tears, and reached for the teapot. He was right, of course. Everything would work out in time. There was nothing to be done but to carry on.

"Does it hurt very much?" I asked.

"Not anymore." He flashed a smile at me, as though to distract me from the grim experiences those words held. "And my left leg was one of my least charming parts, at least."

I gave a strangled little laugh, trying to regain my composure. "That may be, but all the same . . ."

He gave the metal a rap with his knuckles. "It's below the knee, so there's not much damage done. I was never a champion runner, anyway."

"I'm terribly sorry."

"There's no reason for you to be. It happens. Men have come home with worse, and a lot of them haven't come home at all." He grinned. "And at least I'm still dashingly handsome."

I gave a little laugh, a genuine one this time. Leave it to Felix to think of something like that.

"That you are," I agreed. "Though you didn't have to go to such lengths to make me admit it."

He did indeed have the kind of face that drew the female eye, and he was forever giving one looks that clearly warned he was up to no good but drew one in like a moth to the flame nonetheless. He had always reminded me a bit of Douglas Fairbanks, Jr., though, when I had said so once, Colm and Toby had laughed and teased me until I blushed.

He drained the second cup of tea in one long drink.

"Thank you for that, love. Seeing you was the best medicine I've had in months." He set his cup and saucer down on the table. "Alas, I suppose I'd better go. I've got an appointment to look at some lodgings. My landlady rented my place as soon as I enlisted. In the meantime, I'm staying at a hotel. Let me give you the number."

He scribbled his number on a piece of paper from his pocket and handed it to me.

"Are you . . . are you all right, walking?" I asked.

"Certainly. This leg services me nearly as well as the other one did."

I thought I might offer to go with him, to help, but I knew he wouldn't let me. Felix had never been the sort to rely on anyone, and he would be even less likely to do so now.

"Is the old man home?" he asked, putting on his hat. "I came to see you first, but I'll stop at the house if he's in."

"No, Uncle Mick is out at the moment," I said. "But do come back soon. He'll be glad to see you."

He nodded. "I'm glad you were here. I've missed you, Ellie."

"I've missed you, too."

He gave me a wink, chasing away any heavier sentiments either of us might have been feeling, and turned toward the door. He walked carefully but very upright, the limp noticeable only now that I knew it was there.

After he had gone, I sat on the sofa looking at his empty teacup on the table. His visit had been like a taste of old times, but that taste had been tainted with the bitterness of what life had become.

War had already changed so many things, and there was no end in sight. I felt suddenly the weight of helplessness fall upon me.

No, I was not quite helpless. There was my work with Major Ramsey. Whatever I thought of him, some good could come of our association. Perhaps I might, in my own small way, have the chance to make some sort of difference.

I rose from the sofa and moved to the coatrack, where my jacket from the previous evening was hung. Reaching into one pocket, I found the piece of paper Major Ramsey had given me.

I hadn't forgiven the man, of course, and I didn't relish the thought of working for him. But I reminded myself that we must all make sacrifices if we were to win this war.

And, on the selfish side of things, a short time working for him was better than a year or two in prison.

Picking up the telephone, I rang the number. A young man answered on the second ring.

"May I speak to Major Ramsey?" I asked.

"Who is calling, please?"

"Ellie McDonnell," I said, wondering what I should say if he challenged me.

"One moment please."

I was prepared for a long wait—police and their ilk liked to leave one dangling like a worm on a line whenever possible—so I was surprised when he picked up a moment later.

"Major Ramsey."

"This is Ellie McDonnell," I said.

"Yes?"

He sounded almost impatient, as though I was wasting his time, and I fought the urge to say something quite rude. Instead, I thought of Uncle Mick and quelled my temper.

"You told me to ring you," I reminded him.

He rattled off an address. "Eight o'clock tonight. Wear a hat with a veil."

And then the line went dead.

I rolled my eyes. It was all so ridiculously clandestine that it felt like something out of a bad film one might see on a slow week at the cinema.

As I had suspected, working with Major Ramsey was going to be very trying.

CHAPTER SIX

It was raining when I arrived at the address the major had given me, the sky spitting out cold, hard pellets of water.

I had left early for fear of being late, and I now found myself standing outside at half past seven with an umbrella unequal to the slanting rain and wet stockings inside soggy leather shoes.

Looking up at the sign above the door, THE BELL AND HARP, I realized I knew the place, and I was a bit surprised the major would've chosen to meet there. It was a pub that catered to the working class. Uncle Mick and the boys had stopped here for a pint often enough. It wasn't exactly the type of establishment I would've thought a toff like Major Ramsey would frequent.

Of course, that was probably the point.

A large drop of rain hit my hat and rolled down the black veil that hung over my face before dropping onto my chest. As I lowered my head to look at it, another hit me squarely on the back of the neck, cold water trickling down between my shoulder blades. It was enough to make me go inside.

Cold, wet, and cross, I closed my umbrella and stepped into the pub, casting my eyes around the dim interior for a place I might sit until the major arrived.

The inside of the pub felt warm and cozy after standing out in the rain. It was fairly typical as far as pub décor went—all wood paneling and furniture, wide-planked wood floors, yellow lights shining out of sooty sconces, and a long bar, a glittering array of bottles displayed behind it—and filled with a typical array of working-class men and women, enjoying a meal and a pint after a long day's work. I felt soothed by the atmosphere in some way I couldn't quite name.

Glancing around, I was surprised to see the major already sitting at a table in the corner, not too far from the fire that crackled in the large stone fireplace. He gave me a short nod as I entered, and I made my way across the room toward him.

He rose when I neared the table. It was the first time we had stood side by side, and I realized that, in addition to his well-built frame, he was quite tall. A fine figure of a man, Nacy would have called him. He did indeed have an impressive physique, I admitted to myself grudgingly. As though he needed another reason to feel superior.

"Good evening, Miss McDonnell. I trust you're well?" He reached out to help me out of my damp coat.

So we were going to play at politeness, were we? Well, I could do that well enough.

"I'm very well, Major. Thank you." I managed not to sound as insincere as I felt.

He set my dripping coat aside and pulled out my chair as I brushed at a few stray rain spots that dotted my gray dress.

He must have arrived before the rain began, for his uniform was dry and spotless. Despite myself, I felt a bit self-conscious in my rumpled state and three-year-old dress. For all the safes we had emptied over the years, we had never made ourselves rich on it, and fashion had never been very important to me. The things I owned were serviceable and stylish enough for my tastes.

It was only when I had been dressing to meet the major, looking for something to go with the gray felt netted hat, that I realized I had very little in the way of fashionable clothing. Not that it mattered, especially not in wartime, but I never liked to feel at a disadvantage.

I took a seat and the major resumed his.

"What would you like to eat?" he asked.

The question caught me by surprise, and I was prepared to refuse him when I remembered I'd had nothing since the cup of tea and buttered bread I'd had for breakfast that morning.

"I . . . whatever's on hand," I said.

He motioned over the waitress and ordered a pot of tea and steak and kidney pies. I realized suddenly that I was absolutely famished. I had, in fact, eaten very little since breakfast the day before. I was always too on edge to eat before a job, and, after getting arrested and the surprise of Felix's return, I hadn't taken time since for a proper meal. I hoped the thought of food wouldn't set my stomach to grumbling and remove whatever dignity I might have left.

"You needn't keep the veil over your face," he said, when the waitress had gone away. "It was merely a precaution."

"A precaution against what?" I lifted up the veil and, as it was all quite damp, removed my hat altogether and set it aside.

I could only imagine what state my hair was in. It had a natural wave to it, which was convenient when it decided to cooperate. Alas, it had rebelled against the pins this evening, and I suspected it appeared as unkempt as the rest of me.

The major, however, was either too polite or, more likely, too uninterested to notice.

"Against anyone taking note of you."

"Then oughtn't we have met back at your dungeon instead of a public place?"

"My dungeon?" he repeated.

"Where you're keeping my uncle."

For the first time since I had met him, I saw a glimmer of amusement in his expression. "I can assure you your uncle is being well cared for. He has had to face neither the rack nor the wheel. But you don't have to take my word for it."

He reached into the pocket of his jacket and withdrew an envelope. My name was written on the outside in Uncle Mick's familiar hand. It was ridiculous, but my throat clenched at the sight of it and I had to fight to keep tears from springing to my eyes.

I took the envelope and slid it into my pocket.

"Don't you want to read it?" he asked.

"I'll read it later."

"Very well. And, to answer your question, it's perfectly safe to talk freely here. Sitting in this corner of the room, it's difficult to be heard unless one is quite near."

I glanced around, realizing now how perfectly chosen the pub was as a place to have a quiet conversation. There were several people eating and drinking, and the sound of talk and laughter and utensils against plates filled the room. Added to this was the steady patter of rain against the roof and the cracking and popping of wood in the fireplace.

No one was paying the least bit of attention to us. Well, some of the women were looking at Major Ramsey, but I was fairly certain that interest went no further than the superficial.

Was he married? I wondered suddenly. I glanced at his hand. There was no ring, but that was neither proof nor disproof that there was a Mrs. Ramsey somewhere, waiting for him to come home tonight.

I tried to imagine what sort of woman might willingly tie herself to a man like this. He had more than his fair share of good looks, it was true. And from his polished demeanor and elevated rank, I guessed there was probably money and breeding, too. But what was all of that when measured against his callous superiority?

And, anyway, what did it matter to me if he was married? Nothing at all.

"Will you tell me more about the job now?" I asked.

"In good time."

The waitress brought our plates and the tea then, and I was suddenly very eager to eat. It seemed the major was happy to see the food as well, for he cut into his pie at once. I poured the tea.

We ate for a while in a comfortable silence. I supposed each of us were lost in our own thoughts. One might have assumed, given the circumstances, that the meal would be unpleasant, but the food was good, the fire was beginning to warm me, and I had proof that Uncle Mick was all right. All things considered, it was a fairly cheery scene.

As for the major, it was easy enough to ignore him when there was a hot steak and kidney pie before me, and no doubt he felt the same way.

After a few minutes, though, he pushed aside his plate and turned his attention to me.

"As you know, I've asked you here this evening to discuss the operation. We're working on a limited time schedule, so we'll have to be quick. I trust you're ready to go to work?"

"I'm at your disposal," I said. If he detected the trace of sarcasm in my words, which he probably did, he gave no sign of it.

"Our target date is Friday."

This was Wednesday. It was sooner than I had imagined it might be, but I was sure Major Ramsey and his people had done a good deal of the research for me. If they could get me in and out, I could get into the safe easily enough. Besides, the sooner I did it, the sooner Uncle Mick would be free.

"What are the specifics?" I asked him.

"I'm afraid there isn't much information I can share with you."

I didn't bother to withhold the annoyed sigh that came to my lips. "For pity's sake. Can't we dispense with all this hugger-mugger business and get down to facts?"

He looked at me, and I was momentarily distracted from the matter at hand. In the light from the fireplace I suddenly saw that his eyes weren't merely blue; they were nearly lavender, a violet cast to them that called to mind the most perfect shade of twilight sky. They were stunning.

It took me a moment to remember he was scolding me.

"This may be a game to you, Miss McDonnell, but I can assure you it's deadly serious."

I rallied quickly. "The freedom, if not the very lives, of myself and my family rests in your hands, Major Ramsey. I can assure you I understand how serious it is. But if you want me to do a job two days from now, I need to know something about what's expected of me."

We frowned at each other for a long moment. I supposed he wasn't accustomed to being challenged, but I thought he'd better get used to it if he intended to keep ordering me about.

At last, he gave a curt nod. "Fair enough. I can give you the bare details for the time being. Anything else will be on a need-to-know basis."

"I suppose that will have to do," I said ungraciously.

"As I told you last night, there is a set of documents we would like you to retrieve. They rest, at present, in the safe of a man who has no idea that we suspect him of possible collusion with the enemy."

"A German spy?" I asked.

"For the moment, we shall merely call him a man on the fence."

"And this man on the fence is in possession of some important documents the Germans would like to get their hands on."

"Yes."

"How did he come by them?" I asked.

"I'm afraid I can't tell you that."

"Can't or won't?"

"Won't," he amended remorselessly.

"But you're certain they're in the safe?"

"We have good reason to believe so, yes. We don't just want you to remove the documents from the safe, however. We want you to exchange them for another set without the switch being detected."

I considered this for a moment. "So if he does pass them on, the information the Germans get will be false and you'll know you've caught a traitor."

"You've a quick grasp of the facts, Miss McDonnell," he said, in the first words from him that might have been a compliment. "Yes. Once we know the truth about him, we can proceed from there."

"Arrest him or continue using him to feed useless information to the enemy, you mean."

The barest hint of something like a smile touched his lips. "Brava."

"But won't your man notice that the papers have been switched? I mean, isn't he aware of their contents?"

He paused as if considering how much to tell me. "These are rather technical documents. He isn't likely to have perused them in depth."

I was intrigued. I wanted to know just who this man was and what these documents that he possessed were, but I understood the importance of secrecy in wartime and I would just have to learn to live with not knowing. At least for now.

"It all seems straightforward enough," I said.

He nodded. "Do you think you can do it?"

"Of course."

"As easy as all that, is it?" He was looking at me closely, trying to gauge where I was on the scale between skill and empty bravado, I supposed.

"I didn't say it would be easy," I replied. "But I have great confidence in my abilities."

He nodded. "Confidence is an asset in work such as ours. One might even say it is a vital necessity."

If that was the case, no wonder Major Ramsey was succeeding so well, I thought snidely. It was, I realized suddenly, what set me so on edge about him. He somehow managed to be both very on his guard and yet completely at ease at the same time. That sort of supreme confidence was off-putting. I liked a man who could admit that he might not always be right.

"We've made sure the house will be empty Friday night. What else will you need to ensure your success?"

"The combination would be ideal," I said.

Again, a flicker of amusement. "We had considered that as an alternative to abducting a safe-cracking gang, but it seems the combination remains a secret."

"A gang now, are we? We've gone up in the world."

"Criminals are criminals, Miss McDonnell," he said, apparently caring not a whit if he offended me. "But desperate times call for desperate measures."

"And so you must work with thieves." I'll admit, there was a certain satisfaction in pointing this out to him.

"Alas," he said, "His Majesty's government does not have a great deal of safecrackers at its disposal."

"I suppose not," I conceded. "Not people of our caliber at any rate."

He tipped his head in mock acknowledgment.

"It would help, though, if I knew in advance what sort of safe it was," I said.

"I'll see if that can be arranged."

Another thought occurred to me. "Will I be going into that house alone?"

"I will accompany you."

Inwardly, I sighed. Of course, he would.

I tried to imagine what it would be like creeping into a house with Major Ramsey instead of Uncle Mick. Somehow, I didn't think the major would be much good at creeping. He seemed to me the sort of man who always went striding into rooms, shoulders back, head held high. Was he even capable of stealth?

I assessed him. I supposed that he might be, if he tried. I thought he would probably be decent at most things he set his mind to. His type usually was.

"Where is the house?" I asked.

"You needn't worry about that."

"We're used to investigating houses ahead of time, finding the best ways to get in."

"I can appreciate that, but we're going to employ methods a bit different from yours."

"So I've noticed," I agreed tartly. "My criminal gang would never think of kidnapping anyone."

He ignored me. "Is there anything you need to get the job done?"

"Just some scratch paper, to work out the combination."

"Why don't you tell me about the process."

I hadn't expected him to ask this, but I supposed he wanted to know if I was as capable as I claimed to be. Well, I could at least set his mind to rest on that score.

"You understand how safes work, I assume?" I wasn't being facetious. I genuinely didn't know how much he might understand about how the process worked. The average person had very little idea what went on inside that little mechanism.

"I understand the basics," he said. "But perhaps you had better give me a brief tutorial."

I studied him for just a moment to see if it was he who was being facetious, but he seemed to be in earnest. I nodded.

I thought for just a moment about the best way to go about explaining it. Uncle Mick had taught me at such a young age that I didn't exactly remember the lessons. It just felt like something I had always known and, quite naturally, had not had much opportunity to share with others.

"This is quite simplified, but you'll get the idea," I began. "Inside the safe, there's something called the drive cam, which is connected to the exterior dial with a spindle and turns with it. The cam has a notch in it called the gate. The bolting mechanism of the safe is attached to a lever. When the lever's nose drops into the gate, the rotation of the cam pulls the lever and retracts the bolt, and the safe will open."

He nodded. So far, so good.

"The security feature comes in with something called the wheel pack, a set of wheels between the door and the cam. Each number in the safe's combination corresponds to one of the wheels, so the number of wheels determines how many numbers are in the combination. Obviously, the fewer wheels, the easier things are."

"Obviously."

"The bolt's lever has a little bar, perpendicular to the nose, called a fence. Each wheel has its own notch, and unless the wheels are lined up in the correct configuration, the fence hits the wheels and stops the nose from dropping into the gate so that it can't be engaged. Are you following me?"

"Yes."

"Now we go back to the drive cam. As it rotates with the turn of the dial, there is something called a pin that will catch on a tab on the nearest wheel called the fly, engaging the wheel and making it turn with the cam. After another rotation, a pin on that wheel will catch the fly on the next wheel, picking it up, too. That is, causing it to join in the rotation. This is done until the wheel farthest from the cam is put into the correct place for the fence to fall into it.

"Reversing the direction breaks the cycle, releasing that first wheel while it's in the right place, and allowing the next wheel to be moved until its notch lines up with the first. This is how using the correct combination lines up the wheels so that their notches are in a row. Then the fence can fall into them and no longer stops the nose engaging with the gate, and the safe can be opened. That's how the combination works."

"And if one doesn't have the combination?" he asked.

I smiled. "That's where the skill comes in. A good safecracker

can turn the dial and feel the slightest differences in resistance de-
pending on where the fence is in relation to the wheel gates. If one
gate is in the correct position, there is a different feel than if none of
them are. Turning the dial to the left and right lets us feel the contact
points of the nose on either side of the cam gate."

"And what does that tell you?" he asked.

"Due to the manufacturing inconsistencies, the wheels are not
precisely the same size. The fence, therefore, will rest on the biggest
wheel. If one finds the gate on the biggest wheel, the fence will drop
ever so slightly to rest on the next biggest wheel. This means the
nose will also drop lower into the drive cam and will hit the contact
points on either side differently. By trying a succession of numbers
on the dial, one can work out the first number."

He appeared to be following me, which was a point in his favor.
It was a lot of information to drop on someone all at once.

"How is that done?" he asked.

"Many people create a graph of the contact points, which will
show a noticeable dip when the gate of the biggest wheel is beneath
the fence. In my case, I make notations of the relevant numbers as I
come to them. Uncle Mick does it all mentally."

"Does he? An impressive skill."

I met his gaze. "Are you sure you wouldn't rather have him do
this?"

He didn't answer my question. "What's the next step in the
process?"

"Once you have the first number, you can begin to work out the
others. What I refer to as the 'first' number is not necessarily the first
number in the combination, mind you. Just whichever corresponds
to the largest wheel."

"Which you cannot know from outside the safe."

"Correct."

"What then?"

"Once you've found one number, you can use that number and

then work with it to follow a similar pattern. A good safecracker can detect those minuscule changes in the distance between contact points and use them to narrow down the combination."

I realized I had been warming to my lesson and was leaning forward. He, in turn, was watching me intently, giving me his undivided attention.

"And that's it in a nutshell," I said, sitting back. "I've simplified things, of course, and there are variations by safe, but those are the basics."

He nodded. "Thank you. That was quite clear and concise. I'm glad we decided to enlist skilled professionals for the task."

I didn't know why I felt oddly satisfied by this small show of approval. He was just the sort of person I didn't want approval from. After all, he represented a great many of the things I hated: the haughtiness of wealth and privilege, the unmerciful arm of the law. Then again, perhaps it was just that fact that made me glad he realized my talent. I knew he looked down on people like me, but now he was aware how much skill was required to do what we did.

I picked up my teacup and took a sip of the now-cold liquid. At least it was still very sweet.

"Shall I order a fresh pot?" he asked. The politeness caught me off guard, but I supposed he was feeling generous now that I had spilled my secrets. "Or would you, perhaps, prefer something a bit stronger?"

"No. Thank you," I said. "In fact, I suppose I'd better be getting home, if it's all the same to you." Nacy would be wondering where I was.

"Certainly," he said, rising. "Shall I have my driver take you home?"

I shook my head as I finished setting my hat atop it. "It's not far. Besides," I said, drawing the veil down over my face. "It's better to take precautions, isn't it?"

He didn't answer, but picked up my coat and helped me on with it.

"Thank you for dinner," I said, and then felt awkward about saying it, as though we were on a date.

"I'll send a message Friday morning with a meeting time and the location of the rendezvous point."

That had certainly never been said to me on a date before.

"Very well."

I left the pub with mixed emotions. It had gone better than I had thought it might. I didn't exactly like the idea of Major Ramsey accompanying me on the job, but I supposed there was no help for that. At least he seemed to be the sort of man who wouldn't get in the way now that he knew what was involved. I thought back over my tutorial. Really, it had been a fairly vague explanation, all told, but it was difficult to describe the process without a demonstration. And he would get that soon enough.

CHAPTER SEVEN

I spent the next day preparing as I would for any other job. Or perhaps that's not quite accurate. It wasn't the same as any other job. For one thing, I didn't know any of the specifics. The major himself had rung up to tell me, with a terseness that surely boded ill for his subordinates, that his men had not ascertained the make of the safe in their reconnaissance. So I would be going in blind, which was against every cardinal rule of Uncle Mick's.

My uncle was one of the most jovial, spontaneous fellows you would ever meet, but he had always stressed the importance of preparation and serious focus when it came time for business. I knew this job was that much more important since our freedom—to say nothing of the fate of England—was at stake. I tried not to let those little details bother me. *Only think about the pertinent things,* Uncle Mick would say. *Don't get distracted.*

He had said as much in the letter he had sent with the major. I had opened it when I returned home. It was short, but it brought tears to my eyes:

All is well here, Ellie girl. Don't worry about me. Focus on the task. You've all the skills you need. There's not a doubt in my mind that you'll succeed.

I was glad he had written to me. It was just the added boost of confidence I needed.

The morning after my dinner with Major Ramsey, I got up early and drank a strong cup of tea with a bit of toast and marmalade. Then I went to Uncle Mick's workshop.

It was a small building where he kept his locksmithing tools, as well as the tools of his less legitimate enterprises. The place had always been something of a magician's lair to me, a land of enchantment where Uncle Mick worked his wizardry on locks that gave up their secrets to him with a wave of his hand.

One entire wall was covered in pegs, each of which held a key spanning every imaginable size and description. As a child, I had always loved to run my hand along the wall and hear the tinkle of the metal as the blades knocked against one another. I still thought it the grandest musical instrument I could imagine.

Along the other wall there was a rolltop secretary where Uncle Mick did his bookkeeping, and a tall, wide wooden cupboard with many small drawers that contained a vast assortment of tools and lock parts: wrenches, picks, pins, tweezers, plugs, springs, cylinders, clay for impressions, metal pellets for casting, and just about anything else you might care to name, plus more besides.

The center of the room held a long worktable that was even now scattered with a few projects on which he had been working.

But it was none of these items I had come for. I moved through the crowded but tidy space and to the back corner of the room. There against the wall was an old safe that had been there for as long as I could remember. I'd asked Uncle Mick once where it had come from, and he had said he'd picked it up at an auction before I was born.

I'd been quite young when I'd taken to playing with it. I suppose, in the beginning, it was merely a matter of my wanting to mimic what I saw my uncle do as I sat for long, happy hours watching him work. I would turn the knob, feel the clicks of the wheel. Sometimes I would place my ear against the cool metal and listen to the little sounds inside. I must have come by my talent naturally, for there was a certain sort of instinct in me, a feeling I had as I felt and listened to those tiny changes in pressure and sound.

Uncle Mick had eventually taught me how it all worked and urged me to use a paper and pen to chart out the differences on the dial. Then one day the lock gave way and the safe opened beneath my hand.

"It seems the trade runs in your blood, Ellie girl," Uncle Mick had said with a gleam in his eye. I'd never felt prouder.

I think I knew, even as a child, that my uncle wasn't exactly what you'd call a paragon of virtue. There'd been hints, conversations almost spoken in some sort of code between him and my cousins, Colm and Toby, that they were involved in something that they didn't want others to know about.

But it wasn't until I was perhaps twelve or thirteen that Uncle Mick had let me know the full scope of their activities. I hadn't been shocked, as one might expect a proper young lady to be. Indeed, it was almost as though I had known all along, and I had been eager to join them in their work.

I supposed, if examined objectively, it might not be considered the ideal environment for a young, impressionable girl. But most orphans never had a better family nor a better home life. Despite the unconventionality of it all, I had never lacked for material things or for love and support.

It could be argued that Uncle Mick might have protected me from all of this, set me upon the straight and narrow. Nacy had suggested often enough that I should be sent to boarding school to learn to be a lady rather than following in their criminal footsteps. But Uncle Mick had always shook his head and said that he'd taken me in with the intention of making me as much a part of the family as his own children were. And safecracking was what this family did.

I smiled at the memories as I walked to the safe in the back corner. It was a Chubb safe from the Victorian era, black iron with brass trimmings. I ran my hand across the smooth top with as much affection as one might pet a favorite dog.

"Hello, Mr. Chubbs," I said. From the first, I had taken to calling the safe by the name on the manufacturer's plate on its door, and now I would never dream of greeting him with less respect than he deserved.

Then I sat down on the floor and began to work.

There is an art to safecracking, as there is to most things that are a mixture of talent and practiced skill, and I needed to fine-tune it before I went to work. Granted, this safe was familiar to me and not the most perplexing of a challenge, but I suppose a pianist might practice just as well on a pub instrument as on a Steinway. It's the practice that enhances the skill, not the quality of the instrument.

And so Mr. Chubbs and I played our little tune again and again. It was nearly dusk by the time Nacy found me in the workshop.

"Scheming again, are you?" she asked, looking down at where I sat before the safe, an expression on her face that I recognized from when she'd caught the boys and me doing something we oughtn't.

"I don't know what you mean."

She clicked her tongue. "Don't try that innocent face with me. I know when something's afoot. And it's been a good while since you've been out here, spending time with your Mr. Chubbs."

"But, Nacy . . ."

She held up a hand. "I won't ask you what it is, Ellie. You know that I've never meddled in your uncle's business. And you're a grown woman now. If you choose that way of life, I'll not try to stop you. But . . ." She paused, and I was surprised at the tears that glimmered suddenly in her eyes. As caring as she was, she had never been a woman given to emotion, and I could count on one hand the times I'd seen her cry.

"But please be careful," she said at last. "I . . . I couldn't bear to lose you all."

"Oh, Nacy . . ." I stood up and reached out to embrace her. She held me tight, and for just a moment, enveloped in the scent of talc, rose water, and, faintly, baked goods, I felt that childhood sense of security, when everything had seemed right with the world.

"I've done my best to care for you all," she said when she released me. "But you've got to do your part in keeping safe. Once you've left the henhouse, I can't help you fight the foxes."

"I know. But you mustn't worry. Everything is going to be all right. Truly." I offered her the kind of flashing smile that reminded me of Toby. "Besides, there's a bit of the old fox in all of us."

She nodded and then reverted to her own particular brand of affection. "Come and get something to eat, Ellie," she said.

"All right. I'm half-starved." I followed her from the workshop, my body stiff from long hours of sitting but my fingers nimble with practice.

I was as ready as I would ever be.

I dressed all in black for the night we were going to do the job. I didn't know if it would be appropriate, as I knew very little of what we were actually going to do. It was a bit unsettling, to be so thoroughly in the dark where something like this was concerned. I liked to know the lay of the land, so to speak, especially if there might be danger involved.

Of course, I would have Major Ramsey with me this time. And I had the sneaking suspicion that, unlike Uncle Mick or my cousins, he would be armed. I didn't really know if this was a positive thing or not. The possibility of violence wasn't at all comfortable. But I supposed if there was someone who was going to try to do violence to us, at least we were capable of defending ourselves.

We had arranged to meet on a corner a few streets away from the Bell and Harp. The major had offered to send the car for me, but, in the end, we had agreed it would be for the best if we didn't draw unnecessary attention to me or my residence. Besides, I wasn't worried about being alone. I had always been able to take care of myself.

And so I slipped out of my flat not long before midnight and began the walk toward the corner where he would pick me up. I said nothing to Nacy about this adventure, and I sincerely hoped that I would be alive and back in my bed by morning.

The streets were eerily quiet. I didn't know if I would ever get used to the darkness that blanketed everything. London had always seemed so very alive to me, so bright and full of life. Now, suddenly, it was like the city had closed its eyes and fallen into a deep sleep. I reminded myself that asleep was better than dead. Sooner or later, we would wake up again.

I encountered only three or four people in the whole of my walk, and none of them paid me the slightest bit of notice. They were likely going to or from jobs, their minds preoccupied by what had passed or what lay ahead. I supposed the same could be said of me.

I reached the rendezvous point, as Major Ramsey had insisted on calling it, at Sloane Square in plenty of time. The night air was cool, and I stood still in the shadow of the Royal Court Theatre, currently a cinema, breathing it in and listening to the unusual quiet of a city gone dark.

I had heard that some thieves were intensely focused right before a job, that they trained their mind to think of nothing else but the task ahead. I wasn't among their lot. Oh, I was focused enough, and I was aware of the dangers the night held, but I didn't allow myself to dwell on them. I would face my challenges as they came and not conjure them up beforehand.

I heard the car before I saw it. There weren't many on the roads in this area at this time of night, with petrol rationing such as it was and the blackouts making the whole process that much more hazardous.

When the car pulled into view, I couldn't help but scoff at its utter lack of subtlety. It was big and black and quite official looking. No subterfuge here. The thing might as well have had "His Majesty's Government" written on the side of it.

It pulled up to the curb and the back door opened. Major Ramsey's solid form emerged from the car. He was dressed all in black, too, I noted as I stepped from the shadows to meet him. If he was looking to keep from calling attention to himself, though, I didn't think he'd done a good job of it. The dark clothes gave him a somewhat menacing air, but I supposed it was less conspicuous than his uniform would have been.

"Good evening, Miss McDonnell," he said, as politely as you please. If we hadn't been on the way to commit a burglary, he might have been picking me up for an evening on the town.

"Good evening," I said.

I got into the car and he slid in beside me. Then we pulled away and rode along in silence. I glanced again at Major Ramsey, wondering if he might say something about the mission, as he liked to call it. But he didn't even look at me.

I tried to gauge his mood. I didn't detect any tension in him, not more than usual anyway. From what I had seen of him thus far, he was never completely relaxed. I had begun to realize, however, that this wasn't a mark of tension, exactly. It seemed to be more a constant state of readiness, as though he was waiting for whatever might spring up. I supposed it was a good trait for someone in his profession, and it would definitely be useful if we encountered any trouble tonight.

The driver seemed to know where we were going, but it was difficult for me to see in the darkness, and I found it hard to maintain my sense of direction. After a while, we reached a part of town with which I had no familiarity, but which I pegged as probably somewhere in South Kensington.

The car stopped suddenly, and Major Ramsey opened the door and stepped out immediately, motioning for me to follow him.

I got out, and, almost before the major had closed the door softly behind me, the car drove away.

Without hesitation, Major Ramsey took my arm and led me

into a nearby alleyway. It was almost completely dark in the narrow space, most of the moonlight obscured by the buildings on either side, so I found myself glad that his hand remained on my arm as we moved forward. I wasn't sure how he was seeing his way in the dark, but I trusted his instincts and allowed him to pull me along after him.

A few moments later, we came out on another street, stopping in the shadowed mouth of the alleyway, where we couldn't be seen. With the buildings no longer towering overhead on either side, there was a bit of light from the night sky, and I could make out the layout of the street.

It was a posh area, that much was certain. The houses were large and imposing, and there was an air of grandeur that seemed to permeate even the trees and iron gates. Not Belgravia or Mayfair, but certainly plummy.

As I was casing the neighborhood, the major was looking up and down the street, and at last he nodded, taking my elbow again, and led me out into the street.

"I'm not going to run from you, you know," I said, looking down at his hand on my arm.

"Of course not. But if anyone happens to come along, we'll merely look like a couple taking a walk."

It wasn't the best of plans; I was sure anyone with half a brain could see that we weren't a couple, not with him dragging me down the street by the elbow.

"Then perhaps you'd better let me hold your arm rather than the other way around," I suggested sardonically.

He looked at me for just a moment and then, dropping his hand, held out his arm in an exaggerated gesture of courtesy that was all the more ridiculous for the fact that we were standing in the middle of the street dressed all in black, preparing to break into a house.

But I slipped my arm through his, noting in a disinterested sort of way the hard muscle beneath the smooth fabric of his shirt.

We walked at a steady pace, not leisurely enough for a couple out for a romantic evening stroll. Neither of us spoke, and I knew that, if we were being observed, we must make a strange picture. We saw no one, however, and I hoped that it was late enough for us to avoid detection.

Finally, he stopped in a patch of shadows before an iron gate. "This is it," he said in a low voice.

I looked at the imposing residence. It was an impressive three-story building of gray stone, adorned with carefully cultivated ivy.

"This house will have staff," I said.

He glanced at me.

"It's much too grand not to."

"Don't you think we've thought of that?" he asked.

I pulled my arm from his, annoyed at his supercilious tone. "I don't know what you've thought, since you haven't told me anything."

He was unimpressed by my irritation. Without responding, he moved along the gate toward the back of the house. I stood still a moment in silent protest and then followed him.

The side gate was open, and we moved through the garden toward the back door.

I wondered briefly if he would need me to pick the lock. If so, I had come prepared. But so, it seemed, had the major. He moved without hesitation to the door and inserted a key he had apparently drawn from his pocket.

We slipped into the house, and he closed the door behind us. We didn't turn on our torches but stood in the stillness, listening. Everything was dark and quiet.

The house was, as he had said, empty of both residents and staff. I ought to have trusted that the government would be capable of getting information that was accurate, but I had never had a great deal of trust in the government.

"This way." Major Ramsey led me through the house without

pause. Either he had been here before, or he had done a thorough going-over of a map of the place. I followed behind him. I had worn soft-soled shoes, and so there was no sound, even as we walked across the polished wooden floors.

I glanced around as we made our way through several rooms, decorated in a wealthy though not extravagant manner. I surmised the owner of the house might be a bachelor gentleman, for there were none of the gewgaws that were usual to a house occupied by ladies. I supposed the paucity of decorative trinkets was a trait I recognized from my own upbringing. Uncle Mick had cleared away a good deal of Aunt Mary's things in order to put the memories behind him, and Nacy wasn't a woman who tended toward knickknacks.

But this house had gone beyond that. There were very few personal items at all, I realized. It was strange and a bit disappointing, for I had been hoping to be able to surmise the identity of the mysterious document holder. It was likely, of course, that most of his possessions had either been stored or removed from London for safety.

We went up the stairs then. It was a handsome wood staircase with a gleaming bannister. There was a rug along it that looked fairly new, as though the occupant of the house did not do a good deal of going up and down the stairs. This wasn't a primary residence, perhaps? Or perhaps he was a busy man and was seldom at home. Whatever the case, the house was kept in very good order, for none of the stairs creaked as we made our way upward. I almost wished they would have. Everything was so intensely silent.

Major Ramsey, to his credit, moved like a cat in the darkness. Despite the sturdiness of his frame, he was light on his feet and moved with easy assurance through the dark hallway ahead of me.

I appreciated that he didn't turn around to be sure I still followed. He trusted that I was keeping up with him in the darkness, though my steps were as silent as his.

At the end of the hallway, he stopped before a door. Reaching out, he tried the knob. It gave and the door opened ever so slightly.

I had begun to grow accustomed to the darkness, and, as I looked at his profile, I saw there was a flicker of a frown that crossed his brow. Had he expected the door to be locked?

He pushed the door open farther and stepped into the room. I followed. Like the rest of the house, the dark room was made darker with blackout curtains. I would have to see the safe to work on it, and I'd rather not walk through a strange room without any knowledge of what furniture might be lying in wait to trip me.

"Shall I turn on my torch?" I asked.

"Wait a moment." His voice, appearing suddenly, practically in my ear, was so quiet I might almost have imagined it.

I hadn't realized he had moved so close. He had made absolutely no noise. I couldn't even hear him breathing now that he stood beside me, but I could feel the warmth coming off him in the cool room, and I found it distracting. I wasn't used to working this way, with someone literally hovering over my shoulder. Did he intend to trail behind me all the way to the safe on the wall?

We stood like that for a moment, still and silent. I didn't know what, exactly, we were waiting for. Surely the alarm would have been sounded by now had our arrival been detected. But this was his operation. We could play it his way. Within the hour, if all went well, my part of it would be done, and Uncle Mick and I could go back to our lives.

I knew I still had to face the safe, but I didn't foresee that being a problem. It was normally the entry into the house that worried me. That and the exit, but I supposed that Major Ramsey would be able to get us out of here as easily as he had got us in. It had all been rather simpler than I thought.

So now I had only to get into the safe, replace the papers, and we could be on our merry way.

At last, Major Ramsey spoke. "All right. Turn the torch on."

I removed a torch from my pocket and flicked it on, flashing the beam of light across the walls. The wall before us was a bank of covered windows. My light moved to the right wall. It was bookshelves, floor to ceiling, no room for the safe. I flashed it to the left, taking an automatic step in that direction.

Then I stopped suddenly, the beam from the torch shining against the wall.

There was something wrong. The door of the safe stood in plain view against the pale blue paint, and it appeared to be open. Surely that couldn't be right.

The major went over to the wall and looked inside the safe. I thought I heard him curse beneath his breath.

I moved toward him, my torch lighting on a painting on the floor, the one that had concealed the safe, no doubt. The gold frame was broken, as though it had fallen from the wall.

Then I saw something from the corner of my eye. Swinging the torch in that direction, I focused the light on a spot behind the sofa a few feet from the safe.

I barely stifled the gasp that rose to my lips.

A man lay on the floor, a thick, black pool of blood spreading beneath him.

CHAPTER EIGHT

I hadn't had what you might call a genteel upbringing, and I wasn't a shrinking violet by any means, but the unexpected sight of a man lying dead on the floor gave me quite a shock.

I stumbled backward, nearly dropping the torch and only barely managing to keep from crying aloud by pressing a hand to my mouth.

Major Ramsey had apparently caught a glimpse of the body in the flailing light of my torch, for in a moment he was at my side, a steadying hand on my arm.

"Don't scream," he said in a low voice. It was a stupid thing to say; if I was going to scream, I would have jolly well done it already.

He reached down and took the torch from my hand. His fingers as they brushed mine were perfectly warm. My own hands felt as though they had turned to ice.

"Perhaps you'd better look away," he said, as he shined the light back at the inert figure on the floor.

"I . . . I'm all right," I whispered, though I was lying through my teeth. My entire body was shaking, and I felt very much like I might be sick. Still, my eyes followed the beam of light to the body. It was horrible, yes, but there was something so shockingly out of the ordinary in seeing a man in a dinner jacket laid out on the floor of a library that I couldn't quite seem to make enough sense of it to lose my head.

It seemed he had been dead for some time, for he was very stiff. All the color had leached out of his face, leaving it a mottled gray, and his eyes were staring up at the ceiling. The blood beneath him had congealed into a thick, treacly puddle. I clenched my teeth against a wave of nausea.

Despite the ghastliness of it all, however, some coolheaded part of me took note that he hadn't been dead longer than a day or so, for there was no smell of death in the room. There was, though, now that I noticed it, the faintly metallic odor of blood. It wasn't strong enough to have called my attention to it before, but I was certainly aware of it now.

I wondered if that was why Major Ramsey had paused for as long as he had when we first entered the room. As an army major, the scent would no doubt be more familiar to him.

In the time it took for all of these thoughts to charge through my head, the major had moved to the body and crouched beside it. I thought, at first, he was going to check, just to be sure, if the man was dead, but instead he made a brisk but thorough search of the man's pockets. The beam of his torch moved once across the man's face, and I caught another glimpse of his staring brown eyes. I felt a little lurch in my stomach and turned my gaze away.

"How . . . how did he die?" I asked, though I was fairly certain I didn't want to know.

"His throat was slit," the major replied evenly.

I gasped. I wasn't completely a stranger to death, but I had never witnessed something so wretchedly violent. No matter what the man had done, no matter what his loyalties, I couldn't help but feel he hadn't deserved to be killed in this brutal way and left on the floor in a puddle of his own blood.

His search of the body apparently complete, Major Ramsey rose and moved to the big desk in the center of the room. With quick efficiency, he began moving things about and opening drawers to sift through them. Reaching into the final drawer, he drew something out and placed it in his pocket.

Then he crossed the room to me and took my arm. "Come," he said. "We need to leave."

"The papers aren't here?" I asked, though the answer was apparent enough.

He glanced at the open safe in the wall. "No, they're not here."

No, of course not. Why else would someone have killed this man? Someone had beaten us to the papers.

His hand still on my arm, Major Ramsey led me out of the room and back down the stairs. He was still holding on to me when we slipped out of the house and moved down the street, and I was glad of it, for my head was spinning just a tad.

We went a different way than we had come, going down several dark alleyways and across a silent green that might have been cheery with its leafy trees in the daylight but seemed somehow sinister in the damp darkness of night.

At the edge of the green, a safe distance from the house, he stopped near a row of hedges, which concealed us from the street, and turned to me. There was enough moonlight now that we could see each other. "Are you all right?" he asked.

The question surprised me. So did the look of concern that crossed his face as his eyes searched mine. My thoughts had been focused, as I assumed his had been, on our exit from the house. I hadn't stopped to take stock of my emotions, but I did so now, the intensity of all of it hitting me at once.

"Yes, I'm fine," I said faintly.

Then I turned and was immediately sick in the hedges.

It was rather embarrassing, but the major, to his credit, appeared to take it all in stride. He stood beside me and waited patiently.

"I . . . I'm sorry," I said at last, when I was sure I was once again in control of my digestive system.

"No need to apologize," he said, handing me a handkerchief. "I know what we discovered was rather a surprise."

I let out something like a strangled chuckle. "It certainly was that."

"Are you all right now?"

I nodded. It had been an ugly thing to come across and had clearly upset me more than I realized in the moment. Overall, though, I supposed I wasn't much the worse for wear from the experience. I hadn't known the man, after all.

"Was . . . was that your man on the fence?" I asked.

"It was, though someone seems to have given him a decisive shove off of it."

I was still a bit too shaken to appreciate his grim humor, but I noticed he didn't seem exceptionally surprised by this turn of events.

"Are we going to . . . call the police or something?" I asked.

"And tell them what?" he replied dryly. "That we broke into the house and discovered a dead body?"

I should have considered that, of course. How would we explain it? We couldn't very well tell them we had been there on government business, that the man had been involved in the transfer of secret documents to the enemy.

Now that my head was beginning to clear, another question occurred to me. If the man had been willing to hand over the papers, why had he been killed? To silence him? Or was there some other reason?

I didn't ask those questions, though. Something in the major's expression told me he wasn't in the mood for speculation. Instead, I asked what was foremost in my mind. "What do we do now?"

"That seems to be the question," he replied.

He said nothing further, but turned and, moving along a path through the hedges, began walking down the street. I followed, and a moment later the car pulled up out of the fog as if by magic and we got into it.

We went back to the dungeon. Wordlessly passing the young man at the front desk, the major led me down the long hallway, past the room in which he had questioned me the night Uncle Mick and I had been caught, to a room at the end.

He opened the door and motioned for me to precede him. I stepped into the dark room and he switched on a light and came in behind me. It was his office, I realized, glancing around. From his general bearing and demeanor, I would have guessed it would be spartan and utilitarian, but this room, while tidy, had a cozy sort of air to it. The furniture was large and comfortable looking, the clearly expensive rug was well worn, and there was a fireplace with recent ashes still in the hearth.

There were also papers in stacks on the desk, maps on the walls, and stacks of books set here and there. I had the impression that this was a room much lived in; though very different from Uncle Mick's shed, it had the same sort of atmosphere.

"Sit," he said, motioning to one of the leather chairs before his desk. The kindly manner he had shown me in the park had apparently been overruled by his training as an officer, and he had begun to speak in commands. "Come here." "Do this."

If it continued, I would have to remind him I wasn't one of his soldiers, but I supposed now was not the moment to challenge him. And, anyway, I found that I was suddenly very tired. I supposed the shock had had more of an effect on me than I had realized.

I was still a bit annoyed with myself for having been sick, and I determined that if I ever again encountered a murder victim, I would keep my composure. I was nothing if not adaptable.

I went to the chair and sat. Major Ramsey didn't follow suit. Instead, he began moving around the room in measured steps that would've been called pacing if he hadn't been keeping himself under tight control.

He was terribly angry. I could tell that much. Maybe most people wouldn't have put that particular emotion to his actions, but I had always been good at reading emotions. And Major Ramsey was livid. His posture was even more rigid than usual, his jaw tight, his eyes hard.

I knew he was going over the details of the mission again and probably figuring out how he was going to report our failure to whoever his superiors were.

I realized something else, too. Though he hadn't gone into tonight expecting to discover a body, it wasn't the murder that was bothering him. I supposed it was natural given that he was in the military, but the bloody scene hadn't shaken him in the least.

Indeed, I thought by now he had probably dismissed the murdered man from his mind and had turned his attention to the matter at hand. What would be done now that the papers were gone? Who had them and was it still possible to retrieve them? That would be what concerned him.

It occurred to me that I could ask to go home. I had done my part, after all. What further need could he have of me? But I was curious. And some part of me, the part that was used to succeeding at what I did, felt the same frustration the major was experiencing. So I sat and waited.

There was a tap on the door. The major ignored it, but a moment later the door slid open and the glum-faced man who worked at the front of the office looked in. He'd been sitting there tonight when we'd come in, though I think one look at the major's face had been enough to keep him from asking us any questions.

"I've made tea," he said, pushing the door open a bit more. I saw that he was holding a tray.

I glanced at Major Ramsey, but he didn't acknowledge the young man.

So I rose from the chair and went to take it from him. "Thank you."

He nodded, his gaze moving back to the major before he stepped out of the room and closed the door behind him. I had an impression he was afraid of Major Ramsey. Not that I entirely blamed him at the moment. The major did look fierce. I suspected he might be something of a tyrant when crossed.

Well, I wasn't afraid of tyrants.

I set the tray on the corner of the desk and poured myself a cup of tea. I gave myself one large spoonful of sugar and then, after a slight pause, another. I supposed the government owed me that much after what I'd been through tonight.

"How do you take yours, Major?" I asked. I'd been too focused on my steak and kidney pie at the pub to notice if he liked milk or sugar.

He turned and looked at me as though I had lost my mind. "I beg your pardon?"

"How do you take your tea?" I repeated slowly.

"I don't want any tea," he snapped, turning his back to resume his pacing.

This was a very different side of Major Ramsey. Always before he had been calm and composed. This tightly wound gentleman was something else altogether. I found I was more comfortable with this version of him than I was with the other. High temper I knew how to deal with. I'd had enough practice with Uncle Mick and the boys over the years.

"You're not going to do any good to anyone by wearing out the rug," I said.

He stopped and turned, his pale gaze boring into mine. I recognized it was his way of giving me a setdown without saying anything.

Obviously, Major Ramsey was not much used to criticism. I supposed this came from his military rank and what seemed to be a natural confidence, probably inherited along with those good looks and a good family name. With all of that at a man's disposal, most people were bound to bend to his will.

Most, but not all. "I know you're angry," I said, "but pacing won't do you any good and tea will."

He stared at me. "I'm . . . angry?" he repeated.

I nodded. "It's been a rubbish night, but I know anger is the foremost emotion in your mind. You don't like having your plans foiled."

He swore beneath his breath at my analysis of his character. To be fair, I probably would have done the same if the situations were reversed.

"The fate of our country may hang in the balance," he said, his voice severe.

"So you mentioned," I said. "But there's nothing to say that we can't get the papers back."

"Oh, we'll get them back." There was a different set to his mouth now, something harder. "I had just hoped we would be able to do things the easy way."

I knew what he meant. They would have to kill to get them back.

I found I wasn't shocked by the idea. Maybe I should have been, but I knew well enough what was done in times like these, that lives were taken much more easily in wartime than in a time of peace. And, after all, whoever had the papers now had already killed to get them.

"Perhaps there's still a way," I mused. "To do it without anyone knowing."

"After what's been done, it isn't likely we can maintain the element of surprise or substitute the false documents without the Germans knowing about it. At best, we can hope to prevent the originals from getting into the wrong hands. Somehow our plan has been blown all to pieces, and it's left for us to collect the bits and make some sense of them."

"Who do you think killed him?" I asked. "Was it a German agent?"

If that was the case, it seemed the papers were already lost. After all, the murdered man had been dead some time; the killer could be well on his way back to Germany with the documents by now.

He shook his head. "No, not a German agent. We've heard through our networks that a drop is planned with a German agent for sometime next week. This was another traitor."

"You said the dead man had divided loyalties. You think he decided not to turn the papers over to the Germans, after all, and another traitor killed him and took them to deliver to the Nazis?"

"It seems so."

"Do you have any idea who it might be?"

He seemed to be considering, and I had the impression that he was not thinking over my question so much as how he wanted to answer it. At last, he said, "Yes, there are a few people it could possibly be. We'll find our man."

Something in his tone made me quite sure he would.

"What about the dead man?" I asked.

He looked at me. "What about him?"

As I had suspected, the man was no longer of any interest to him.

"Surely his death can't remain a secret for long?"

"No, but it will be ruled a case of robbery. You know, better than I do, that there are a great many thieves on the loose in London at present."

For some silly reason, the reminder smarted.

There wasn't anything malicious in the comment; he simply stated it as fact. But it made me see myself in a way I had never really done before. Oh, I knew well enough what we were. There had never been any wool over my eyes about our profession. Uncle Mick had never tried to make it out as though we were a merry bunch of noble thieves.

But I didn't like to be lumped in with violent criminals. And perhaps, I admitted, a part of me wanted to be something more.

"I feel a bit bad we left him lying there," I said.

He looked up at me, as though he had never considered that particular aspect. "He'll be discovered soon enough."

"Yes, but it seems rather . . . cold somehow."

"There are a lot of things we have to do that would probably seem cold to you, Miss McDonnell."

I wasn't sure what he meant by that grim statement, but I nodded.

The major moved to take the chair beside me, rather than the one behind his desk, and stretched out his long legs. I noticed suddenly that he looked tired. There were creases in the bronzed skin along his eyes that I had never noticed there before, and, in the lamplight, I could see the golden gleam of stubble beginning to rise on his jaw. He suddenly looked human, which was disconcerting in a way I couldn't quite name.

It was on the tip of my tongue to tell him he should get some rest, but it certainly wasn't my place. What was more, I knew he wasn't likely to rest anytime soon, not until he got things sorted and he had decided what our next course of action was going to be.

Our next course of action. I was surprised by the thought. Did I mean to go on helping him? After all, I had done as he asked. By rights, Uncle Mick and I should be on our way home now. Somehow, however, things felt unfinished, as though there was some part I still needed to play.

"I take my tea black," he said suddenly.

Of course, he did.

I poured him a cup of tea and then, before handing it over to him, stirred in a bit of sugar. "You could use some sweetness," I said.

He took the cup from me without reply and took a sip of it. In addition to being sweet, it was scalding hot, but he didn't seem to notice.

"You kept your cool tonight," he said. "That was well done."

I turned to look at him, shocked at the compliment. This mild approval, coming from the source it did, seemed high praise indeed.

"I was sick in the bushes," I reminded him.

"Not until after. It's in the moment that coolness is necessary, and you held up when it counted."

"A cool head is a necessity in safecracking," I told him. "We've had some close scrapes before."

He nodded. "All the same, a lot of people would have gone to pieces upon discovering a body. If you'd have screamed, we might have been in trouble."

"I'm not given to screaming at surprises," I said.

"No. I don't suppose you are."

He took another sip of tea.

"What's going to happen now?" I asked.

"That is something we're going to have to consider," he said. "I'll speak with my superiors in the morning and see what course of action they recommend."

He rose from his seat, setting his cup and saucer on the corner of his desk. "You may as well go home, Miss McDonnell."

"What about my uncle?"

He seemed to consider this. At last, he nodded. "You've fulfilled your part of the bargain. I'll have your uncle released in the morning."

"Then . . . that's it?" I asked, trying not to let the disappointment creep into my voice.

"As far as I can see, yes. You're free to go."

For some reason, I didn't like the easy way he dismissed me from all of this. I knew perfectly well I was nothing more to him than a tool in this plan, but I was a useful tool nonetheless. Not something to be cast aside.

"I'm in it this far," I said before I could think better of it. "Isn't there something else I can do to help?"

He looked down at me. I couldn't tell what he was thinking, and it was a moment before he spoke. "It depends, I suppose, on where we go from here."

"If there's anything I can do, I'd like to see this through." It wasn't until I said the words that I realized how true they were. I wanted to be a part of this, not because I had to, but because, for the first time in a long time, I felt as though I was doing something good.

He studied me for just a moment. Then he moved to the door and pulled it open. "It's been a long night. Go home and rest. I'll be in touch."

I rose from my chair. It wasn't exactly promising, but I knew there was no use arguing. He was right; it had been a long night. And strong tea or no, I could do with a rest.

I paused as I reached the door, wondering what I should say. Nothing clever came to mind. "Good night, Major Ramsey," I said.

"Good night, Miss McDonnell."

CHAPTER NINE

True to Major Ramsey's word, Uncle Mick was home by breakfast.

I was at the house when he arrived, having just finished eating a bowl of Nacy's delicious porridge with eggs and bacon. I had been too shaken up by the night's events to sleep much after getting home in the early hours of the morning, and now, as Nacy cleared away the dishes, I sat at the table lost in thought.

The matter of the murder and the missing documents was still very much on my mind. I didn't know why I should be so concerned about all of it. It wasn't my problem to solve, after all. But there was a strange, unsettled feeling that hung over me anyway. A traitor had killed a man in cold blood and was giving our secrets to the enemy, and it made me angry.

The major had been so tight-lipped about it all, but surely there was a way around his cageyness. Perhaps an avenue or two I could pursue on my own.

"Penny for your thoughts, lass."

I looked up at the sound of a voice in the doorway.

"Uncle Mick!" I jumped from my chair and hurried to him, embracing him tightly. Though I prided myself on being a capable and independent woman, there was no denying that the sight of him was a weight lifted off my shoulders.

Releasing him at last, I stepped back to look him over, just as I had done to Felix when he had appeared at my door. Uncle Mick was a bit bedraggled and in need of a shave but none the worse for wear, all told. It had only been a few days, of course, though it seemed much longer.

"I'm so glad you're home," I said.

"You oughtn't fret so, Ellie girl," he said, patting my head, an affectionate gesture that had carried over from my childhood. "It's not as though I'd have languished away there. It was almost like a fancy hotel, lass! Had a gourmet chef, I'd expect, for the food was excellent—though not up to Nacy's standards, of course—and a bed so soft it might as well have been made of clouds."

I smiled. How like him to find the silver lining. "That all sounds rather luxurious," I said, "but it might have ended in a serious charge. We're lucky things worked out as they did."

He shrugged. "I wasn't worried. It'll take more than something like that to keep your old Uncle Mick down. Is that breakfast I smell?"

That was also very like Uncle Mick. He never took anything as seriously as he ought. It was a charming trait at times, and it made life seem much less vexing when viewed through the lens of his good humor. But there were other times when he ought to have been a bit more solemn, and I felt barely escaping a lengthy prison sentence was one of them.

"First, tell me what the major said to you," I said, glancing over my shoulder to make sure Nacy had not returned to the dining room. I hadn't yet told Nacy the nature of our ordeal. She was sharp and knew that something was amiss, of course, but I supposed she knew I would reveal everything in time. I had never been any good at keeping secrets from Nacy.

"I didn't see the major," Uncle Mick said. "They came to my room and told me I was free to go. You can bet I didn't stand around to ask questions."

"No," I agreed. I didn't know why, but I was a bit disappointed

Uncle Mick hadn't seen Major Ramsey. I supposed I was curious to know what he would have had to say about our adventure. And I also wanted to know if he intended to let us continue helping.

"It came off all right, then?" Uncle Mick asked. "The job, I mean."

"Not exactly," I said.

In a low voice, I related to him the details of what had happened. It was strange to me now, as though it had all happened a long time ago. It seemed impossible that it had only been the night before. Even the grim element of having found a body seemed like the dregs of some bad dream that had faded with daylight.

He let out a low whistle when I had finished. "A body, was it? It seems this is a serious business."

I nodded. "It's quite serious, I think. The major didn't confide in me, of course, but I had the impression this was a blow to their plans."

"What's the plan now, then?" Uncle Mick asked.

That was the question, wasn't it? For some reason, I was reluctant to tell Uncle Mick how much I hoped we might continue to be involved. It wasn't that I thought he would object. After all, he had argued that it was our duty to do our part. Why, then, did I already feel as though there was a tug-of-war between my life a few days ago and the one now?

"Major Ramsey said he would contact me," I said at last.

He looked at me, his gaze sharp, but when he spoke his tone was light. Focus on what's before you and wait to see what comes. That was his motto, and he proved it again when he spoke.

"Going to contact you later, is he?" he said. "Then I guess there's naught to do but wait. Where's that breakfast? I'm half-starved. Prison works up a man's appetite."   /

I could tell that Uncle Mick, for all his cheer and good humor, was tired, and I soon left the house so that, indulged with good food and a comfortable bed, he could get some rest.

Nacy was working in our garden, and I went to help her. She'd kept a kitchen garden even before the war, but it was bigger now, every available space given over to rows of vegetables. With the Germans marauding their way across Europe, the supply lines to Britain were tightening. We had all quickly realized that it was necessary to do as much as possible to help ourselves.

I looked at the neat rows, which had produced tomatoes, lettuce, onions, radish, cabbage, turnips, peas, and other fresh produce over the past few months. There was a beauty in it, in the symmetry of the rows and the way the greens glistened with dew. There were birds chirping happily as they pranced and flew around the garden. Even with the noise of cars in the background, it was like a bit of the country in the middle of the city.

"Your uncle hasn't learned his lesson, I take it," Nacy said, as she pulled up an encroaching weed.

"What do you mean?" I knelt in one of the rows, the wetness of the dewy vegetation seeping into my skirt, and pulled at the weeds there.

"I know that twinkle in his eye. Whatever he's gotten into, he plans to get further into it still. It'll lead to trouble, I'm sure. It usually does."

"Oh, I don't . . ." I began.

She waved a gloved hand, covered in dirt. "You needn't start with your excuses, Ellie. I know well enough when there's something going on beneath my nose, something out of the usual, I mean. None of you could hide a thing from me since the day you were born, so don't try now. I suppose you'll tell me about it in good time."

It wasn't a rebuke. Nacy had always known that there were certain things she was better off not knowing. She didn't ask questions unless she was sure she wanted to know the answers.

Pulling at the bits of green growing up around the vegetables, I wondered if she was right. Was Uncle Mick as eager to go on with all of this as I was? I had been a bit disappointed that he hadn't had any information to give about Major Ramsey and his operation. He had had very little to relate about his time in custody at all, as he had remained in his makeshift cell. He had been kept out of the operation, but, like Nacy, I had the impression he intended to go forward, not back.

We finished the weeding in a comfortable silence, and then I rose, brushing the dirt and bits of greenery from my clothes.

"Do you need help with anything else, Nacy?" I asked.

"No, go and get some rest, love. I can see you're all in."

I hadn't been able to hide that from her either.

Returning to my flat, I put the kettle on. I was tired, but I knew I wouldn't be able to rest. Not yet. I almost wished that Felix would show up again, as I could use some of his charm to distract me.

I had just finished drinking my tea when there was a knock at the door. Had Felix read my mind? It wouldn't be the first time he had done such a thing.

When I opened the door, however, I was not met with Felix's smiling face. Instead, an older man in a dark suit stood on the step. "Miss McDonnell?" he asked politely. In just those two words I caught the hint of an unfamiliar accent.

"Yes," I answered cautiously.

"Major Ramsey sends his regards and asks that you accompany me to his office."

I somehow suspected the major hadn't put the request exactly in those polite terms, but this gentleman was too kind to phrase it as the command it was. He was somewhere around sixty, with a shock of white hair and a merry twinkle in his brown eyes that couldn't be disguised by his formal bearing.

"If you'll give me just a moment . . ." I said. I had, of course, bathed and dressed before eating breakfast, but my hair had begun its revolt early today, aided by the breezes in the garden, and I certainly hadn't applied any makeup.

"Certainly, miss. Take your time."

He turned and went back to the front of the house, and I spent a few moments making myself presentable, running a brush over my hair and putting on a bit of lipstick. Then I left a note for Nacy or Uncle Mick on my table where they would be sure to see it if they came looking for me. I felt as though the major might have telephoned me rather than sending someone, but I supposed it had been his intention to make it a difficult request to refuse.

The car was parked in front of Uncle Mick's house, not the same big black car in which we had ridden last night, but still conspicuous enough.

"Did he ask for me and my uncle?" I asked, as I reached the driver. It occurred to me that, if we were going to continue to aid the major, he might want to see both of us.

The driver opened the door for me, and I could see that Uncle Mick was already in the backseat. "Looks like the adventure continues, eh, lass?"

"I suppose so," I said.

I got into the car, and the driver closed the door.

"Looks like rain," Uncle Mick said to the driver as we pulled away and began the drive toward the major's office.

I was glad he had taken up talking to the man. I wasn't accustomed to being chauffeured about, and it felt strange to either talk to Uncle Mick and ignore the man in the front seat or to ride in silence with someone else at the wheel.

"Yes, sir. That it does."

"We're not used to having a driver," I said. "We used to drive ourselves, before all this started."

"Got an old car, but we don't need it enough to use up the petrol," Uncle Mick said.

The driver nodded. "I'm afraid the war has changed a great deal for many of us."

I still could not place his accent. "You've come to London recently?" I asked.

"I come from Poland," he said.

"Oh," I said. There was not more I could say, not when I knew that his homeland had been so ruthlessly overrun by the Germans.

"My wife and I, we left before the Germans come," he went on. "Many we knew were not so fortunate."

"Yes, I imagine so," I said, my heart going out to him.

"My sons . . . I do not know what has become of them."

"I'm sorry," I said softly.

"One of my sons is missing, too," Uncle Mick said. For the briefest moment, there was the heaviness of shared loss around us.

"But we hope for the best, don't we?" Uncle Mick added in that cheery, genuine way of his. "If there's one thing we've a lot of in this country, it's hope."

The driver smiled at us in the mirror. "That we do, sir."

For not the first time since this dreadful war had started, I had the sensation that I was bound to people who might otherwise have been perfect strangers, that we were all connected by some invisible strings that pulled us together in ways we might never have imagined.

"My name's Ellie, and this is my uncle, Mick," I said. "What's your name?"

"Jakub," he said.

"I'm glad to have met you, Jakub," I told him, and I meant it.

We reached the major's office. It was the first time I had seen it in the daylight, and I thought that, for all their pretenses of being a secret organization, they didn't seem to be all that secretive in their movements.

Then again, this was not the sort of building that would call attention to itself. That is, it was no more ostentatious than any of the other houses in Belgravia. Several of these buildings had been lined with sandbags, and there was nothing to much differentiate this particular house from any other. I supposed one never knew what went on behind closed doors.

We bid Jakub farewell and made our way up the front steps. The door was locked—one had to take some precautions as a clandestine government agency, I supposed—but when I rang the bell it was opened almost immediately by the same glum young man. I wondered when it was that he slept. Perhaps that was why he always looked down in the mouth. They ought to let the poor boy rest.

"The major's asked to speak to you alone, Miss McDonnell, before he speaks to both of you."

I glanced at Uncle Mick and he gave a shrug. "Waiting is something I'm good at."

The young man looked relieved, as though he had expected us to protest. I had the impression he was always waiting for disaster.

"We haven't been properly introduced," I said, extending my hand. "I'm Ellie."

He looked surprised but instinctively reached out to shake my hand. "Miss McDonnell."

I shook my head. "Ellie. We're friends around here, aren't we?"

He gave me the barest smile, the first I had seen on his face. He looked suddenly very young. "If you say so. My name's Oscar. Oscar Davies."

"It's good to meet you, Oscar."

Uncle Mick introduced himself, too, and I felt we were now all one big, happy spy family.

"If you'll just follow me," Oscar Davies said, immediately falling back into his role as nervous secretary. I knew the way well enough, as I had been here not twelve hours before, but I let him lead me to the door at the end of the hallway. He knocked on it once.

"Enter."

He pushed the door open. "Miss McDonnell to see you, sir," he said, without fully entering the room. Then he stepped aside and left me standing in the doorway.

Major Ramsey had risen from behind his desk.

"Miss McDonnell. Good morning. Come in, won't you? And close the door. Davies is always neglecting things."

I looked behind me and saw that the young man had disappeared. Hopefully Uncle Mick would be able to put him at ease. He had a knack for that.

I entered the room and pulled the door shut behind me.

"Please, sit down," he said, motioning to the chairs before his desk. I moved forward and took the seat I had used earlier this morning. It seemed days ago that we had sat here discussing the murder and the missing documents, as though sleeping and breakfast had faded the memory into something hazy and indistinct.

The major, on the other hand, looked as though he hadn't slept, and if I'd had to bet on it, I'd have laid odds he hadn't eaten either. He had, however, shaved. He'd changed his clothes, too; he was back in uniform now, though his jacket hung over the back of his chair and he had loosened his necktie.

The tea items from last night had disappeared, and there was a pot of coffee on the desk. I could smell how strong it was from where I sat.

He made to take his seat and then, apparently realizing his informality, reached for his uniform tunic. I waved my hand. "Please don't bother with that for me."

He paused for just a moment before leaving the jacket where it was and settling into his seat. The slightest easing of his ramrod posture and the loose tie at his neck were the only concessions he seemed to be making for what was clearly a lack of sleep. His expression was alert as ever, so I don't really know what gave it away, but I could sense he was tired.

"Do you want some coffee?" he asked, motioning to the pot.

I shook my head. I couldn't abide the stuff. If and when we ran out of tea in this country, I would be prepared to go to battle with the Germans myself.

"There's been a development," he said without further ado.

My heart picked up the pace. "What is it?"

He opened the top drawer of his desk and pulled out a small, thin black book, which he tossed on the desk between us. "That," he said.

It was on the tip of my tongue to ask what it was, but then I remembered him taking something from the drawer in the dead man's desk last night and putting it into his pocket. No doubt it had been this book.

"May I?" I was already reaching for it as I asked. After all, if he didn't want me to handle it, he shouldn't have put it within grabbing distance.

I opened it and was a bit disappointed to see that it was a common datebook. The man had led a busy life, by the looks of it, because most of the pages were filled. When I flipped through it, though, I realized that I couldn't make out any of the words. Another language, perhaps? But no, the letters were all wrong in a way I couldn't quite name.

"Either his handwriting is atrocious, or it's coded," I said, looking up at the major.

"Quite possibly both," he replied. "Although, we've deciphered it."

"That was quick work," I said, impressed. While I had been pulling up weeds in the garden, the major and his people had apparently not stopped to rest.

"It wasn't a complicated cipher," he said. "I think our man was fairly confident he had the upper hand and wasn't overly concerned about being caught."

"A costly mistake," I said, blinking back the memory of the man's brown eyes staring, unseeing, from the bloody puddle on the floor. What had been the last thing that crossed his mind, as he lay there dying? Had he thought of his killer? Of his country? Of someone that he loved?

The major's gaze met mine, pulling me out of my grim day-dream. "In times like these, any mistake may prove costly. That's why we've got to move with care."

We? My heart pounded a bit at the word, but I forced myself to remain calm.

"Most of the entries in that book are of little use, but there is one thing of interest. He's scheduled a meeting with a contact for to-morrow night. The notation seems to indicate an exchange is going to be made."

"Then you know who the traitor is?" I wondered why I felt vaguely disappointed. Perhaps I had thought the matter would not be solved without my help. Well, this seemed easy enough if they had a name and place.

"Not exactly," he answered.

I waited. There was a long moment of quiet that was finally bro-ken when the major's chair creaked as he sat forward, his forearms leaning on the desk. I couldn't help but notice the way his uniform dress shirt outlined the muscles of his upper arms. He clearly hadn't spent all of his time in the military at a desk.

"I've spoken with my superiors about you."

My brows went up slightly.

"I've been given permission to take you into my confidence, to a degree."

"How flattering," I couldn't resist replying.

"I've told them that you did very well under pressure and that you may prove valuable in the next stage of the operation."

"How so?" I asked warily.

"The datebook indicates the dead man was to meet 'X' at a party hosted by Sir Nigel Randolf."

I let out a low whistle as Uncle Mick might have done. Sir Nigel Randolf was a bigwig, a newspaper tycoon who was as famous for his volatile temper as he was for the strong opinions he ran in his paper. He'd loudly voiced his support for German appeasement before the war and had been facing backlash ever since with all the good humor of a rabid bulldog.

"So, with our man dead, both the murderer and the contact are likely invited to the party."

"It would seem so," he said. "I've obtained a list of who was invited and we've narrowed it down to a few key players."

"But how does that help us? Surely we can't just barge into a party?"

"I've secured an invitation," he said.

Of course, he had. I didn't bother to ask how he had managed that. I was beginning to realize that Major Ramsey let very little stand in his way.

There was, however, one aspect of all of this that wasn't entirely clear to me.

"Where do I come in?"

"There is the possibility that Sir Nigel is in on the scheme himself."

He was watching me closely for a reaction, but there was little to see. I didn't find it hard to believe that a prewar German sympathizer might retain some of those feelings even after the fighting had started.

The next bit was more of a surprise. "I'd like you to open his safe during the party," he said.

"A tall order, isn't it?" I asked, trying not to show him how alarming I found the suggestion. Sneaking into an empty house was one thing; breaking into a safe during the middle of a party at a rich man's mansion was something else altogether.

"A job worthy of someone of your caliber," the major said, and I didn't miss the challenge inherent in his turning my words back on me. Fair enough.

I gave a short nod.

"Then you're willing to help?"

It might have been wise to think it over for a moment or two, but I'd already known what I was getting into when I came here. "Of course," I said. "But how am I supposed to get into the house without being seen in the midst of a big event like this? Do you plan to open a window for me to slip into or something?"

Those blue-lavender eyes of his locked onto mine. "Nothing so clandestine, Miss McDonnell. You'll walk in like all the other guests, as you'll be accompanying me to the party as my date."

CHAPTER TEN

I almost laughed at the thought of it, but I was fairly sure that wasn't a reaction he'd appreciate. I took a moment to collect myself, as it seemed things were spiraling rapidly out of control.

That was why he had asked to speak to me alone, then. He wanted to make sure I would accompany him before we heard Uncle Mick's protests. It was a clever bit of strategy, I had to admit.

"Will anyone you know be at this party?" I asked slowly.

"Yes," he replied.

"Then it's not going to work," I said lightly. "No one who knows you will believe for a moment you'd date a girl like me."

He studied me. "Why do you say that?"

I raised an eyebrow. "Isn't it obvious?"

"There's nothing overtly objectionable about you," he said.

"You oughtn't say such sweet things to me, Major Ramsey," I replied tartly. "It's liable to go to my head."

A hint of a smile crossed his lips. "Do you suppose you can manage to keep that sharp tongue of yours in check for the duration of the evening?"

I shrugged, knowing my eyes still held mischief. "I can generally manage to accomplish what I set out to do."

"Yes," he said. "I imagine that you do. Which is why I don't think you'll have any difficulty fitting in at this party, no matter what your background."

I stiffened a bit at this. "I know how to mix with swells, all right," I told him. "I've had a proper education, and this won't be the first time I've mingled with a high society set. You needn't worry that I won't know which forks and glasses to use."

"I didn't mean to insinuate any such thing," he said. "I only meant that I've noticed there's a certain gentility to you that would not be out of place among the upper classes."

I felt sure there was an insult in there somewhere, but I couldn't exactly put my finger on it. Nevertheless, he was right. Uncle Mick had made sure I was properly educated and that I knew the ins and outs of good society. I hadn't gone to university, but I'd worked hard—and excelled—at my schooling and served a term at finishing school for good measure. My accent, while obviously not as cut-glass as the major's, was polished enough for elegant company. I might not be a proper society lady, but I'd learned to pass for something close to one. It was better that way when we were trying to do a job, to be able to blend in. It was important to be able to insert oneself into the mind of the quarry.

Prepared or not, though, the thought of attending such an event made me just the slightest bit uneasy. I would never have admitted that to the major, of course, but I felt it all the same. It wasn't that I didn't think I could do it. There had been few times in my life when I had doubted my capabilities. I hadn't been raised that way. Growing up, I had seen Uncle Mick accomplish everything he had put his mind to, and it had never occurred to me that I wasn't capable of achieving the same things. He had never treated me differently because I was a girl—not much differently, anyway.

But it was one thing sneaking into a dark house in the dead of night to open a safe. That was something I knew how to do. I knew—or had at least thought I knew—what to expect. It wouldn't be the same at a party. There would be a house full of people, eyes on us from all angles.

And there would be a killer in our midst.

If the major noticed my hesitation, however, he didn't acknowledge it. "I'll pick you up tomorrow evening at nineteen hundred hours."

That was it. No pleasantries, no options. He would pick me up, and he would expect me to be ready. I mused that it was probably the way he conducted all his dinner dates.

I gave a little sigh. "All right."

His gaze swept over me in an assessing way, as though taking in the quality of my clothes. "We'll get you an appropriate evening gown," he said.

My chin tipped up a bit at what he seemed to be insinuating. "What makes you think that I don't have one already?"

"Have you?"

I had challenged him defensively, automatically, but now I thought of the dress that hung in my closet, the one I had always worn to dances and the like. It was nice enough, but I had a feeling it wouldn't pass muster at an event held by Sir Nigel Randolf. It might be a difficult situation to remedy, especially in the next twenty-four hours.

He seemed to be following my train of thought, for he said, "It's all right if you haven't. We'll get something sent over."

"I should hate to be in your debt." It was a polite turn of phrase, but I meant it. I didn't want to owe Major Ramsey any more than I already did.

"We'll take it out of your wages, shall we?" he asked.

I thought he was teasing me, but then I realized that he was serious. "What wages?"

"You're going to be paid for your work, of course. You didn't expect to do this for free?"

"I thought I was doing it to *remain* free," I replied.

"That was the initial inducement, yes, but you fulfilled that part of the bargain. As you are choosing to remain in our employ, you'll be paid for your services. You'll need something to live on now that there will be no more thievery in the foreseeable future."

This was something I hadn't counted on, and it took me by surprise.

"We'll put your uncle on the payroll as well," he said. "He will doubtless be of use to us. I'll discuss the particulars with both of you in a few moments."

"That's . . . that's very kind," I said.

He went on without acknowledging me. "You can leave your measurements with Davies before you go, and he'll see to it that they get something sent over to you by tomorrow. I assume you have the appropriate . . . cosmetics and the like?"

I nodded. "I can even manage to control my hair when I set my mind to it."

His gaze flickered almost imperceptibly to the black waves framing my face. Out of the corner of my eye, I could see an errant curl making an escape near my temple, but I suppressed the urge to push it back behind my ear.

"I am certain you'll be quite presentable," he said, in that charming way he had of hovering right between compliment and rudeness.

"Now," he said, rising from his chair. "We'll discuss things further with your uncle."

He went to the door and pulled it open. "Davies," he called. "Send in Mr. McDonnell."

I heard an indistinct sound at the end of the hallway. Davies hopping to, no doubt.

Major Ramsey came back to his desk. "Difficulties with the telephones," he said. "I can't ring Davies from here at present."

That was as good an opening as any to ask what I'd been

wondering since the first night I'd been brought here. "What sort of operation is this, anyway?"

"What do you mean?"

"I mean this," I said, waving my hand to indicate the house in general. "This clearly isn't a government building."

"No," he said. "It's a private residence that's been requisitioned."

"Whose residence is it?" I asked.

There was a brief pause. "Mine."

The door opened and Uncle Mick came in before I could reply.

I ought to have realized. After all, his office had a comfortable, settled feeling to it, and he moved about as though he owned the place. Then again, he moved about that way everywhere he went.

Still, I had to adjust the category into which I'd placed him in my head. I had guessed he was probably from a well-off family, but, somehow, a Belgravia residence was a level or two up from what I'd assumed.

"Good morning, Mr. McDonnell," he said.

"Good morning, Major."

The two of them acted as though they hadn't been prisoner and jailer a few short hours ago. How quickly we adapt in wartime.

Uncle Mick took a seat and accepted a cup of the major's sooty coffee, and then we got down to business.

"I've informed Miss McDonnell that we have further need of your . . . unique set of skills," Major Ramsey said. "You'll both be asked to sign the Official Secrets Act, and you'll be paid for your services."

"We'll do what you need us to, Major, but for our country," Uncle Mick replied. "Not for money." I recognized that slight lift of his chin. My uncle was a proud man. We might not always be honest, but we worked for what we had nonetheless.

The major was, as usual, unmoved. "All the same, it is preferable for us to pay you than to have you make your money . . . elsewhere."

It was clear enough what he meant, but he decided to make it clearer. "What I'm saying is this: if I hear of any illegal activities occurring, I won't hesitate to turn either of you over to the proper authorities."

I nodded. Perhaps I was growing accustomed to the major's rough edges because I didn't even feel annoyed by the threat. Deep down, I knew we were fortunate to get this chance. I felt, for once, grateful to the major rather than antagonized by him. It would be a weight off to know we had a bit of money coming in.

Uncle Mick seemed to feel the same way, for a small smile crossed his lips and he gave the major a jaunty salute. "Righto, sir."

"Now that that's settled, we'll get back to the matter at hand," the major said as he sat back in his chair again. "The man whose body we stumbled across was called Harden. He was the owner of a factory, at which weapons are currently being produced."

My senses prickled at this newest bit of information. It didn't take a genius to make the obvious inference. "Then the documents were weapons information," I said.

The major tipped his head. "He had a meeting scheduled to pass them off tomorrow night, if his datebook is correct."

He gave Uncle Mick a brief summary of what he'd told me about the party at Sir Nigel Randolf's house, casually dropping in the fact that I'd be attending as his date. Uncle Mick glanced at me at this point but said nothing. I supposed he'd have something to say later.

"How do we know whoever killed him wasn't who he planned to meet at the party, surprising him early, so to speak?" Uncle Mick asked.

It was a fair point. "If they already have the documents, they'll have no need to turn up at the rendezvous point," I pointed out. Rendezvous point. Two days in government service, and I was already beginning to pick up their lingo.

"There would be little reason to kill him in his home, not when the papers were coming to them at the party," Major Ramsey said. "It would have been an unnecessary risk. I don't entirely discount it for one reason, which I will address in a moment. However, I believe Harden had an accomplice, and that it was this person who double-crossed Harden, possibly to claim whatever compensation they were offered for himself. That accomplice no doubt knew about the meeting and will keep it in order to pass off the information as originally planned.

"Frankly, we're not as concerned with who the killer might be as to who he contacts," the major went on. "One of the people at the party is planning to pass the documents off to the Germans. We need to discover who that person is and substitute the false documents if possible. Or stop them at the very least."

"A 'party' is a big group," Uncle Mick said. "You say you've narrowed it down a bit?"

"Yes," the major answered. "There are five people we suspect may be involved."

Uncle Mick settled into his chair. "Give us the rundown, then."

The major hesitated, as I was beginning to realize he usually did before revealing a new piece of information. He liked to get it settled in his head first, I supposed, to organize what and how much information he was going to give up. I suspected he'd be a marvel at cards.

"The dead man, Harden, and the suspected German collaborators all belong to the same collector's club. We believe that it may be a front for a pro-German group that has been operating in this country since before the war. It is, after all, an excellent way for a disparate group of people to meet without attracting too much attention. As I mentioned, there's Sir Nigel himself. You know he owns *The Old Smoke*?"

"Yes. And he wasn't exactly subtle about his associations with Germany," I said, drawing on what I knew of the man's politics.

The major nodded, that glimmer of approval I was beginning to recognize in his expression. "He agreed with Chamberlain on appeasement, and has made no secret about his dislike of Churchill, both in and out of print. We've had our eye on him for some time, due to some of his prewar German connections, but, for such a vocal man, he's been very careful not to go too far, not to do anything that might incriminate himself or push him beyond the pale."

"The cleverest ones are always the best at that sort of thing," Uncle Mick said. "And Sir Nigel is clever, to be sure."

"Nevertheless, it's only a matter of time before he makes the wrong enemies in our government. It's possible he's lining things up with the Germans in the event he needs to leave the country."

"Or in case the Nazis arrive here," I said vaguely.

"They won't," the major said. He sounded very sure of himself, and for once I found comfort in his confidence. I thought of my cousin Colm, working on RAF planes in Torquay, so close and yet so far. Like so many other valiant Englishmen, he'd fight to the death before allowing our shores to be overrun. But I didn't know how I'd bear it if I lost him, not when Toby was already missing.

I pushed these thoughts away, rallying inwardly. We had a job to do, and focusing on doing it well was in the best interests of those I cared about as well as my country. I turned my attention back to the major.

"I mentioned one reason why it's possible the contact might have killed Harden," he went on. "There is a man in Sir Nigel's employ by the name of Jerome Curtis. He functions as a majordomo of sorts for Sir Nigel, but his main duties are ensuring Sir Nigel's safety and making sure people comply with his will, by violent means, if necessary."

"An enforcer," Uncle Mick said.

"Precisely," the major said. "There's precious little background information to be found on the man, but he ran with a racketeering gang for a while in his youth, had a short and exceptionally brutal boxing career, and there are rumors he was something of a mercenary before he joined Sir Nigel's permanent employ, selling his services to the highest bidder."

"Then it's possible he may have killed Harden for Sir Nigel," I speculated. "Which is why you think the documents may be in Sir Nigel's safe."

The major nodded. "It's certainly a possibility. One we need to rule out."

Uncle Mick gave a whistle. "It's shaping up to be a fine group of miscreants."

"We're just beginning," Major Ramsey said. "The next person of interest is Leslie Turner-Hill. He is the director of Bothingham's. You're familiar with the establishment?"

"Yes," I said. The auction house was one of the oldest in England. We had an acquaintance who had sold several pieces of art in its illustrious auctions. They were all forgeries, of course, so I thought it best not to mention it at the moment.

"He did a steady trade with members of the German high command before we got into the war," Major Ramsey was saying. "Men who fancy themselves art collectors. Goering and the like. It's quite possible he formed connections that will continue to prove beneficial to him throughout the war."

Uncle Mick swore beneath his breath.

"It's distasteful, of course," I said, "but isn't it a stretch between doing business with such people before the war and handing over government secrets to them now?" Even as I asked the question, I knew the answer.

"Money's caused men to do worse, Ellie girl," Uncle Mick said.

I wanted to be shocked that people like these could put monetary gain before the good of their country, but I found I could not be. Uncle Mick was right. While our family had always held themselves to certain standards, I had encountered a good many of Uncle Mick's less savory associates over the years, men who would be willing to betray their own mothers for a few pounds.

"Money isn't the only motivation, however," the major went on. "The next potential conspirator is Matthew Winthrop. He's a poet, of sorts. His father is in government, but, apparently, he's formed some strong ideas of his own. He was in an underground political club with some of his school chums, a club that tried to mimic many of the policies put into place in Germany by Hitler."

I made an expression of distaste. "But he's committed no crime?"

"No. Not as far as we know. And, in all honesty, even if he—or any of them—had, it has been in our best interest to let many of these individuals continue to move about freely in society, so long as they're being monitored."

"Yes, I can see how that might prove to your advantage," I said.

Uncle Mick nodded. "Keep your friends close and your enemies closer."

"Precisely." He sat back in his chair. "The final person who might have reasons to conspire with the Germans is Jocelyn Abbot. She's a socialite. You may have seen her name in the society columns?"

"I don't often read them," I said honestly. While other thieves might have scanned the pages of the gossip rags for information on potential targets, we had always chosen ours for their lack of notoriety. We weren't after publicity or the kind of influence that would bring the law down hard on our heads.

"She's from a very wealthy and well-connected family."

"Of German heritage?" I guessed.

"Yes. Her grandfather was connected with Kaiser Wilhelm's government, though they moved to this country before Miss Abbot's father was born. Her family has given the impression of being staunchly pro-British ever since, but sometimes heritage runs deep. And there is another factor of interest. She is engaged to Barnaby Ellhurst."

My brows rose. I knew the name well enough. Barnaby Ellhurst was an RAF pilot who had made a name for himself during the Battle of Dunkirk. His bravery and skill in battle had been lauded by Churchill himself. But he had disappeared while on a mission over France a month before, and no one had heard what had become of him. It was widely assumed he had been captured, though the Germans had made no such claims.

"You think she might have had something to do with his being shot down?" I said, leaping to the logical conclusion. "That she gave them information of some sort about his flight to France?"

"I think it's possible."

"But surely her fiancé's life and freedom would mean more to her than Germany's cause," I said. "I find it incredible she would do something like that to a man she loved."

"A declaration of love is not proof of it." His voice was bland as he said this, but his expression hardened ever so slightly. Interesting. I tucked this observation away to ponder later.

"So you believe Harden stole the documents, intending to pass them off to one of these people who will, in turn, pass it off to a German contact. But Harden was murdered, perhaps because he got cold feet, and his killer will turn up at the party to pass the documents off instead," I said, summing things up.

"Yes. The suspected conspirators will all be at the party, since it involves their collector's group."

"Birds of a feather, in more ways than one," I said. "What sort of collecting do they do?"

"Chinese porcelain."

"How sinister," I said dryly.

"They've all been rather keen on it for years. It's the purpose of this party, in fact. Bothingham's has some new pieces going to auction, and Sir Nigel has arranged a private viewing at his house so that the collectors might look them over."

"And are you a collector?" I asked, wondering how the two of us would manage to fit unobtrusively into this group of eccentrics.

"I'm not, but my uncle is interested in such things. It was on his behalf that I arranged the invitation."

Major Ramsey was a man of many layers. It was clear now that he was very posh indeed, but I found it strange to think that he had an uncle somewhere with glass cases of ancient porcelain. What was more, I couldn't exactly picture him haggling with collectors over the price of a vase or plate. He knew better than I did what needed to be done, however, so I would just have to trust him on that score.

I realized that I had been studying him rather intently and collected my thoughts.

"Just those five, then?" I asked. "How many people do you suppose will be at the party?"

"It's going to be a large group. Sir Nigel can't afford, after all, to invite only German sympathizers to his parties. The collector's group has been expanded to include several other interested parties. Now, with many wealthy people out of the country, is an excellent time to get good prices."

"A bit cheeky, to bring fragile collectibles under his roof with Messerschmitts buzzing overhead, isn't it?"

"The rich and powerful stop for no man—or machine."

"A bit like Nero playing his fiddle while Rome burned, eh?"

The corners of his mouth tipped up. "Not a bad comparison."

"So we'll need to watch these five and wait to see if someone, a collaborator, tries to pass off the papers to them."

"Yes. Of course, it's possible the German contact is someone we have overlooked, but that's a chance we'll take."

There was something in the way he said it that made me think he relished the challenge. So the stoic Major Ramsey had an adventurous streak, after all.

One thing was certain: it was going to be an interesting evening.

CHAPTER ELEVEN

Uncle Mick, it turned out, had his own part to play in our little drama. He and one of the major's men were going to enter Leslie Turner-Hill's auction house while the rest of us were at the party. It was just possible, the major thought, that Mr. Turner-Hill was using artwork to smuggle information out of the country. Uncle Mick and the major's man would do a thorough going-over of the auction house while we were at the party.

We discussed the whole plan in more detail when we were back in the privacy of his workshop.

By rights, Uncle Mick should have gone to bed when we returned home, but I knew he wouldn't rest. No doubt his fingers were itching to get to work after days in captivity. He was not the sort of man who had ever enjoyed sitting still for long. His mind was always whirling, his hands ready to be at work. I had never seen him idle.

"What do you think about it all, my girl?" he asked, when he had settled himself at his worktable. There was an array of locks spread out before him, his tools scattered across the table in a configuration that would have looked random to anyone but him.

I sat on the desk chair.

"I think we'll be lucky if it works," I said. "It seems to me the whole thing hangs on a lot of hopes."

"Hopes make the world go round, love," he said cheerily.

He was bound to be cheery now that he had a job ahead. Uncle Mick thrived on this sort of thing. He loved locks, and he loved them twice as much when he was opening ones that weren't his to open.

In some ways, I wondered if his task might be more dangerous than mine. After all, I would have the major with me. We knew little of who Uncle Mick's companion on the raid of the auction house would be.

I wished there was some way that we could've brought Uncle Mick to the party with us, but I knew that would never work. Uncle Mick was a lot of things, but he'd never pass for a high society gentleman.

"The party sounds like a grand time," he said. He was watching me carefully. "But you'll be careful, won't you? These people have killed before, and I'm sure they won't hesitate to do so again."

I nodded. "I'll be careful. I don't really think they'd do anyone harm at a party like this. After all, it's going to be a fairly large event."

"Just mind you watch your back," he said. He was never one to fuss, so I knew the fact he had cautioned me twice in the space of a few moments meant he was worried. I moved to his side and placed a hand on his arm.

"I can look out for myself, Uncle Mick. And Major Ramsey isn't likely to let any harm come to me if it can be helped."

"You trust him, then."

His words took me by surprise, and I considered them for a moment. "Yes," I said at last. "I suppose I do."

He nodded. "I've always been a good judge of character, you know, and I think he's an honest man."

"We've never had much use for honest people before this," I said with a little smile. Major Ramsey was just the type of person we would have avoided like the plague. Obviously, our connection with him was only the result of a set of circumstances beyond our control.

It might even be fate, if one believed in such things.

"No, but we should always welcome honorable men as friends," Uncle Mick said with a wink. "They're useful people, in their own way."

"I wouldn't say the major is a friend, exactly," I said. "But at least he's not an enemy."

"Your opinion of him has improved, I see." There was a twinkle in his eyes.

"I don't hate him quite as much as I did, if that's what you mean."

Though I didn't want to admit it, he was right; the major was growing on me. I'd thought him a coldhearted brute upon first meeting, but I was beginning to believe that at least his motives were pure. After all, we had excused our own behavior based on noble motives before this.

Uncle Mick seemed to interpret my unspoken words correctly, for he grinned. "You spoke to him alone. Did he tell you what the next step will be if all of this goes wrong?"

I shook my head. "He's being very tight-lipped about it all."

"That's not such a great surprise. It's very hush-hush stuff, after all. And, whatever happens, I'm sure he has a plan."

"I suppose you're right," I said. "Whatever else he is, he seems to be terribly competent."

"He's a good-looking chap," Uncle Mick said with a sly glance in my direction.

I gave him a sharp look. "I suppose. If you don't mind stuffed shirts."

"Though I don't suppose a government man would make a very useful addition to the family," he mused, still teasing me.

"We don't need an addition to the family." I knew I sounded sulky, but I couldn't seem to help it. I wasn't finding all of this as amusing as Uncle Mick was.

"I know this particular bloke may not be your cup of tea, but I wouldn't rule it out just yet, my girl. Perhaps this will be our opportunity to turn over a new leaf."

I knew he meant well, and what he was saying was true. Perhaps now, if we veered onto the straight and narrow, I might have the chance to live a bit more normal of a life. Or at least as near to it as the McDonnells could get.

There had never been much opportunity for me to date; Uncle Mick and my cousins had seen to that. They were a merry enough bunch, unless you crossed them. Everyone knew that, and the local blokes weren't keen on making them angry and steered clear of me for the most part. I'd been out with a fellow or two in my time, but there had never really been a man I had fancied above the usual. At least, unless you counted Felix. But now wasn't the time to think about that.

There was an expression on Uncle Mick's face that I didn't care to try to interpret. I suspected he intended to tease me about the major, but I didn't feel it was a joking matter. Perhaps it was because I knew that the major would never in a million years deign to look at a girl like me as anything other than a useful cog in his machine. Not that I wanted him to, mind.

"This is serious business, Uncle Mick," I reminded him.

He nodded, though his expression was still amused. "You know what I say, Ellie girl. Prepare as best you can and be ready for whatever else may come."

It wasn't a long walk to the Colindale Newspaper Library the next morning. The weather was pleasant, and it was good to be out and about in the sunshine and cool breeze. I felt a bit as though I had been living in some dark bubble the past week or so, everything done in the shadows and in secret.

I had never had call to visit the Newspaper Library before, though I had spent many a happy hour in the London Library. We were a bookish lot, though one might not have thought it to look at us. I had fond memories of Uncle Mick reading to me and the boys as we sat before the fire, adventure and mystery stories mostly, things like *The Adventures of Sherlock Holmes*. Uncle Mick liked crime stories. The irony appealed to him, I think.

The Newspaper Library was a sturdy brick building that had the air of knowledge about it. I went inside and was greeted by the scent of paper and ink.

A cheerful young woman was only too glad to assist me with what I was looking for, and within a few minutes I was sitting at a long wooden table in the reading room with bound copies of last month's issues of *The Old Smoke, The Times,* and two or three of the lesser-known papers before me.

It was the idea of learning more about Chinese porcelain that had brought me here. It had occurred to me that, in addition to re-searching pottery, it might be useful to learn what I could about some of the people who we were to encounter at the dinner party.

Major Ramsey had given me the basics, of course, but he was the sort of man who only revealed what was absolutely necessary, and I was certain there was more to be learned. I wasn't accus-tomed to working without doing my research. Just because I had agreed to help the man didn't mean that everything was going to be done his way.

I wouldn't uncover any deep, dark secrets within the pages of these papers, certainly, but at least I wouldn't be wandering into the lion's den blind.

Flipping through the first paper, it quickly became apparent this wasn't going to be an easy task. There is a great deal of news pub-lished in London, and much of it is dreadfully dull.

I looked first for information about Mr. Harden's death. It didn't take me long to find it, though there wasn't much hullabaloo made about his passing. MAN KILLED IN HOME ROBBERY, the headline read. The article was sparse in detail, and very little seemed to be said about the man or his grisly demise. "Thomas Harden was killed in an apparent robbery at his home, the killers making off with the contents of his safe. It is a reminder that, in these dark days, we must be vigilant."

It was true enough, I supposed. After all, Uncle Mick and I had been taking advantage of "these dark days" ourselves. For the first time in a long time, I felt a little pang of conscience. We would never have dreamed of harming anyone, of course, but it seemed a bit shabby to use the war to our advantage.

There was no mention of Mr. Harden's connection with the weapons factory, though, of course, those things would not have been made known to the public. There was a great deal happening in London these days that would not be found in the newspapers.

Included in the article was a small photograph of the man. I looked at it closely, pushing aside in my head the image of his dead eyes staring up at the ceiling in his office. It wasn't a quality photograph, but I had a good memory for faces, and I was fairly certain I had seen his before. When he was alive, that is. Perhaps if I thought about it for a few moments, it would come back to me.

As for the suspects we would be meeting tonight, I had decided to start with our first, and host of the party, Sir Nigel. Since he owned *The Old Smoke*, I assumed there would be a good deal to learn about him. I was wrong on that score. It seemed that he took care to keep himself out of the papers. When one owned a section of the news, I supposed one could dictate what was newsworthy.

It was, however, easy to see the way that Sir Nigel's interests lay; he didn't make much of a secret about his leanings in the sort of articles he published in his paper. I asked for the papers from a year ago and saw that he was particularly keen on keeping relations with Germany on steady footing. The articles in the paper went on at length about the benefits to be gained from a peaceful relationship and all that we had already gained since the last war. There was little doubt of *The Old Smoke*'s position when it came to hostilities with Germany.

I couldn't help but wonder what motivated that position. After all, no one was keen to go to war, but it had become increasingly obvious that it was going to be difficult to avoid a conflict. Why had he been so opposed to it?

I could only think that there must be some reason he was particularly invested in promoting Germany's interests.

There was one article that was of particular interest that was not in *The Old Smoke* but *The Times*. It wasn't about Sir Nigel, but about his nephew, John Myron, who had returned from Germany, where he had been in diplomatic service. The article insinuated that Mr. Myron was relieved to leave Germany behind him, but I wondered what the true connection was there. Did sympathy for the country run in the family?

I flipped through several more papers before I saw a headline that gave me pause: JOHN MYRON KILLED IN AUTOMOBILE ACCIDENT.

I skimmed the lines below. The accident had taken place a month ago. "John Myron, former aide to the ambassador to Germany, was killed in a car crash Friday night returning to London from Torquay, where he had been staying at Larksong, the seaside home of his uncle, Sir Nigel Randolf. Police believe the hooded lights on his car prevented him from seeing the curve in the dark road until it was too late."

Curious. Had it really been an accident? Or something more sinister?

There was nothing to be learned about Jerome Curtis, Sir Nigel's majordomo, as the major had referred to him. I assumed that, as Sir Nigel's bodyguard and enforcer, he would take care to keep himself in the background. I did recall what the major had said about Curtis being associated with racketeers and having a short boxing career, but I could find nothing relevant and I soon gave up the chase.

Next, as part of my search for Jocelyn Abbot, I found articles dating back to around the time I remembered hearing about the fate of the RAF pilot Barnaby Ellhurst. If Miss Abbot's missing fiancé was another victim of her entanglement in espionage, I felt I should learn more about him. It wasn't long before I came across articles about his heroics. He had flown a Hawker Hurricane and shot down a number of German planes. Even after his aircraft had begun to malfunction, he had managed to stay in the air long enough to stop a Messerschmitt before it could strafe a boat deck full of soldiers.

The young man was impressive, all right. In perhaps the third or fourth article I found about him, there was a picture of him with a woman. A quick glance at the article told me this was Jocelyn Abbot.

I studied the picture. She was tall, blond, and very beautiful. Chicly dressed and expertly coiffed. One could almost smell her expensive perfume looking at her. In the photo, she was clutching Barnaby Ellhurst's arm as she looked at the camera. He was looking at her.

I wouldn't necessarily have put them together. Barnaby Ellhurst was handsome in a rugged sort of way—unruly dark hair, angular features, sharp eyes—but he didn't seem to be the kind of man that would draw a socialite. I noted that they hadn't become engaged until after he'd made a name for himself. Was that why she had formed the connection? Perhaps she had been instructed to get close to one of Britain's most illustrious young pilots. After all, his disappearance had been a jolt to the nation's morale.

There was another article in one of the smaller, more gossipy papers about Jocelyn Abbot after he disappeared. TWICE THWARTED IN LOVE? the headline read. "After a broken engagement with one of London's most eligible bachelors, Miss Abbot is now confronted with tragedy in the form of a missing fiancé, Flight Lieutenant Barnaby Ellhurst." The article described how, on a flight mission over France, both he and his plane had disappeared without a trace. It was presumed that he had been shot down, but whether he was dead or merely captured was unknown.

The article was accompanied by a photograph of Miss Abbot

looking appropriately distraught in a tailored black suit, the veil of her hat angled just so.

There wasn't much else of interest to be found about her, though her name was scattered often enough throughout notices of society events, plays and parties, and the like. It was a bit surprising to me that she hadn't left London now that things were so uncertain. But perhaps that was because she had been ordered by her spymasters to stay.

The auction house director, Leslie Turner-Hill, appeared here and there in the papers, always in connection with Bothingham's. He seemed to be the sort of man who lived on the fringes of high society, moving around in that world but not really a part of it. It might be the ideal situation for creating antipathy and even resentment. If he couldn't be a part of the world he wanted to be in, then maybe he was hoping to make his way in a different sort of society.

There was an advertisement for Chinese porcelain and an upcoming auction. "Several fine specimens recently acquired from European collectors." I wondered who these collectors were and if they might have any bearing on the party tonight. I supposed there was no way to know.

Despite much searching, I didn't find a picture of Turner-Hill, so I would have to have the major point him out to me.

I didn't find anything about society man and aspiring poet Matthew Winthrop at all, not a word. I would have thought there would at least be a society column mention of him if he was in with Sir Nigel and his crowd, but I supposed that he had been interested in staying out of the papers, especially if he was the ringleader of some sort of underground political group. Could a small group of fascist university students really be involved in something that might endanger the entire country? Small stones cause big ripples, as Uncle Mick always said.

"Finding everything you need?" the young lady asked me, pulling my mind back to the present.

"Thank you, yes," I said, looking up, feeling a bit as though I was coming up from a deep dive underwater.

The way I've told it makes it sound like it was a matter of minutes to find these articles, but a glance at my watch confirmed I'd been sitting in the reading room for more than four hours. As it was when I was working on a safe, I'd lost track of time. I felt I had accomplished my goal; I had discovered what I could about the backgrounds of Sir Nigel, Jocelyn Abbot, and Leslie Turner-Hill. Matthew Winthrop and Jerome Curtis, Sir Nigel's henchman, both remained something of an enigma, but I intended to keep an eye on them at the party. I didn't think there was much more information to be gleaned today.

I rose from my seat, stretching my neck as I stood. It had been a long day, but I felt that now I was ready to face whatever—and whoever—the evening had in store.

It was at that moment that I suddenly remembered where I had seen the dead man, Thomas Harden, before. And I knew who it was that might be able to help me.

CHAPTER TWELVE

Maudie Johnson and I had grown up on the same street, and we had remained casual friends. Toby had always had a bit of a crush on her, which was why I had noticed when I saw her out with a dapper gentleman one evening a few months before. Now I knew who that gentleman had been: Thomas Harden.

It was just possible that she knew some of what was going on in his life. At the very least, she might have noticed if he was interacting with any suspicious-looking characters. It certainly couldn't hurt to ask.

Her flat was on my route home from the Newspaper Library, so I took a chance and knocked on her door.

"Oh! Hello, Ellie," she said, smiling brightly. She had always been one of the prettiest girls in the neighborhood, with her heart-shaped face, glossy blond hair, and big blue eyes.

A dancer from a young age, she was now a chorus girl at a local nightclub. It was probably where she'd met Thomas Harden.

"Hello, Maudie. How have you been?"

"Oh, all right. How about you? I . . . I heard about Toby."

I nodded. "We hope to hear something soon."

"I'm sure you will."

I had decided before knocking that I would just have out with my question, so I stuck to the plan. "I . . . well, it may sound a bit odd, but I've come to talk to you about Thomas Harden."

Her smile faltered ever so slightly. She glanced around, past my shoulder, and then pulled the door open. "You'd better come in."

I followed her through the entryway into the flat's living room. It was decorated in a very modern style, with satin and floral-patterned furniture. Very fashionable.

"Would you like some tea?" she asked, when we were settled on a comfortable pair of rose-printed chairs.

"No, I'm fine, thank you. I don't mean to intrude. I just . . ."

"What do you know about Thomas Harden?" she asked. Her tone wasn't sharp, but there was a certain wariness in her.

"I saw in the paper that he'd been killed by burglars, and I remembered that the two of you were going together."

"I stopped seeing him several weeks ago," she said. It was meant to put an end to the conversation, I think, but I had the sense she wanted to say more.

"Well, you have my condolences, all the same. It's always a shock when someone one knows dies suddenly."

Her eyes met mine. "A lot of people are going to die suddenly in this war."

It was a grim truth, but it was clear there was a deeper meaning in her words. She was speaking in riddles and waiting for me to solve them.

"But Mr. Harden wasn't going to war," I said, trying to edge her forward.

She shook her head. "He had an important job. He worked at a factory up north."

"Oh?" I asked. I was sure this wasn't common knowledge, and I didn't intend to show my hand.

"I . . . he wouldn't tell me anything, of course. But I think they were making something up there . . . related to the war effort."

I leaned forward slightly as though we were exchanging secrets.

I knew now what she was getting at, which was, of course, what I had been waiting for her to say all along. "You don't suppose that had something to do with why he was killed?"

Now it was she who leaned forward, though I didn't know who was likely to hear us in her empty flat. "There were strange things that happened several times we went out together."

"Like what?"

"Like people following us. More than once, we dodged them in his car, though he tried not to let on that's what was happening. And then there were strange, secretive phone calls Thomas would receive. I thought at first he had another girl, but I picked up on the other phone once and it was a man."

"What were they talking about?"

She looked abashed. "Something to do with the factory, I think. I hung up because I didn't want to hear anything I oughtn't."

I nodded, and she continued.

"Then once we were out to dinner, and he excused himself from the table. He took his time about coming back, and when I went to look for him, he was talking to a man."

I felt suddenly on the cusp of discovery. "What did the man look like?" I asked.

She shrugged. "His back was to me, so I didn't get a good look at him. He was a tall fellow in a dinner jacket. Dark hair."

It wasn't much help.

"Anything else?" I realized I was pressing her rather hard, but now that she was revealing her secrets, they were coming fast and loose.

She shook her head. "I didn't think too much of it all, at the time. I figured it was to do with the factory work, things he couldn't tell me. We weren't very serious, after all. But when I'd heard he'd been killed, I began to wonder . . ."

There was more coming. I held my breath and waited.

"Once, after one of those phone calls, he asked me something very odd. He asked how recognizable I thought handwriting was. If I could compare two letters and tell the differences."

"Handwriting?" I repeated, perplexed. That wasn't what I'd expected. "Did he show you two letters to compare?"

Maudie shook her head. "He asked it in kind of a philosophical way. I didn't go on seeing him long after that."

"Perhaps that was for the best," I said. In more ways than one.

We chatted about the old neighborhood and our mutual acquaintances for a while after that, and at last I took my leave. I needed to get home to prepare for the party.

I wasn't sure that I had learned anything important, exactly, but it was something to think about. And I would keep my eye out for tall, dark-haired gentlemen among our potential suspects. And possibly those with an interest in graphology.

"At least I look the part," I muttered to myself, as I stood in my flat a few minutes to seven o'clock that evening.

I felt a bit like Cinderella on her way to the ball, if Cinderella had been primarily focused on committing a burglary.

I did one final turn before the mirror, taking in my appearance. The gown had been waiting for me when I arrived home from my visit with Maudie Johnson. It had been delivered in a large white box, and I had gasped when I pushed aside the wrapping to pull it out.

It was a much prettier gown than anything I'd ever owned before. It was made of a deep burgundy velvet and had a fitted waist and long, flowing skirt with an extra bit of fabric to the side that was held in place with a glittering pin at my hip.

It hugged me in all the right places, drawing attention to my curves. The square neckline was a bit lower than one I might have chosen for myself, but I couldn't deny that it made me look rather glamorous. It was low-cut enough to "allude to my bosom," as Nacy would say, and the thick straps across my shoulders called attention to the skin of my neck.

They'd even sent along a beautiful pair of satin heels and real silk stockings. What luxury!

My hair, for once, had turned out just the way I intended, with a soft wave across the front and a perfectly smooth chignon fastened with a crystal barrette. I looked older with my hair this way, which I thought suited me.

As I didn't own any good jewelry, I went without. I had a few decent costume pieces, but the people I would be mixing with tonight would know the difference. Anyway, the gown was elegant enough to stand on its own.

I'd gone a bit heavy on the mascara, and I'd chosen a lipstick that matched the oxblood color of the gown. All told, the effect was striking with my black hair and pale skin.

What would Major Ramsey think of it all? This question sprung to my mind before I realized it was going to, and I felt irritated with myself. What did it matter what he thought?

If I was honest, though, I was glad that I looked well. Every other time he had seen me, my appearance had been a bit of a mess, and I was vain enough to want him to know that I could be pretty when I chose to be.

Besides, he was a good-looking man in a city where men were scarce. Surely I could acknowledge the fact without attaching any particular significance to it.

I had just spritzed myself with an expensive Parisian perfume Felix had given me for Christmas last year and gathered my coat and handbag when there was a rap at my door.

Opening it, I was greeted by the major. He was attired in his dress uniform, and I couldn't help but admire how well he looked. Now that I had decided that it was perfectly reasonable to find him attractive in a vague, indifferent way, I took a bit more notice of the way the khaki-greenish uniform seemed to emphasize his height and long legs, the leather Sam Browne belt accentuating the breadth of his shoulders and trim waist.

He was looking me over as I looked him over, I realized. His eyes ran from top to bottom and back again, and I was fairly certain I didn't imagine that they lingered a bit on the places where the dress hugged me just right. I felt a hint of gratification that he had seemed to notice me as a woman, though I was not at all sure that he would think of me in those terms. After all, he had made it very clear in the past that I was primarily a thief in his eyes.

"Shall I do, do you think?" I asked.

I half expected him to say something rude, but instead he nodded, his expression difficult to read. "You'll do," he said. And then, after the slightest pause: "You look very nice, Miss McDonnell."

I had been prepared to come back with a smart retort, so I was a bit at a loss for what to say in the face of a compliment. "Thank you, Major. So do you." Inwardly, I grimaced. It hadn't been quite what I meant to say.

"May I?" he asked, indicating my coat.

"Thank you." I handed it to him, and he helped me into it.

Then he motioned to the waiting car. "Shall we?"

Jakub was our driver. He opened the car door for me as I approached.

"Good evening, Jakub," I said, smiling brightly at him.

"Good evening, Miss McDonnell."

"Ellie," I corrected him.

He nodded, returning my smile. "Good evening, Ellie."

"Watch your skirt, Miss McDonnell," Major Ramsey said as I slid into the car, and I pulled the velvet fabric in before he closed the door. I wasn't exactly accustomed to formalwear.

"Don't you suppose you'd better call me Ellie?" I asked, when he got in on the other side.

He shook his head. "I think I'd better call you something else entirely. It's better that we don't use your real name so you can't be traced when all of this is over. What would suit you?"

"What's the relationship between us meant to be?" I asked, wanting to know what my part would be before I decided what I should be called. "Exactly how well are we meant to know each other?"

His eyes met mine, and I felt a silly little jolt in my stomach. Probably embarrassment, as I supposed he thought I'd meant the question suggestively. I hadn't, but, now that I thought about it, I did need to know if I was meant to pass myself off as a casual date or a mistress.

"I don't suppose you have any experience with secretarial work?" he asked.

He meant me to be his *secretary*? For some reason, this was very disappointing.

"I can take shorthand and type." I had taken a course in the basics a few years back, to learn how to better organize Uncle Mick's business. He was as sharp as a razor when it came to locks, but paperwork and billing had never been his strong suit.

"Then perhaps we can say you work at a business close to the War Office and we met one day over lunch."

"Slumming it a bit with an office worker, aren't you?" I was unaccountably glad that I was meant to be a proper date. Now he wouldn't expect me to follow him around taking notes all evening.

He ignored my quip. "I asked you to dinner, and we struck up an immediate romance."

"Are we very much in love?" I asked cheekily. I was trying to see how we were going to play this, if he would be willing to soften some of those edges to banter with me. I had a sneaking suspicion it was going to be very difficult to flirt with Major Ramsey.

"This is our fourth date," he said, not in the least flustered by my provoking behavior. "Your feelings are unclear, as you've been playing hard to get."

The corner of my mouth tipped up, and I clicked my tongue. "Have I? And with such a shortage of men in this country, too."

"It's not entirely your fault," he said. "My personality takes a bit of warming up to."

I laughed outright at this. "And so you mean to woo me with Chinese porcelain?"

"Desperate times, Miss McDonnell."

"You've got to stop Miss McDonnell-ing me," I said. "You're liable to forget and use it tonight."

"All right. Who would you like to be?"

I considered. "I suppose as close as possible to my real name might be easiest to remember."

He nodded. "We wouldn't want the name to be completely foreign to your ear."

"How about Elizabeth Donaldson?" I suggested.

"Very well. Elizabeth."

"Don't you suppose you might call me Lizzie by the fourth date? Or Bess, or Betsy?"

He shook his head. "I disapprove of diminutives."

"What?"

"Diminutives. Pet names."

"I know what they are," I retorted. "Why do you disapprove of them?"

"I feel as though one should be called what one is named. Otherwise, what's the point?"

I gave a little laugh. "You're very much a man who lives by the rules, aren't you?" I asked.

"That's what rules are for, aren't they?"

I shrugged. "I don't know. I find that it's always been more fun to flout them a bit."

He looked as though he was about to say something and thought better of it. For just a moment I had the impression that there had been a time in his life when he had flouted the rules and had met with disaster, and I wondered what it had been.

Despite myself, I felt another flicker of interest in Major Ramsey and his past.

I realized suddenly how very little I knew about him. "And what about you?" I asked. "What's your given name?"

"Gabriel."

I considered this. It seemed appropriate that he might share a name with the archangel: impressive, intimidating, and firmly on the side of good. With that fair, handsome face he looked a bit like an angel, or a marble bust of one.

"I hadn't taken you for a Gabriel, but it suits you," I said after a moment. "I assume your friends don't call you Gabe?"

"My friends call me Ramsey," he said. "No one calls me Gabriel."

"Not even women?" I pressed. There was, I realized, the risk he might think I was actually flirting with him, but I was trying very hard to break down some of his barriers.

I had thought I might throw him off a bit with this question, at least rattle his very proper demeanor, but he met my gaze evenly. "I don't have a lot of time for women at present, Miss McDonnell."

For some reason I found this difficult to believe. I didn't have a great deal of experience with men, but I had enough to know that a man like Major Ramsey could have his pick of girls with very little effort.

"Well, I won't call you Ramsey. It's much too formal. So Gabriel it shall be."

"That is your prerogative," he said flatly.

Of course, if he was always as much of a pompous prig as he was when talking to me, it could very well put a damper on things where women were concerned.

I found myself wondering what he was like in his regular life. Surely he smiled and laughed and talked of silly things with the people close to him? I couldn't imagine that he went through life with his shoulders squared and that grim face all the time. Of course, the persona seemed very natural to him, so perhaps he did. In any event, it was never going to make any difference to me one way or the other, so I needn't worry about it.

"Is there anything else I need to know before we get there tonight?" I asked.

He looked at me. "Like what?"

I shrugged. "I don't know. You're the man with all the information."

"You know nearly as much as I do about what will happen tonight. Just keep your eyes open, and tell me if you see anything suspicious. Don't put yourself in any danger."

"I don't intend to." I found it almost a bit sweet that he was concerned with my well-being.

"During the display of the porcelain, there will likely be an opportunity for us to slip away and get to the safe. You must follow my instructions at all times. I know you're used to working on your own, but, for all intents and purposes, you are now under my command."

So much for sweet talk.

I suppressed my instinctive desire to contradict him and instead answered primly. "Yes, sir, Major Ramsey."

He didn't say much else as we drove, and I didn't press him. I could already tell that we weren't likely to fool anyone into thinking we were romantically linked, but there was no helping that. He certainly couldn't say I hadn't tried.

A short time later we pulled up in front of a massive sandstone mansion. Even the sandbags and blackout curtains couldn't dampen the effect.

Jakub opened my door and I stepped out of the car, looking up at the magnificent structure and preparing myself for whatever lay ahead. To be honest, the thought of interacting with a bunch of society people was daunting.

"Ready, Elizabeth?" he asked, extending his elbow to me.

I slipped my arm through his. "Ready, Gabriel."

Together we walked up the front steps and into the building.

CHAPTER THIRTEEN

I had been prepared for grandeur, but Sir Nigel Randolf's Mayfair house was a study in opulence. It was all white marble floors and pillars, golden moldings, and glittering chandeliers—everything so bright it almost hurt the eyes.

The house was also massive. The foyer alone was large enough to host a ball, our footsteps echoing on the gleaming floors and up, up into the ceiling three stories above us. This, I thought, was perhaps the ultimate symbol of the decadently rich: huge amounts of space devoted to nothing in particular.

"Vulgar, isn't it?" the major said in my ear.

I looked up at him. "It's certainly extravagant."

I didn't have anything against the rich, particularly. I had learned early on that life isn't fair. Why be angry that someone else was dealt a better hand of cards? Of course, my family had never been above cheating a bit.

"And more crowded than I expected," I said, noting the handsomely dressed swells moving in and out of rooms, drinks in hand. "Are all these people really interested in Chinese porcelain?"

"Most of them are more interested in seeing and being seen," he replied. "Sir Nigel is known for his parties, even in wartime."

"Will you point out our quarries to me?"

"Here comes one of them now," he said in a low voice. "That's Sir Nigel."

I turned to see a gentleman in evening clothes approaching with a purposeful stride.

Sir Nigel was just how I had expected him to look. He was a gentleman of advancing years, gone a bit heavy with good living. He had a face that was not unhandsome beneath a head of thick gray hair, though the worries he was hiding seemed to have taken their toll, for his face had a tired cast to it, despite his best efforts to hide it. He was dark beneath his sharp, pale blue eyes, and his skin had that unhealthy hue of someone who drank too much and slept too little. Of course, drink and sleeplessness were common enough afflictions in London these days.

There was no hint of tiredness in his manner, however. He was too good a fraud for that.

"Ramsey!" he said in the booming voice of a man accustomed to having his opinion matter more than other people's.

He came forward and clasped the major's hand. "Glad to see you back in the country. North Africa didn't agree with you, I take it?"

"It agreed with me fine," the major replied. "But I must go where I'm sent."

North Africa, was it? That explained that bronzed cast to his skin. Had they sent him back for this mission in particular, or was there some other reason?

"Of course, my boy. Of course," Sir Nigel said, his gaze coming to me. "And who is this lovely young lady?"

"This is Miss Elizabeth Donaldson. Elizabeth, Sir Nigel Randolf."

"How do you do?" I said. He took my hand in his. His grip was tight, and his eyes fastened on my face. There was something assessing in the way he looked at me, but I wasn't worried; I knew I looked the part tonight. As if to back up this opinion his eyes dropped, for just a moment, to my low neckline before he pulled them back to my face again.

"It's a pleasure to meet you, Miss Donaldson," he said. "I thought I knew all the most beautiful women in London, but it seems I was mistaken."

I smiled. "You're too kind, Sir Nigel."

"I'm not kind at all." His smile was suddenly wolfish, and I believed him. "In fact, I'm known to be something of a lecher. Ramsey had better keep an eye on you."

"I intend to," Major Ramsey said with a smile that was not quite friendly. One hand moved to rest, ever so lightly, on my lower back. Perhaps he would be better at playing his part than I had originally thought.

Sir Nigel laughed. "Then I think you're safe, Miss Donaldson. I wouldn't dare challenge the major here. But come to the drawing room, will you? There are a few people I'd like you to meet."

"Certainly," Major Ramsey said.

I was a bit surprised that Sir Nigel was making so much of the major. I thought we would blend unobtrusively into the gathering, but Sir Nigel was treating him almost as an honored guest. I had the feeling there was something I was missing, likely something that Major Ramsey hadn't felt it necessary to tell me.

Sir Nigel led us across the foyer and through an open pair of wide wooden doors.

I stepped into the room, the major's hand under my arm, and looked around me. It was my habit to take in as much about a room as possible upon entering it.

He had called it a drawing room, but this was a grand room, all high ceilings, carved molding and crimson wallpaper, and careful arrangements of antique furniture. There was a gigantic marble fireplace on the opposite side to where we had entered, a fire roaring. I could hear the crackling from where I stood, though it was probably a cricket pitch away.

We moved farther into the room, Major Ramsey nodding at the people we passed as we went. I saw a few eyes move to me as we passed through the crowd, and I wondered what kind of speculation I was inspiring in all their elegant, gossipy heads.

Sir Nigel led us to a little group of six or seven people who sat on the furniture clustered near the fireplace. They stopped their conversation as we approached.

"Ramsey's arrived at last," Sir Nigel said to the group. "And he's brought this lovely young lady, Miss Elizabeth Donaldson. I've brought them over to present to you."

He made introductions all around then, but I paid attention to only two of them.

One was Leslie Turner-Hill, the director of Bothingham's. He was tall, thin, and very pale, with thick spectacles. He looked like just the sort of man who spent all his time in a gloomy cellar looking at pottery. His hair was dark, so it was possible he was the man Maudie had seen talking to Thomas Harden.

At the moment, however, I was more interested in the woman, based on a rather unexpected flash of surprise across her face as we approached. Or, to be more precise, as Major Ramsey approached.

"This is Jocelyn Abbot," Sir Nigel said, glancing at the major. "But you know Jocelyn, I think, Ramsey?"

Even if there hadn't been a slightly malicious gleam of amusement in Sir Nigel's expression, I would have noticed the least pause in conversation as the major and Miss Abbot looked at each other. There was a history here, I realized at once. Missing pilot fiancé or no, she and Major Ramsey clearly had been more than mere acquaintances. Well, wasn't that interesting.

"Hello, Jocelyn," the major said blandly.

"Hello, Gabriel." So women did call him Gabriel, after all. Her voice, in contrast to the crispness of his tone, was soft and warm.

I looked her over as she and the major relived whatever memories they were sharing. As in the photographs I had seen of her in the society pages, she was a tall, lovely woman, with golden hair and piercing dark eyes. She was dressed to the nines in black satin, and she was very thin. Worried about the fate of Barnaby Ellhurst—or something else?

At last, those eyes turned to me. She greeted me politely enough, but I saw her taking my measure at once, her gaze running from my hair and down my dress. It was a thorough appraisal, and I supposed she might have examined my legs to see if the silk stockings on them were real if she had been able to.

I felt a bit smug about my stockings. They could have the gown back when all this was over, but the stockings I could use.

Sir Nigel finished his introductions, and the group began to chat about the two topics of most interest to Londoners: the weather and the war.

We then broke off into smaller groups, the pleasant hum of conversation mingling with the cracking of the fire.

"Do you have much of an interest in Chinese porcelain, Miss Donaldson?" Leslie Turner-Hill asked, turning to me. I was fairly certain he was being sarcastic. Perhaps he resented ignorant intruders at his educational event.

"I think the Ming pieces are quite lovely," I said. "Especially the Xuande period. Although, I confess I'm more fascinated by the hunping jars of the Han dynasty. So intriguing, aren't they?"

He blinked. "Er. Yes. Quite so."

"Of course, I don't know much about it," I said with a smile. "I just do a bit of reading here and there. But I'm quite interested to see the pieces you'll be discussing tonight."

I happened to glance at Major Ramsey just then and saw that his brows had risen ever so slightly at my sudden display of knowledge. Our eyes met briefly and the faintest smile—could it actually be approval?—crossed his lips.

Mr. Turner-Hill left me alone after that, though I kept my eye on him as he moved away from our group.

I watched the major, too, intrigued to see that this social side of him was much different from the rigid way he normally carried himself. Of course, there was no reason why he should have revealed that side of himself to me when he was playing the commanding officer, but I found the change in him to be interesting. For one thing, he seemed much more relaxed. It wasn't that he had dropped his stern demeanor, but there was something added to it, something more polished and pleasant. A different kind of confidence. He even smiled occasionally, which revealed a beautiful set of white teeth.

Everyone seemed to enjoy his company and go out of their way to speak to him. Everyone except Jocelyn Abbot, that is. It seemed to me that the two of them were ignoring each other while trying very hard to pretend that they weren't.

I had the strong impression that there was some sort of unfinished business between them. What had their relationship been, and when had Barnaby Ellhurst come into it? I remembered suddenly the article I had read, a broken engagement with an eligible bachelor. But surely that hadn't been *Major Ramsey*? I had a lot of questions to ask him when this evening was over.

The major paid me very little attention as I conversed with the other guests, so I was surprised when he suddenly appeared at my side, put a hand on my back, and leaned in close, his warm breath whispering across my neck. "Don't look now, but Matthew Winthrop's just come in. The dark fellow in the gray suit."

I nodded and smiled as though he had said something very amusing. Then I turned my head to look up at him. He was still leaning toward me, and I found that his face was much closer than I had expected it to be. There was an odd little jolt of surprise in my stomach as our eyes met. He held my gaze for a moment before his hand dropped from my back and he turned away.

When I looked away from him, I saw that Jocelyn Abbot was watching us.

I glanced toward the door to see the man the major had indicated. Matthew Winthrop was a surly young man with dark hair and eyes. He skulked into the room looking so obviously suspicious that I wondered if he could possibly be guilty of anything. Surely the Nazis would recruit better spies than that?

It was just then that I noticed, for the first time, a rather large, hulking gentleman standing alone in one corner of the room, his eyes playing over the gathering. Jerome Curtis, Sir Nigel's henchman, I presumed. His watchful face was characterized by several scars and a misshapen nose, and, from where I stood, his dark eyes looked like shining black holes in his face.

He looked just the sort of man who would slit a throat. Good lord, did these people recruit directly from the villain warehouse?

Well, anyway, I now had all five of our quarries in sight.

Let the games begin.

Things got rather boring after that. The next hour or so was a mind-numbing blur of introductions, small talk, and speculation about the pottery we would be viewing later in the evening. I could mingle in society well enough, but I found it awfully tedious to make conversation with strangers about things that were of little interest to me. And, despite the newspapers I had skimmed on the topic the night before, I didn't have much interest in Chinese porcelain. Clearly Major Ramsey had misrepresented things a bit when he had called this a party.

At least the food, which was served on a long table buffet-style, was good.

The major and I, by design, moved about different sides of the room, keeping an eye on the five suspects. I tried not to think about the silly physical reaction I'd had to the major. Just because he was attractive did not mean I was attracted to *him*. The two things were entirely different.

I pushed the thoughts away and attempted to focus on the conversation I was having with an elderly gentleman about whether

London would fall to the Germans. I offered my opinion that, as Churchill had said, we would fight in the street before that happened, as my gaze followed Sir Nigel.

He moved with ease through the room, chatting with his guests, laughing with the men and flirting with the women, the consummate host. I distrusted him instinctively. There was something off-putting about that kind of superficial charm.

Of course, just because he was egotistical didn't mean the man was a Nazi spy.

As though sensing that I was watching him, Sir Nigel moved away from a group of guests and came up to me, handing me a champagne glass.

"Enjoying yourself, Miss Donaldson?"

"Very much," I said brightly. I accepted the glass but didn't drink from it. I wasn't entirely sure I trusted the man, and, even if I had, I needed a completely clear head tonight.

"I'm afraid things might get dull once we get around to discussing the porcelain," Sir Nigel said. "Unless, of course, you're a collector yourself?"

"I have a mild interest in such things, though I certainly don't know much about it."

"It's a strange hobby to outsiders, I suppose. But there's something magnificent about fragile objects that have stood the test of time."

"Yes," I agreed. "Appearances can be deceiving."

His gaze settled on my face for a moment.

"How long have you and Ramsey known each other?" he asked at last.

I almost suspected he was trying to throw me off guard with the sudden change in topics, but I had been prepared for questions. I was glad the major and I had gone over our story together. At least we wouldn't be telling people different versions of how we met.

"Only a few weeks, but it seems like much longer."

He smiled. "Yes, when one is young it always does."

The words might have sounded sentimental, but I already knew Sir Nigel well enough to recognize the cynicism and the condescension in them.

"Everything happens faster in wartime, don't you think?" I replied.

"I suppose so."

I realized that I shouldn't overdo it. After all, anyone who knew Major Ramsey would know that he wasn't a "love at first sight" sort of fellow.

"Of course, I'm speaking only of myself," I said. "I don't really know how Gabriel feels. It's difficult to tell with him, isn't it? Do you know him well?"

"I've known the family for quite a long time."

I spoke aloud the first thought that came to my head. "Do they all have such frightfully good posture?"

He laughed heartily. "That's excellent, Miss Donaldson. Yes, I'm afraid they're all a bit stiff upon first acquaintance, but you needn't let that worry you. Lord Overbrook will like you very much indeed."

"Lord Overbrook?"

Sir Nigel's smile widened. "Ramsey didn't tell you, did he? Of course not. He's never been one to flaunt the connection. His uncle is the Earl of Overbrook."

Since it was obvious I hadn't known, I didn't bother to hide my surprise. "No," I said. "He didn't mention that detail."

The nephew of an earl. So Major Ramsey was upper crust indeed.

"I suppose an earl must have very good posture," I said with a smile.

"Ramsey's never been one to make use of his family connections, of course," Sir Nigel said. "Though, I've no doubt it was his uncle's influence that got him out of North Africa before things began to heat up too much. A desk is much safer than the desert, after all."

I don't know why I felt the need to defend the major against this insinuation, but I did.

"I don't think he wanted to come back," I said, though I, of course, knew nothing about the matter. "He'd much rather be in the field than behind a desk."

"Oh, of course. But Overbrook is the sort of man who gets what he wants. And, after all, Ramsey's a clever chap. I'm sure he'll make his mark on things here in London."

Sir Nigel seemed to be the sort of man who enjoyed making offhanded snide remarks, but I knew that if he thought the major had been recalled due to family connections, others must, too. And surely Major Ramsey must realize that people thought it. I knew it would be grating to him, to have people believe his uncle had pulled strings to get him a desk job safely away from the front lines.

"I'm sure Gabriel will acquit himself admirably in whatever he's called upon to do." I let just the faintest hint of irritation edge my tone, as it would have if this man had said such a thing about a man I was dating.

He smiled at me, a bit patronizingly, I thought. "No doubt. Now, as much as I hate to leave your charming company, I'm afraid I must go and speak with Turner-Hill about the proceedings."

"Of course."

He left me alone, Jerome Curtis following him like some great, ominous shadow, and I was still thinking about this newest revelation about Major Ramsey as my gaze began to move around the room again. It was a good thing I was accustomed to using both my mind and my eyes; if I hadn't been paying attention, I would have missed the fact that one of the waiters serving champagne had unobtrusively slipped a piece of paper to Matthew Winthrop.

CHAPTER FOURTEEN

Matthew Winthrop took the piece of paper and, glancing quickly around the room, turned his back to the crowd and opened it, his eyes scanning the paper. Then he slipped it into his pocket. All very suspect behavior.

I looked around for Major Ramsey, but he was nowhere to be seen. That was all right, I supposed, for I would be better at this particular job anyway.

I set down the glass of champagne Sir Nigel had given me. Then I sauntered in a leisurely way to where Mr. Winthrop stood at the edge of the room, his back to the wall. He had the appearance of someone who was here against his will, and I knew it wasn't unlikely he would make a break for it at the earliest opportunity. I needed to act quickly.

Despite his gloomy air, I was confident I could warm him up. We McDonnells had never been short on charm.

"Hello," I said when I reached him.

He glanced at me dismissively, but then decided to take a second look. It appeared he didn't entirely dislike what he saw.

"Hello," he answered, his frown letting up ever so slightly.

"Are you enjoying the party?" I asked.

He shrugged. "Well enough, I suppose."

I extended my hand to him. "I'm Elizabeth Donaldson."

He took my hand. "Matthew Winthrop."

"Pleased to meet you, Mr. Winthrop. I don't know many people here, and, when I saw you standing against the wall, I thought it looked like a nice out-of-the-way place."

"I'm not much of one for large gatherings."

"Neither am I," I said. "Did you come alone?"

"Yes." He looked at me with growing interest. "Did you?"

I sighed. "No. I came with someone, but he's wandered off."

"That was remiss of him," he said with a faint smile, something slightly friendlier in his tone. There. We were making progress.

I nodded. "He thought I might be interested in looking at the porcelain. His uncle collects the stuff, I think. I don't know much about it. Are you a collector?"

"In a manner of speaking."

I gave him a teasing smile. "You don't have the look of a man who's interested in ancient porcelain."

He was warming to me. I could tell. He had turned his body toward me, and there was now something very close to a smile hovering on his lips. "What sort of look do I have?"

I pretended to look him over and consider even as I remembered what the major had said about his being an aspiring poet. "You look as though you would write poetry," I said at last.

He gave a little laugh. "I do write poetry."

"Do you?" I tried to sound delighted. "How wonderful!"

"Do you like poetry?"

At least this I could answer honestly. "I like it very much. It's always seemed like magic to me, the way poets can put into words thoughts and feelings that seem almost impossible to express."

He nodded. "It's what makes poetry such a challenge, but there's nothing like the satisfaction of when it turns out the right way."

"I can imagine. Is it very difficult to write poems?"

"Sometimes it's a Herculean task. Sometimes it's the easiest thing in the world." There was a slightly dreamy quality to his voice now; it was like I had turned a key and a door had slid open before me.

"Fascinating," I said. "How often do you write poems?"

"The muses are erratic, I'm afraid. There is no telling when they might strike, but it's often at the most inconvenient times."

"Is that what you were doing standing here all alone when I interrupted you? Thinking about poetry?"

"I . . . ah, yes." He was a bad liar. That was noteworthy.

"Do you just make up the lines in your head?"

I didn't miss the enthusiasm that flashed in his eyes at my questions. It was the same look Uncle Mick got when he was going to start talking about locks. "As a matter of fact, I keep a notebook on me at all times."

"Oh, really? Do read some of it to me! I'm fascinated with the creative process." It was an effort to keep myself from rolling my eyes at my own malarkey. The last thing I wanted to do was hear this young fascist's poems. It seemed he was buying what I was selling, however, for a flush had spread across his cheeks.

"It's really just a bunch of rough lines. I write the poems themselves on a typewriter."

"Perhaps you can recite something from memory." I hoped the government appreciated the service I was doing them.

"I'm not much accustomed to reciting aloud. I mostly put together collections to be read."

"Couldn't you make an exception?" I stepped closer, brazenly placing a hand on his arm and leaning in closer. He didn't seem to mind.

"Well, I suppose . . . I have one called 'Lark's Song in the Evening.' It's . . ."

"Excuse me." I looked up to see Major Ramsey approaching. He had that commanding officer look on his face again. I felt Mr. Winthrop's posture stiffen beside me.

"Hello, Gabriel," I said brightly, dropping my hand from

Matthew Winthrop's arm and easing back ever so slightly from him. "Mr. Winthrop, this is Major Gabriel Ramsey. Gabriel, this is Matthew Winthrop. He's a poet. He's just been telling me the most fascinating things about . . ."

"How do you do," Major Ramsey interrupted coolly. "Elizabeth, may I speak to you?"

"Yes, in a moment."

"Now." There was a beat of silence before he added, "Please."

There was nothing I could say to that without making a scene, and I didn't suppose that would be useful. Though, if a man had talked to me that way in other circumstances, I would have let him know what I thought of it.

I gave Matthew Winthrop an apologetic look. "Perhaps I'll see you later? I would so like to hear your poem."

He nodded. His face had closed up upon Major Ramsey's arrival. I had a feeling, however, that he wouldn't object to picking up the conversation again.

Without further ado, the major took my arm and led me away to a secluded corner of the room. "What are you doing?" he asked in a low voice as I turned to face him.

"I was talking to Mr. Winthrop. What are you doing?" I asked this, though it was clear that what he was doing was reading me a lecture.

"This wasn't part of the plan," he said. "I told you to follow my instructions. You were not to approach the suspects."

I realized he still held my elbow, so I pulled my arm from his grasp. "I'm capable of holding a conversation without putting myself in danger." My tone was mild, but I could feel my temper beginning to simmer below the surface. I clearly wasn't cut out for military service; I instinctively resented orders.

"Stop frowning," he commanded. "People will notice."

"They'll think we're having a lovers' quarrel," I retorted. "After all, you did just drag me away from another man's side."

He gave a quick glance around the room. "Yes, you were quite close to his side. What did you intend to do from there?"

I had been going to tell him about the message I had seen Mr. Winthrop receive, but he was making me angry, and I never felt like being cooperative when I was in that frame of mind.

When I didn't answer, he leaned forward, his eyes on mine, and dropped his voice so there was no chance of being overheard. "I've recruited you to open safes, Miss McDonnell, not seduce the enemy."

I gritted my teeth, and my fists clenched at my sides. *Don't lose your temper, Ellie. Don't lose your temper.* I drew in a breath through my nose and let it out slowly, but I was losing the battle. I could feel the blood pounding in my ears as I glared at him, not trusting myself to reply.

"Oh dear. I hope I'm not interrupting at a bad time." We dragged our eyes from each other and turned to see Sir Nigel walking toward us, a smile on his lips. He knew perfectly well that he was, and neither of us bothered to reassure him.

Major Ramsey stepped back slightly from me, his expression once again bland.

"A lovers' quarrel, is it? Well, 'the course of true love never did run smooth.' Isn't that the saying?" Sir Nigel asked. He was enjoying this. "Alas, Miss Donaldson, I have to side with Ramsey on this one, I'm afraid. I wouldn't leave you alone with Winthrop for long either. Despite the boy's gloomy countenance, he has a reputation."

So he'd been watching, had he? Well, at least we had made a good show of it.

I managed a tight smile. "I can look after myself, Sir Nigel." The man was beginning to irritate me, and there was only so much a fine gown and silk stockings could do to hold down an Irish temper.

He grinned, and I wondered if he sensed how difficult it was for me to remain civil. Somehow, I thought he did. "I don't doubt it, Miss Donaldson. Not for a moment. I merely hope you aren't too cross at Ramsey here. He means well."

I glanced at the major. His expression was impossible to read.

"Were you looking for me, Sir Nigel?" he asked.

Sir Nigel smiled. "Yes, I ought to mind my own business, oughtn't I? The real reason I came over was to tell you Turner-Hill is about to begin his presentation, if you care to come to the ballroom. We've chairs set up there."

"Yes, we'll be there in a moment," Major Ramsey said.

"Don't muck it up, old boy," Sir Nigel said, patting the major's shoulder as he walked away. "Women like Miss Donaldson don't come along every day."

He left us alone and the major turned to face me again. Whatever Sir Nigel's intentions had been, he'd defused the situation effectively enough. The intensity of a moment before had fizzled out, and, though I was still irritated with the major, I no longer felt as though steam was coming out of my ears.

It was then Major Ramsey surprised me. "I apologize if I've offended you," he said. "I'm merely concerned for your safety."

I hadn't expected an apology, and it caught me off guard.

"I appreciate that," I said. "But if we're to work together, I'd appreciate a bit of trust in my abilities."

"I don't doubt your abilities," he said. "If I did, you wouldn't be here."

Was he trying to throw me off by complimenting me? I wouldn't put it past him. Whatever the case, I still had a few grievances to be aired.

"Yet you've been keeping secrets from me," I said in a low voice. If I had hoped this would startle him into some sort of admission, I was hoping in vain. He didn't so much as blink at the accusation.

"I keep secrets from everybody," he replied, his gaze moving around the room.

"You didn't tell me you're the nephew of an earl."

He turned back to me and let out an irritated breath. "Because it doesn't signify."

"I'm meant to be your . . ." I paused and settled on the least offensive word I could think of. "Sweetheart. We're supposed to give the impression that we've been seeing each other, and keeping such things secret makes it look as though I know very little about you."

"It's our fourth date. You're not likely to know much about me."

"Is that also why you didn't mention your history with Jocelyn Abbot?" I asked.

This got his attention. He turned his pale eyes to me. Winter twilight, I realized. That was the shade of his eyes. The color of an evening sky descending over a snowy field.

For pity's sake, Ellie, I thought. *Now's not the time to make poetry about him.* I was getting as bad as Matthew Winthrop.

"Who told you that?" he asked.

"The two of you aren't exactly subtle."

I think this, more than anything I had said that evening, annoyed him.

"We saw each other socially for a time. It was over long before any of this started, and it has no bearing on anything." As usual, he was understating things; it had clearly been much more than a social acquaintance. I supposed, however, that now was not the time to discuss it.

Still, I couldn't resist adding, "If I'd had a relationship with any of the suspects, I think you'd have been quite put out that I didn't make it known."

"Now is not the time to discuss it," he said. Though I had just had the same thought, it irritated me to hear him say it.

"I know it's none of my business. Or wouldn't be, under normal circumstances, but I think I have the right to know what I was getting into."

He seemed as though he was about to make some sort of retort but thought better of it. He paused for just a moment and then looked me in the eye. "You're right. I'll make an effort to do a better job of keeping you informed in the future."

I eyed him suspiciously.

"Shall we be friends again?" he asked, holding out his hand.

My brows went up. "Were we ever friends?" I questioned.

He gave me a look.

I sighed. "Fine. Friends."

I placed my hand in his. I thought he would shake it briefly and release it, but he held on for a moment. His grip was firm and warm.

"And, in return, you'll stay away from the suspects," he said. It wasn't a question.

I tried to pull my hand away, but he was holding it too tightly. He'd tricked me into a handshake.

"I'll make an effort," I said, throwing his words back at him.

"Good." He released my hand.

"But, if you hadn't been in a strop," I went on, "I would have had time to tell you that I had a very good reason for talking to Matthew Winthrop."

"Oh?"

"Yes. I was watching him from across the room, and I saw one of the waiters pass him a note. He read it surreptitiously and put it in the pocket of his jacket."

He let out an irritated breath. "And you're just telling me this now."

"You didn't give me much of a chance before," I retorted.

"And that's why you decided to approach him," he said, his voice having lost the conciliatory tone of a moment ago. "What? Did you suppose that if you talked with him for a while, took an interest in his poetry, that he would take the note out and show it to you?"

He really was an insufferable prig at times.

"No," I replied, holding up the folded piece of paper that had been clutched in my left hand throughout all of this. "I thought I could take it from his pocket."

CHAPTER FIFTEEN

The major stared at me for a moment, as though trying to decide how he should react to this newest proof of my criminal tendencies.

"A pickpocket, too?" he said at last. "Your talents are diverse."

"It's more of a parlor trick than a useful skill, but it proved useful enough tonight, didn't it?"

He didn't answer and, before I could protest, had reached out to take the paper from my fingers.

I wanted to snatch it back. After all, it was I who had retrieved it. We had, however, called enough attention to ourselves already tonight.

He glanced around the room. Most of the party had begun to move toward the ballroom, where Leslie Turner-Hill was to begin his lecture. We would have to go ourselves soon or be missed.

Turning his back to the room, the major opened the piece of paper, his eyes scanning it. I couldn't tell from his expression what he thought, but when could I ever?

I leaned forward to examine it. It was written in black ink in a style that made the handwriting unexceptional. It was also complete gibberish.

"Is it the same code as the one in Harden's book?" I asked.

"It appears so," he said. He tucked it into his own pocket. "I'll have someone look at it. In the meantime, we'll keep a close eye on Mr. Winthrop."

"Don't you think he's bound to miss the note eventually?" I asked.

"Probably, but he won't know when or where he lost it."

"Can we rule out the others then?"

"I don't think we can rule anyone out. I'm still very much interested to have a look in Sir Nigel's safe. Once the lecture has started, we'll slip out and go to his study."

I nodded.

He offered me his arm, and, after the briefest hesitation, I took it and we made our way toward the ballroom. It was the most impressive room yet, and that was saying something. It was a vast space with gold-papered walls, gilded moldings, a row of gleaming chandeliers, and a muraled ceiling with multiple scenes from mythology painted across its expanse.

I looked up at the mural above us. It depicted a woman crossing a dark river in a boat with a grim helmsman, her face a mixture of fear and determination.

"Persephone in the Underworld," the major said in a low voice, following my gaze.

"No," I replied. "Psyche's final task."

He glanced at me, but I said no more as we slipped into two seats near the back.

We were a bit late, as Leslie Turner-Hill was already speaking from a podium at the front of the room, the crowd intent on his lecture.

"As you all know, Blanc de Chine may vary in color," he was saying. "The first piece I wish to show tonight is an exceptional example of Dehua porcelain."

There was a table beside the podium, with several pieces exhibited upon it, and, as he spoke, he began to move along and talk about them. We were too far back, however, to have a good view.

My eyes began to blur a bit after that, almost like a qingbai glaze, one might say. I was interested enough in artifacts and antiquities, but the speech Mr. Turner-Hill was giving was geared more toward fanatics. I noticed that Sir Nigel and Jocelyn Abbot sat near the front of the audience, both smiling appreciatively at all the right points in the lecture.

I stole a glance at the major, waiting for some sort of cue that it was time to go to work. He appeared perfectly absorbed in the lecture, his posture relaxed. I shifted in my seat, my thigh brushing his before I moved it quickly away.

Mr. Turner-Hill moved on to the next piece of porcelain. He made some sort of obscure pottery pun, and the audience laughed.

The major turned his head ever so slightly in my direction then and spoke in a tone so low it was almost inaudible. "In just a moment, go out into the hall, and wait for me in the alcove by the stairs."

I nodded.

As the lecture continued, I rose and slipped past the major, moving unhurriedly out of the ballroom and into the foyer. It was cool here, away from all the closely seated bodies, and Mr. Turner-Hill's voice had faded to a murmur. I took a deep breath, readying myself for the next stage of the operation.

Then I walked toward the large marble staircase. It was across the foyer from the front door and stopped at a wide landing before branching off into two separate staircases that circled upward. Beneath the ground floor staircase there was a little alcove with a velvet settee. I sat on it, waiting for the major to come out.

Was this going to work? I certainly hoped so, though I wasn't entirely optimistic. Sir Nigel seemed to me to be a very wily sort of person, and I wasn't sure that he would keep the papers in a safe. Surely there must be hundreds of hiding places in a house this size.

"Elizabeth." I looked up to see the major standing there. I hadn't even heard him approaching.

He held out a hand, and, without thinking, I rose and went to him, sliding my hand into his.

Without a word, he turned and led me out of the alcove and down a long corridor. "Do you think we'll be missed?" I asked, when I was certain we were out of earshot of the ballroom.

"I doubt it. This crowd seems very absorbed in the lecture. But if we are, they'll assume we've snuck off to be alone for a while." I supposed his leading me away by the hand had been intentional. If anyone had happened to observe us, it might have looked very much as though we were sneaking off for an illicit rendezvous.

I glanced at him. "Are they likely to believe such a thing of you, Major Ramsey?" I wasn't teasing him, not entirely. There was something so very staid about him at all times that I found it difficult to imagine anyone might think we had snuck away for a tryst during the middle of a lecture on Chinese porcelain. Then again, what better time?

"I take it you haven't noticed the way the men here have been watching you tonight," he said. "I'm sure they wouldn't blame me for being tempted."

For a moment I wasn't sure I had heard him right. He wasn't flirting with me, surely. He didn't even glance in my direction. He sounded as though he was serious, and I didn't know whether to be flattered or amused.

This less public part of the house was in keeping with all the other finery on display: all thick carpets and dark walls and gold-framed paintings. I assumed that the major would know the layout of the house, so I followed him without question.

The corridor was dimly lit here, with only select sconces along the hallway alight. Things were much quieter, too, the only sound the very faint swishing of my velvet dress as we walked. I realized the fabric was much better for housebreaking than satin or silk might have been. I would have to keep that in mind for future endeavors.

We reached a door toward the end of the corridor, and the major glanced behind us before opening it and ushering me inside, closing the door. It was almost completely dark until he switched on a lamp near the door he must have seen from the dim light in the hallway.

Even in the soft glow from the lamp, I could see it was a beautiful room, a cross between an office and a library. Three of the walls were covered with bookshelves. The far wall was all made up of high windows, which were currently covered with long, black shades.

The furniture was heavy and beautifully made. A big desk sat in the middle of the room. There were also a set of chairs and a leather sofa that sat to one side. It looked the ideal place to spend an afternoon reading or writing correspondence. Or even hatching plots against one's own government, I supposed.

"The safe is here," Major Ramsey said, moving without hesitation toward a painting on the wall between two rows of shelves. I was no art expert, but I didn't like the picture, and I could see how it might have been chosen to hide something else rather than on its own merits. It clearly wasn't of the same quality as most of the pieces in the house. Somehow, I thought it seemed beneath Sir Nigel's cleverness, but maybe it was some sort of private joke.

The major grabbed the thick gilded frame by one edge and gave it a little tug. It came loose, opening like the cover of a book to reveal the safe in the wall behind it.

"How did you know it was there?" I asked.

"I've done my research," he replied, as usual answering my questions in a manner that gave me absolutely no information.

He moved slightly out of the way and motioned me forward.

I was relieved to see that I was familiar with the model. It wasn't one of the high-quality burglar-proof safes, but something much simpler. The first thing I tried was the manufacturer's combination. I didn't suppose Sir Nigel would be so careless as to neglect to change the combination, but it was worth a try.

A quick check confirmed it had been changed.

"May I have the paper and pencil, please?"

He reached into his pocket and handed them to me. They were

the only tools I had told him I needed, but I had no place to carry them. The dress was decidedly not made for concealing things.

"How long will it take you?" he asked behind my shoulder.

"Longer than necessary if you hover behind me."

He let out a breath and stepped back. I listened as his steps moved toward the desk. The drawer rattled.

"Locked?" I asked, looking over my shoulder.

"I didn't expect it to be open."

"Here, let me." I moved toward him as I reached up and took a pin from my hair. It was the sort of thing that was always being done in books and at the cinema, but it really did work. One just had to have the right angle and know the right sort of pressure to apply.

It was the work of only a few seconds for the lock to give. Really, if more people knew how easily ordinary locks were picked, they would invest in better security for their important things.

The major began sifting through the papers, and I moved back toward the safe.

I tuned him out after that, focusing the way Uncle Mick had taught me to do. For a long time there was nothing but me and the dial, the almost imperceptible changes in give as I found the contact points.

I supposed the major wished the lock was as pliant as the one on the desk drawer had been, but I was enjoying every moment of it. I felt calm, almost relaxed, as I worked, testing the dial and graphing the points in the notebook.

My brain felt sharper and clearer than it ever had. Was it the knowledge that I was using my talent for the good of my country? Whatever the case, I graphed out the combination in what felt like record time.

Turning the dial, I felt it give, and I pulled the safe open. "There," I said softly.

Major Ramsey was at my side in an instant. "Well done, Miss McDonnell."

He pulled a torch from his pocket and shone it inside the safe. Reaching in, he sifted through the contents.

I held my breath.

"No," he said after a moment. "They're not here."

"Are you sure?"

"There are no documents here at all."

I fought down my disappointment. I had known from the beginning that it was a long shot. After all, Sir Nigel was a clever man, and, if it was he who had taken the papers, I thought he might have known better than to put them in his safe. It was still disappointing, though.

The major stepped away from the safe, and I couldn't resist looking inside myself. He was right; there were only a few jewelry boxes inside. It seemed that Sir Nigel kept his valuable documents elsewhere.

"Shall I close it?" I asked the major.

"Yes," he answered, not bothering to look at me.

I closed it and spun the dial, Uncle Mick's words echoing in my head. *Always leave things the way you found them, lass.* I pushed the painting back into place.

Was everything just the same? I went over our movements in my head. No, not quite. There were still the desk drawers to be tended to.

"There was nothing worthwhile in the desk?" I asked.

"No."

"Perhaps he's keeping them somewhere else."

"That doesn't do us any good, does it?" There was an edge to his voice, but I knew him well enough now to know it was not directed at me. He was frustrated with our failure. I certainly couldn't blame him for that.

I went to the desk drawer I had opened and, using the pin I had left on the desk, managed to push the lock back into place. Straightening the bent pin, I pushed it back into my hair. Now no one would ever know that we had been here.

"What now?" I asked, moving to the major's side.

He sighed. "Now we're back where we started."

"We've got the message that was slipped to Matthew Winthrop," I said. "That's something, isn't it?"

He turned to look at me, his expression unreadable. "We'd better go back. I'm sure the lecture is nearly finished by now."

That meant he didn't want to talk about it. He was the sort of man who liked to collect his thoughts before discussion, so I wouldn't press him now. Besides, we were going to be missed if we didn't get back soon.

We had just reached the door when we heard the unmistakable sound of voices in the hallway outside.

Major Ramsey held up a hand, signaling me to be still. It was very annoying when he instructed me to do things I was obviously going to do anyway.

There were two voices outside the room. I recognized the first as Sir Nigel's.

"I don't like it," he said. "I want you to go and look into things."

"I'll leave now."

"No. Wait until after my guests have gone. It will be less conspicuous."

I didn't hear the answer, if there was one, because I was busy thinking over our options.

I cast my eyes around the room. There was only one door. If they were coming to the library, we'd have to either hide or find a good excuse. We had gotten ourselves in a fine mess now. I had the same sensation of unease on the back of my neck now as I had the night when Uncle Mick and I had been caught.

I looked up at Major Ramsey. I could almost see the various scenarios flashing across his eyes as he considered the options. Then he leaned toward me, so close his lips were almost touching my cheek.

"I apologize in advance," he said in a low voice. "But I'm going to have to kiss you."

CHAPTER SIXTEEN

The startling words took me by surprise for just a moment, but then I realized what he meant. Being caught kissing would be much less troubling than being caught snooping around someone's library in the semidarkness. After all, it had been the plan to make it look that way if we were discovered leaving the lecture together.

All the same, it occurred to me a simple embrace wasn't going to be enough to explain our presence here, so far from the ballroom when we might easily have shared a kiss in the alcove or the deserted drawing room. We needed to be convincing.

I glanced around us, at where we stood near the doorway, thinking how ridiculous and implausible it would look to anyone walking in that we might just be standing here kissing.

As whoever was talking stopped outside the door, I grabbed his arm and pulled him over to the cluster of furniture in the center of the room, stopping near the leather sofa.

"Do a proper job of it," I instructed. Reaching up, I quickly unbuttoned the top button of his tunic and reached up to muss his hair. Then, before I could give myself too much time to think about what I was doing, I fell upon the sofa and pulled him down with me.

Whatever else might be said of Major Ramsey, he was a quick

study. He ran a hand through my hair in return, pulled one strap of my gown down from my shoulder, and—in a rather smooth gesture—slid one hand beneath the hem of my skirt and up my leg as the doorknob rattled. I didn't have time to marvel at this exceptionally efficient tousling before his mouth found mine.

The kissing was done as he did everything else: thoroughly and extremely competently. We were meant to appear to be caught in the middle of a passionate embrace, not at the beginning of it, and there was no reservation or hesitation in his manner as we commenced to full-fledged necking. He did a proper job of it, all right, and I had to admit that it was not at all unpleasant. It was all an act, of course, but it was a natural enough thing to wrap my arms around his neck and participate.

By the time the door opened, we were caught in a thoroughly compromising position.

It had only been a matter of moments since the kiss began, but I was still a bit dizzy as he pulled his mouth away, disentangled himself from me, and stood up quickly, turning to face the door. Sir Nigel stood in the doorway. Whoever he had been talking to in the hallway was no longer there. I'd hazard a guess it had been Jerome Curtis.

The major's shoulders stiffened as he adjusted his tunic, calling attention to the buttons I had managed to undo.

I sat up on the sofa, pulling up the strap of my gown, smoothing out my skirts, and patting down my hair, all while doing my best to affect a thoroughly embarrassed expression. I dropped my gaze, and I found it wasn't quite necessary to feign mortification. I had been caught robbing a house, true enough, but I had never been caught on a stranger's sofa with a man's hand up my skirt.

Though I was averting my eyes from Sir Nigel, I caught a quick glance of his expression, and I thought that our little ruse might have done the trick. He didn't look angry or even suspicious; instead, a bit of an amused smile hovered on the corners of his mouth.

"I beg your pardon," he said dryly. "I didn't know the room was occupied."

"I'm sorry, Sir Nigel," Major Ramsey said stiffly. "I'm afraid I've taken advantage of your hospitality and acted very badly."

He stood slightly in front of me, as though shielding me from the brunt of the embarrassment, and I noticed that he didn't offer excuses. Of course, what excuses could one offer for such behavior? I felt a bit smug at how well we had pulled it off.

"No need to apologize, old boy," Sir Nigel said with a smile, his eyes flickering to me for just a moment. "Glad to see you've mended things with your young lady—and that you're capable of getting carried away like the rest of us."

Major Ramsey's posture grew, if possible, a bit stiffer.

"Elizabeth and I . . ." His voice trailed off. "I suppose we'd better get back to the lecture."

He turned and offered me a hand, helping me up from the sofa.

"Of course," Sir Nigel said. "And don't worry about me. I'm the soul of discretion. There's a war on, after all. One might as well enjoy life while one can."

"Thank you," I said in a low voice, still refraining from meeting his gaze.

Major Ramsey took me by the arm, and we made a hasty exit from the room.

My heart was pounding as he led me wordlessly down the hallway toward the foyer. I could hear the sound of laughter and conversation from the front part of the house. Apparently, the lecture was over.

"Wait a moment." The major caught my arm when we were still out of sight of the rest of the guests, and I turned to look up at him. I half expected him to look chagrined after what we'd just been caught doing, but he hadn't lost any of the composure I was beginning to realize he wore like a second skin. "Your hair is . . . untidy," he said.

I reached up and felt that my chignon was indeed lopsided, curls cascading down one side of my neck. That pin I'd bent to pick the desk drawer lock had apparently given way and left me askew. That and the major's fingers in my hair. For some silly reason, I flushed.

I fished into the other side of my hair and pulled out a pin. Rolling up the loose curls, I pinned them back into place as best I could.

"Better?" I asked the major, for want of a mirror.

He studied me. "May I?" he asked at last, motioning toward my hair.

I nodded.

He reached out to smooth the wave at the front of my face and then tucked another errant curl behind my ear. There was nothing tender in the way he did it, but I still felt the skin of my neck go hot. What on earth was wrong with me?

"Thank you," I said, looking up at him. Then my flush deepened. "Oh. You . . . you've got lipstick on your mouth."

He pulled a handkerchief from his pocket and rubbed it across his mouth. "Better?"

"May I?" I asked.

He nodded, and I used my thumb to wipe the remaining smudge from beneath his lower lip. How very strange it was to think that he had been kissing me moments ago. If it wasn't for the ample evidence, I might have thought I'd imagined the whole thing. Not that I had ever imagined kissing Major Ramsey.

"I apologize again for that," he said.

"There's no need," I replied briskly, forcing myself to meet his gaze. "There couldn't have been a better reason for us to be alone in that room together."

"You thought rather quickly yourself," he said, no doubt remembering how I had wantonly pulled him down atop me on the sofa.

I managed an embarrassed smile. "Yes, well, I thought we'd better do a thorough job of it if we were to be convincing."

I saw the corner of his mouth twitch, the hint of that smile that he so seldom let have free rein.

"Sir Nigel is a smart man, but I like to think we were convincing."

"Yes." I tried not to think about his lips on mine and that warm hand on my leg. "You're a good actor, among other things."

His eyes met mine, and I felt a fresh wave of embarrassment realizing that he probably thought I meant the kiss. Well, he had been good at that, too. There was no sense in denying it.

"I think we both acquitted ourselves admirably," he said. "Now I suppose we'd better get back before our absence draws any more notice."

We slipped back into the crowd of mingling guests without drawing much attention to ourselves, and, after a moment, I excused myself to the powder room. Though I was sure the major had done a credible job tucking my hair back into place, I needed to powder my nose and reapply my lipstick.

It was clear that Sir Nigel was accustomed to entertaining society ladies, for the powder room was as elegantly decorated as any I had seen in London nightclubs. On one wall an enormous gold-framed mirror hung atop pink brocade wallpaper. Before the mirror there was a long marble-topped table with several satin-covered stools lined in front of it. As luck would have it, Jocelyn Abbot sat at one of the stools and the one beside her was unoccupied.

Her eyes in the mirror moved my way as I entered, and then she looked away, intending to ignore me, I supposed.

I'm fairly sure she flinched when I brazenly dropped into the seat next to her. "It was a wonderful lecture, wasn't it?" I said, pulling out my tube of lipstick. "It was all so interesting."

Her reflection fastened me in its cool gaze. "Did you think so? You missed most of it."

So she'd noticed that, had she? She had been sitting near the front of the room, so I wondered how she knew. I supposed she had seen

Major Ramsey and I leaving the corridor after the lecture had ended, a bit disheveled despite our best efforts to tidy each other up.

I gave her a vaguely embarrassed smile. "I slipped out for a few moments toward the end."

"How long have you been seeing Gabriel Ramsey?" she asked. Well, now it was all out in the open. I admired a woman who got right to the point.

"Only a few weeks," I said, as I applied my lipstick. "I'm very fond of him already."

I watched her reflection as she said this, and there was a flicker of some emotion in her expression that she couldn't quite hide.

"Gabriel Ramsey is a very fine gentleman," she said at last.

"Do you know him well?"

"Yes. I know him very well." She turned to look at me directly, not in the mirror, as she said this, and I knew that she meant me to take the hint.

"Oh," I said, and I fancy I was even able to work up a bit of a blush. "I see."

She gave a careless shrug, a bit more gracious now that I had been put in my place. "I haven't seen him in some time, however."

"I . . . suppose his being away in North Africa put a strain on things." I intended, with talk of our men at war, to work the conversation around to Barnaby Ellhurst, but I was honest enough with myself to realize there was also a bit of curiosity involved.

"It wasn't the distance. There were . . . other things . . ." Her words faded off and she offered me a strained smile. "Well, it doesn't really matter."

But it clearly did. I recognized that conflicted look in her expression because it was one I had felt myself. It was, I realized, a reflection of my feelings for Felix, a sort of unresolved longing. It was obvious she had loved the major. Perhaps she still did.

So where did that leave Barnaby Ellhurst?

I waited for her to tell me about the daredevil pilot, but she

didn't. I considered that, if she wasn't a spy, it might be too painful for her. Or perhaps she had grown tired of talking about it. I
couldn't blame her for that. None of us like to relive our tragedies
over and over aloud. I had tried to bury mine so deep that a lot of
digging would be necessary to drag them out into the light.

Unfortunately, I had a job to do. There was the possibility she
was a German spy, and that was more important than delicacy at the
moment. I was about to question her on the subject when she caught
me off guard by leaning forward and placing one hand over mine.

"I hope you make him very happy," she said softly, her dark eyes
shimmering. "He deserves it."

Then she rose quickly from her seat. "Have a good evening,
Miss Donaldson."

When I came out of the powder room a moment later, she had
left the party.

CHAPTER SEVENTEEN

Major Ramsey was engaged in a conversation with an elderly gentleman, and so I took the opportunity to pounce upon Leslie Turner-Hill.

Matthew Winthrop was the obvious suspect now since he had received that coded missive, but, since we were here, we might as well be thorough.

I waited for a moment when the auction house director was alone, a group of adoring pottery-lovers having finally left his side, and made my move.

"I enjoyed the lecture very much, Mr. Turner-Hill," I said, approaching him.

He turned to look down at me over his glasses. I wondered if he had noticed the major and me slipping out of the lecture as well. If so, he didn't mention it.

"Thank you. Miss . . . Dolan, was it?"

"Donaldson. I learned a great deal from you tonight. I have a fresh appreciation for Chinese porcelain." I was laying it on thick, of course, but I had judged correctly in assuming he would respond well to flattery.

"I am considered one of the preeminent authorities on the subject," he preened, his thin, angular face suffusing with the glow of a person quite pleased with himself. "Chinese porcelain isn't my only specialty, of course, but it is, perhaps, the one dearest to my heart."

I tried to imagine this effete gentleman slitting Thomas Harden's throat and couldn't quite picture it.

"I suppose people travel from far and wide to purchase your pieces," I said. "Has the war affected that much?"

His face clouded slightly, but, though I was looking closely, I didn't see any sign of guilt in his features. "I'm afraid it has, somewhat. But wars don't last forever."

"No," I agreed. "And whatever way the wind blows, I'm sure you will still find buyers."

I was treading a thin line. The major had mentioned that he had procured pieces for high-ranking Germans before the war. Were there still connections there?

"I suppose you're right, though I have no doubt we will be the victors. England's long and glorious history supports this belief." If Leslie Turner-Hill was a liar, he was a good one. He seemed completely sincere.

"Yes, I'm sure you're right."

"You mentioned earlier the Han dynasty hunping jars," he said, deftly steering the conversation back to his favorite topic. "There were none on display tonight, of course. But we've had one or two in our auctions before. Have you been to Bothingham's?"

"I haven't had the pleasure, but my uncle has."

I thought of Uncle Mick and the major's man creeping about the auction house, perhaps even at that particular moment. Were they finding anything of use that might incriminate this gentleman?

"Indeed. Well, you shall have to attend one of our auctions. I think you'll find that there are few events more . . ."

He went on talking, but I wasn't listening. Out of the corner of my eye, I noticed Jerome Curtis slipping through a set of French doors at the side of the room.

I remembered the conversation I had overheard between him

and Sir Nigel outside the library door. At least, I presumed it had been him.

Sir Nigel had said he wanted the man to look into something. I wondered what it was.

What was more, I wondered if he was going outside to make the document drop. Given the note to Matthew Winthrop we had intercepted, it seemed unlikely. But I wanted to be sure.

I glanced around to see if Major Ramsey was anywhere about. He wasn't where I had seen him last, nor could I locate him anywhere else within easy distance. Well, it seemed it would be up to me.

Luckily, I was spared the task of disentangling myself from Mr. Turner-Hill by a group of bespectacled academics who approached, notebooks in hand, ready to discuss the merits of Jingde-zhen porcelain.

With a vague farewell, I left Leslie Turner-Hill and followed Jerome Curtis outside.

I stepped through the French doors into a small garden. It was very dark—with the blackout curtains on the doors no light shone from inside—and it took a moment for my eyes to adjust.

It was then I saw the hulking shadow of Jerome Curtis standing with his back to the wall. He was watching me from the darkness.

I pretended to be startled. "Oh! Oh, hello."

"Hello." His voice was low and coarse. He sounded just as I had expected him to; that is, the way film villains sound.

"I just came out for a bit of air," I said. "It's rather warm with so many people in there."

He said nothing. I saw the lit end of his cigarette moving as he brought it to his lips.

"Do you have a spare?" I asked. "I'm afraid I've left mine inside."

He reached into the inside pocket of his dinner jacket and pulled out a pack, holding it out.

I stepped toward him and pulled one from the pack, put it between my lips, and leaned forward expectantly, waiting for him to light it. He struck a match, which momentarily lit up his features. He looked even more frightening up close than he had from across the room. I'd known plenty of rough men, as Uncle Mick's friends were a motley crew. But there was something different about Jerome Curtis, and I tried to analyze just what it was.

His face was lumpy and misshapen, but I'd seen boxers' faces before. The scars, too, weren't especially unusual. It was his eyes, I realized. They gave the appearance of being completely black, the pupil indistinguishable from the iris. In combination with the violent past written across his features and his bulky frame, they made him look like some sort of storybook ogre.

"Thank you," I said, taking a drag of the cigarette and blowing out a stream of smoke into the darkness.

We stood there in the quiet for a moment.

I wondered why it was that he had come out here. I supposed it was possible he'd just decided to have a smoke by himself. When involved in spy games, it's easy to forget that some people are behaving without hidden motivations.

"I don't really know that much about porcelain," I said, by way of conversation. "Are you a collector?"

He glanced at me. "I work for Sir Nigel."

"Oh, that must be very interesting."

He gave something like a grunt in reply. Clearly, he didn't want to talk.

We smoked for another moment in silence.

"It's strange, isn't it?" I said at last. "The city so dark like this."

Another grunt.

"I suppose the Luftwaffe will find us anyway. Eventually."

This garnered no response.

"I just hope they don't come by land."

"They all will wish they hadn't."

I was a bit surprised that it was this statement that drew a response from him. I was also surprised by the sinister intonation of it, the clear threat in the words. He clearly didn't have any love for the Germans.

"That's what my uncle says," I told him. "My uncle . . . well, he grew up with some rough characters. Underworld types." I remembered what Major Ramsey had told me about Jerome Curtis being involved with racketeers and thought this might be the key to getting him to open up.

No such luck. He didn't respond to the bait.

I was having a difficult time getting a read on this Jerome Curtis. Maybe it was having grown up around some unsavory characters, but, despite his fearsome features, I realized I didn't feel uncomfortable with him alone in the shadows.

Maybe I should have. But I didn't have the sensation that he posed any threat to me. And, somehow, I didn't feel that he was the type of man who would side with the Germans or do any work for them. Of course, there was still the possibility that he killed at Sir Nigel's behest.

As opposed to Mr. Turner-Hill, I could very well picture Jerome Curtis slitting a man's throat without thinking twice.

The racketeering angle hadn't worked, so I decided to see if the boxing angle would yield something. I remembered a friend of Uncle Mick's, a mountain of a man with a face more battered than Jerome Curtis's and misshapen ears that had intrigued me as a child. He had come to the house several times, drinking and laughing merrily with Uncle Mick while the boys and I sat and listened to his tales of bloody bouts in the ring until Nacy had finally shooed us out of the room.

"Yes, Uncle Laddy says he'll beat the Germans himself if he has to," I said. "He was a boxer once and says he could take on at least a squadron by himself."

He looked at me. "Laddy Malone?"

I nodded, smiling brightly. "Yes! Do you know him?"

"I fought Laddy Malone back in '24," he said.

"Oh, really?"

"Nearly killed me, he did." It was the warmest I had heard his voice yet. "Took me months to recover from that fight."

"I shall have to ask him if he remembers." I hadn't seen Laddy Malone in years, and I sincerely hoped that Jerome Curtis wasn't friends with him and would question the connection. "What's your name?" I asked.

"Tell him Jolly Jerry sends his regards."

Jolly Jerry. I almost laughed aloud.

"I shall. I'm sure he'll be glad to hear you're doing well in life."

"Not as well as the old days," he said. "But I ain't as young as I used to be."

"Yes, that's what Uncle Laddy always says."

"He's right, though, about us fighters. We've still got enough in us to fight the Germans if we need to."

I nodded. "Yes, I believe you're right."

There was a small shaft of light that shone into the garden just then as the French doors opened.

"Elizabeth." I recognized that disapproving voice. The major had found me.

"Yes, coming, Gabriel," I said.

I dropped my cigarette and stubbed it out with the toe of my shoe.

"The major thinks I'm a society lady, born and bred," I said to Jerome Curtis in a whisper. "Uncle Laddy will be our little secret." Then I winked at him before I turned and followed the major inside.

CHAPTER EIGHTEEN

The major gave me one of those ice-blue glares as he led me back into the house, but he didn't say anything. I supposed he knew a lost cause when he saw one.

We didn't stay long at the party after that. The lecture had finished, and we had accomplished our goal of getting into the safe. Besides, Jocelyn Abbot and Matthew Winthrop seemed to have left the party. Leslie Turner-Hill was still there, surrounded by his acolytes, but it didn't seem he'd be passing off any papers in that situation.

We walked out into the cool evening air, and I took a deep breath, feeling that momentary sensation of weightlessness that always accompanied the end of a completed job. It had certainly been a night.

"Did you learn anything useful from Jerome Curtis?" the major asked me when we were back in the car.

"I don't get the impression he's spying for the Germans of his own free will," I said. "If he's killing, it's at Sir Nigel's behest, but somehow I don't think he's involved."

"And why is that?"

"I don't know how to explain it. But I've known men like that, dangerous men, who, oddly enough, have certain lines they won't cross. I think spying for the enemy is one of his."

The major said nothing, and we lapsed into silence as we pulled away from the house and onto the darkened roads. I supposed we were both lost in thought. I'm sure Major Ramsey was thinking about the documents that had not been in the safe and what, if anything, could still be done to locate them. I was thinking about that, too, to a certain extent, as well as my interactions with each of the potential spies.

But the nearness of Major Ramsey in the car's backseat also caused my mind to return to the embrace on the sofa. I didn't like that this useless little thought crept its way into my brain. It hadn't meant anything. Major Ramsey, under normal circumstances, would never look twice at a woman like me. Oh, I didn't doubt that I could be attractive when I set my mind to it, but a man in his position, an officer in the army, never mind an earl's nephew, was accustomed to rules and regulations; I made my living by breaking them. I doubted whether we had two things in common.

As a single young woman in the midst of the taxing circumstances of war, it was perfectly natural that I might be drawn to a handsome man with whom I had been thrown into an adventure. Nevertheless, it would do no good to spend time thinking about it.

The car came to a stop before Uncle Mick's house, pulling my thoughts back to the present.

I turned to the major, unsure of what to say. I settled on something professional. "I'm sorry we didn't find the documents."

"Not for lack of your skills," he said. "You did well tonight, Miss McDonnell. Once again, you held up admirably under pressure."

"And this time I wasn't sick afterward," I pointed out.

He smiled. A full, amused smile, the first one I had ever earned from him. "I shall take it as a compliment that you weren't."

I laughed then, realizing how it had sounded. "What I meant to say is that tonight was infinitely preferable to finding a dead body."

"It was indeed." His eyes caught mine, and I felt the flush creep up on my neck again. I needed to get out of the car before I managed to embarrass myself. Luckily, Jakub opened the door just then.

I held out my hand to the major. "Good night, Major Ramsey."

His warm fingers closed around mine. "Good night."

I got out of the car and went into the house, my head all in a whirl. It had been an eventful evening. We might not have found the papers, but I had proven that I was a valuable asset. What was more, I had to admit to myself that I was beginning to relish the thrill of this job.

It was well past midnight, but I was much too excited to sleep. So I went to put the kettle on. I was surprised when, coming out of the kitchen, I heard a tap at the door.

My heart fluttered for just a moment. Had the major returned? No, of course, he hadn't. He could have no reason to.

I walked to the door and pulled it open, surprised to see Felix standing on the step, hat in hand.

His eyes ran over me and he let out a whistle.

"I was . . . out tonight," I said.

"So I see."

"I've just come home. I've got the kettle on. Will you come in?"

He glanced at his wristwatch. "Do you think I'd better? I didn't realize how late it was, and we can't have the old man making trouble for us. I was just walking by and thought I'd see if you were up. I can come back tomorrow."

I glanced at the darkened house. Had Uncle Mick returned from his own adventure? It seemed likely, for he had started out before we did. I supposed he would give his account of what had happened tomorrow.

"Uncle Mick's gone to bed, and, anyway, he knows he doesn't have to worry about you."

"Are you sure?" Felix asked with a wink. "With you looking like that, I may be hard-pressed to behave myself."

I shot him a look as I pulled the door open fully and stepped aside so he could enter. "I can take care of myself, and don't you forget it."

"I won't," he said with a laugh. "You've landed me a solid blow more than once, after all."

"Not in several years, but I haven't forgotten how," I said as we moved to the sofa. "What are you doing walking around London at this time of night?"

"Stopped at a pub for a pint. I've been walking all over the city looking for a job all day and just happened to be passing." He paused, sighed. "No, that's not entirely true. There's something that's been weighing on my mind. Something I need to talk to you about."

"You know you can talk to me about anything," I said, but I was a bit surprised—even unnerved—by the seriousness of his expression. Felix was usually so cheerful, so completely at ease.

"I've found something out. Or, at least, I may have. I . . ." His eyes came up to mine. "It's about your mother."

There was a moment of silence. Of all the things he might have said, this was the last I had expected.

My family never talked about my mother. She was like something from a history book, a fact from long ago that we knew and brushed aside. A relic of another time that sat in an attic corner covered in cobwebs. There was good enough reason for the way we danced around any mention of her, but sometimes I felt the weight of that history bearing down on me until I thought I might be crushed by it.

One such time, when I was feeling especially weary and heartbroken, I had cried on Felix's shoulder and the story spilled out. He had held me and comforted me in a way that Uncle Mick or the boys couldn't have, as an outsider without prejudice. I had told him what I had never told anyone else, that I believed my mother was innocent of the crime of which she had been convicted.

"What . . . what about her?" I managed to ask.

"It isn't much. But there was a fellow I met in the navy. We'd had a bit too much to drink one night, or he had, at any rate, and he started telling me about his family and how his mother was arrested and spent a year at Holloway. I didn't say anything about your mother, of course. But then he mentioned her case. He said . . . well . . . he knew it was a name I would probably recognize."

I knew what Felix was being too kind to say. My mother's case had the kind of notoriety that most people in Britain were familiar with.

"Anyway, he said that his mother got to be chummy with yours. And that your mother told her things."

I felt oddly cold, numb. When I spoke, my voice sounded strange in my own ears. "What sort of things?"

"He didn't know exactly, or was too drunk to remember. But he said that his mother told him most women in prison claimed to be innocent, but your mother was the only one she ever believed. She said there were facts that didn't come out in court, and that she thought maybe your mother might have proved it in time . . ."

We both sat in silence for a long moment. My mind was reeling a bit, though I tried to tell myself I shouldn't get excited. This was nothing new, after all. Not really. The opinion of a fellow convict wouldn't amount to much in most people's eyes. And the story was secondhand, from a drunk young man who might be misremembering his mother's story. And yet . . .

"Is his mother still alive?" I asked.

"She is. I could write to him for her address if you want to talk to her. I didn't like to mention your connection until I'd spoken with you." He paused. "I didn't even know if I should tell you, to be honest. What are the odds you might be able to learn something after all this time? But then I realized that I couldn't keep it to myself. It's not my information to do with as I please; it's yours."

I met his gaze, my heart swelling with gratitude.

"Thank you, Felix," I said softly.

He reached out to take my hand. "I don't think you should get your hopes up, Ellie."

I nodded. "But it couldn't hurt to talk to her."

He didn't answer.

I went to get the kettle and tea-things then. It was a lot to think about all at once, too much. Between the events of the party tonight and this newest revelation, my head was all in a muddle.

Well, one thing at a time. Focus was the key to success. Focus and prioritizing the tasks ahead. It would take time for Felix to hear back from his shipmate. While we waited, I would continue to do my bit for the government and not allow myself to be distracted.

I pushed thoughts of my mother from my head—an easy enough task after years of training—and put on a recording. We sat comfortably drinking our tea as the familiar strains of "Cinderella, Stay in My Arms" floated into the room. This song reminded me of happier days before the war, when we hadn't known what was coming and life had seemed so full of joyful possibilities. So blissfully without complexity.

We listened for a minute, both of us transported by the music, I supposed, and then Felix turned to me, his eyes moving over me. "Were you out dancing tonight?"

"No. I was at a lecture on Chinese porcelain."

He grinned. "The war's put a bit of a damper on the social scene, eh?"

I laughed. "Something like that."

"You ought to be dancing in that dress." He set his teacup aside and stood, holding out his hand. "Dance with me."

"But . . ." I couldn't seem to help it; my eyes flickered to his leg.

"Don't say it, Ellie," he said softly. "Just do it."

I put my hand into his, and he led me to the middle of the floor. I stepped into his arms, and we began to move to the music.

For a moment, I felt as though the past months had slipped away and we were both the carefree people we had been before. But I couldn't completely forget that there was something different now, a new awareness in the way we held each other. Perhaps it was the realization that life was such a fragile thing. Though he moved with grace, I could feel a slight tension in him whenever his weight moved to his bad leg, and I knew it must be causing him pain to dance but that it would cause even more to stop.

And so we swayed gently to the music, a strange mixture of melancholy and contentment and something more buzzing through me. Major Ramsey and everything else that had happened tonight suddenly seemed very far away.

The recording came to an end, but we stayed where we were, our arms still around each other. I looked up at him and our eyes held for a long moment.

Then he released me and stepped back, his jaw tightening as his step faltered ever so slightly.

"I suppose I should go," he said, mustering a smile. "At least now your lovely gown hasn't gone to waste."

"Stay a little longer." Somehow, I was reluctant to be alone just now. "I've got a new Glenn Miller recording." It had been something we had always loved doing together, listening to music late into the night.

He hesitated then nodded. "All right."

He went back to the sofa as I moved to the gramophone. "You'll like this one, I think."

"Good old Ellie," he said, pulling a cigarette case from his pocket. "Always making me feel right at home."

I took my seat beside him and we sat finishing our tea and listening to the music, without the need to talk. Despite the strange way I'd felt in his arms, I was comfortable and at ease, felt better than I had in ages. I hadn't really realized how much I had missed him, how much I had missed the company of someone with whom I felt I knew where I stood.

It wasn't quite the same with Uncle Mick. He was always his cheery self even with the boys gone, but I knew that he was feeling the strain of Toby being missing and of Colm off fighting. It was hard on all of us, but some part of me always felt the need to protect my uncle, to not let him see how things affected me. I needed to be strong for him.

I had been so lost in the thought that I was surprised when the record came to an end. "Shall we listen to another?"

Felix didn't answer. When I looked over at him, he was asleep.

I knew I should wake him. Uncle Mick had always been an understanding man, but he would never approve of a man staying overnight in my flat. Not even Felix; perhaps especially not Felix.

But I couldn't bear to wake him up. It was cool outside, and he looked so very warm and comfortable there on the couch. Besides, I knew his leg must trouble him a great deal, and, if he could sleep well here, I didn't intend to interrupt him.

And so I took a blanket that Nacy had knitted and gently draped it over him. He didn't so much as stir.

I quietly turned out the light and went to my bedroom.

CHAPTER NINETEEN

Felix left early, before I was awake. It was a shame he left so soon, for I would have been happy to feed him breakfast. It would have created a scandal if he had been caught here, I supposed, but I didn't really care. I was a grown woman, after all. Uncle Mick and Nacy might scold me, but what happened in my flat was my business.

Besides, even if I had been romantically inclined toward Felix, I knew better than to let things go too far with a man who had no serious intentions. And, despite the way he had looked at me last night, Felix's intentions were never serious. At least, that's what I had always thought. Felix was glib and charming, and, despite my attraction to him, I had not thought he meant much by his flirtations. But I had to admit that something was different between us now. It was something more substantial than the fleeting sparks of mutual attraction. We were moving into uncharted territory. It was an added complication to a steadily growing list of complications.

Whatever the case, the sofa was empty when I came out of the bedroom, the blanket I had covered him with neatly folded atop the cushions.

I went to the house for breakfast. I was anxious to talk with Uncle Mick about last night. I hoped he had been more successful than the major and I were.

He was seated at the big table in the dining room with his cup of tea, the morning paper spread out before him. He looked up when I entered.

"Ellie girl," he said, smiling brightly. "How are you this fine morning?"

"I'm all right," I said vaguely, moving to the seat beside him. We hadn't yet confessed any of our doings to Nacy, though it was entirely possible she already had some inkling of what we were up to. Despite her frequent protestations that we needn't tell her anything we didn't want to, Nacy always found things out; I hadn't been able to hide anything from her yet.

She came into the room just then, bearing a plate with sausage, eggs, toast, and tomatoes from our garden.

"Good morning, Nacy," I said.

She set the plate down with a decided thump on the table in front of me. I looked up and saw her grim expression.

"Slept well, did you?" she asked.

"Yes, I slept fine," I said, confused by her manner.

She continued to look at me hard, but her brows moved upward ever so slightly.

And then I realized. She had seen Felix leaving my flat.

Blast. It was just as I had said. There was no keeping secrets from Nacy.

I glanced at Uncle Mick. Though it had all been perfectly innocent—and, really, why should I have to explain myself at all?—it was not a conversation I wished to have at the breakfast table.

Nacy seemed to be of the same mind, for she turned and went wordlessly back to the kitchen. Uncle Mick, who was absorbed in his paper, didn't appear to have noticed the silent exchange.

I took a bite of eggs.

"I've got a job this morning, Ellie girl," Uncle Mick said.

I looked up.

"A legitimate one." He winked. "Would you like to come along?"

"Yes," I said. "I'd like it very much." Especially since it would allow me to question him about his excursion to the auction house last night and also avoid Nacy for the time being.

I ate quickly, and we left the house and began our walk toward the station. It was a fine morning, the sun shining cheerily through a cool breeze. It felt good to be walking among the familiar streets, all the houses and shops as well known as the back of my hand.

In some ways, things were the same as they had been since I was a child, but it was impossible not to notice the changes the war had brought. It wasn't only the sandbags, blackout curtains, and boarded-up windows. There was more of a sense of subdued purpose, evident in things like the kitchen gardens that now took up all the available space on people's lawns. And there were fewer children, too, playing carelessly in the streets.

There had been quite a few in our neighborhood before this, and I found I missed the sounds of their laughing and shouting to one another as they played their games. There were still children to be seen, but there was something a bit restrained about them. The younger ones sensed that something was different, and many of the older ones had stepped up to do the jobs left behind by their fathers who had gone off to war. I hoped it wouldn't be long before they were all able to be children again, but some part of me knew it wasn't likely things would ever return to the way they had been.

"How did things go last night?" Uncle Mick asked as we walked along a quiet street.

"All right," I said. "Though we didn't find the documents."

I told him all about our adventure, though I left out the part about Major Ramsey's kissing me. It just wasn't the sort of thing you mentioned to your uncle.

"Then it seems this Winthrop fellow may be our man," he said.

"Possibly," I agreed. "But what about you? Were you successful last night?"

I was eager to hear how he'd made out in his reconnaissance at the auction house.

He shook his head. "Not to speak of. We got in all right, did a thorough going-over of the place. But there was nothing to be found."

"No documents hidden behind canvases or stuffed into pottery?" I asked, only half joking.

He smiled. "Not that we could find. And the major's man is as thorough as I am. No, I'm afraid if that chap's got secrets, he's keeping them elsewhere."

Then it had been a somewhat disappointing evening all around.

We passed Hendon Park. It was quiet today, very few people out and about. Last month they'd held a large rally there. "Rout the Rumour," it had been called. There were songs and dances and speakers that encouraged us to keep from spreading gossip about the war. It seemed like a very long time ago now.

Passing through the pillared entryway of Hendon Central Station, we descended into the muggy confines of the Tube. I reflected, as I had often done in recent months, how some things were so changed and yet others remained the same.

As we waited for the Northern line train to appear, Uncle Mick smoked a cigarette and told me about the job. It would be easy enough, he said. A man in Piccadilly had rung up that morning to ask him to replace the locks on his doors.

"Not very interesting, but I never turn down a job, you know."

Uncle Mick often received jobs from far-flung parts of the city. He was a man who had built a solid reputation for himself, and it was well known that if you had a difficult lock that needed opening, he was your man.

I felt a sudden surge of happiness in this little bit of normality. I was with Uncle Mick. We were going to do an uncomplicated job. I breathed a sigh of relief that, even just for the moment, all was right with the world.

Alas, that peaceful feeling was to be short-lived.

We were gone perhaps three hours, and I returned to find Nacy in more of a state than she had been when we left. She came out of the house as we approached, clearly having been watching for us from the window.

She started talking before she reached us. "There you are. It's about time. I'll be pleased to have some peace at last. They've been ringing nonstop, and that after they sent that man around three times. A waste of petrol, it was, and I told him so. It's not his fault, of course, but someone ought to do something. I don't know what they're . . ."

"Nacy, what on earth are you talking about?" I interrupted.

She gave an exasperated sigh. "I've told you. They've been ringing."

"Who has?" I asked.

"Someone on behalf of a Major Ramsey. He says you're to come straightaway. Alone."

After a bit of discussion with Nacy and Uncle Mick, assuring them I would be perfectly fine going alone, I returned to the station. It was a bit of a guessing game as to how to get there by the Tube, as I had only been to the major's office in the car. But I had an excellent memory and a keen sense of direction. And, after all, it wasn't as though I was going to run into a rough crowd in Belgravia.

Soon enough I found myself on a familiar street, a short walk from there to the major's office. It was quieter here than it was in Hendon, more reserved. But perhaps that was just the tenor of the street and not a result of wartime.

What did the major want to see me about? Had someone been able to get hold of the papers? But no. He would've called both me and Uncle Mick in that case.

Why had he insisted I come quickly and alone? I was curious, and just the slightest bit uneasy.

Poor Uncle Mick had wanted to accompany me, but if Major

Ramsey had said I was to come alone, there was no sense in provoking him. And, after all, I knew well enough now how to handle the major.

I moved up the front steps, rapping on the door, and Oscar Davies, his face even grimmer than usual, opened it at once.

"The major is waiting for you, Miss McDonnell," he said as soon as I entered. Something in the way he said it made me think it was a warning. "He sent me round to your house more than once this morning."

"So I've heard," I told him.

Rather than look amused by my sarcasm, he looked slightly scandalized.

He opened his mouth as though he was going to say something and then shut it again. He turned as if to lead me to the office, but I stopped him.

"I know the way, Oscar," I said.

He nodded, and I thought he looked relieved that he wasn't going to have to lead me in that direction. Was Major Ramsey really that much of a dragon? It wouldn't surprise me. As Uncle Mick had said, they didn't make men majors without their being able to terrify their underlings. Or something to that effect.

I gave Oscar a little smile and then went down the hall. I reached the door to Major Ramsey's office and knocked.

His voice was muffled by the heavy wood of the door but clear enough. "Enter."

I pushed open the door and stepped inside. He wasn't sitting at his desk. Instead, he stood observing one of the maps on the wall with his arms behind his back. He didn't turn when I came in.

"Good morning," I said, by way of greeting.

"Who is he?"

I was caught off guard by both the question and his tone. "Who?"

He turned to look at me then, and I could see that he was very serious. "The man who spent the night in your flat."

I felt the color creeping over my face at the question and the insinuation that was in it. My first impulse was to make excuses, but I fought it down. After all, what right did he have to ask me such questions? If I hadn't explained to my dear Nacy, I certainly didn't feel obligated to explain to him.

"I don't think that's any of your business," I said lightly.

"I'm afraid you're wrong," he said calmly. "For all intents and purposes, you are still under our jurisdiction twenty-four hours a day. That includes your late-night rendezvous."

"I thought the evening was concluded after the lecture," I said tightly. "Why were you having me watched?"

"As a precaution."

I resisted the urge to make an angry retort. I knew already that anger never got me anywhere with Major Ramsey.

"Who is the man, Miss McDonnell?"

Stubbornness and my rising temper made me want to refuse to tell him, but that would have been childish. Especially when I had nothing to hide.

"He's just a friend," I said.

"His name?"

"I'm surprised you don't know," I retorted. "You seem to know everything else about my personal business."

He continued as though I hadn't spoken. "I can find out, Miss McDonnell. You may as well tell me and save us both time and trouble."

I didn't like it when he got high-handed with me, but I supposed he was right enough. I drew in a breath through my nose, a trick I had for calming my temper. "It's not a secret. His name is Felix Lacey."

"And he's an intimate friend of yours."

I stiffened at the question.

"He slept on my sofa, if that's what you mean." I don't know why I said it. It didn't matter to me one way or the other what Major Ramsey thought, and I was sure that my personal life mattered not at all to him, except for maybe another chance to lord his superior morality over me. Though I found it difficult to believe that a man with his looks was celibate.

"Where he slept is immaterial," he said. "The government doesn't care what you do so much as whom you do it with."

A proper gentleman would have been embarrassed to have this conversation, but Major Ramsey didn't seem at all uncomfortable.

"Felix has nothing to do with any of this. Leave him out of it."

"I need to know who your associates are. Need I remind you that this is serious business? A strange man taking up residence in your flat is bound to put a crimp in things."

"He hasn't taken up residence," I said, doing my best to rein in my quickly heightening temper. "He's just returned home, so he came to see me. He fell asleep on my sofa while we were listening to the gramophone, and I didn't want to wake him."

I was instantly angry at myself for having revealed so much to him, so I added: "I don't think you have any business questioning me about what happens in my flat."

"Your uncle has no objection to gentlemen callers, then?"

I certainly didn't want to admit to Major Ramsey that Felix had skulked out of my house in the predawn hours. Of course, he probably knew this already given that he apparently had my house being watched.

"I'm a grown woman, Major Ramsey," I said, meeting his gaze. "My uncle understands that. As I'm sure you do."

"Of course. And does Mr. Lacey know about your occupation?"

"About the safes, you mean?"

"Yes. Is he aware that you and your uncle and cousins break into houses and steal things?"

"He knows some of it, not all. He's been a friend of our family for a long time. He . . . he's even helped us out once or twice." I wasn't sure I should have said it, but it was the truth. Despite my irritation, I didn't want to hide things from Major Ramsey if possible. He would only find out in the end, and it would just make things more difficult between us.

"Then he's a safecracker as well."

"No. He has . . . other skills."

I was certain Major Ramsey would press me on this, but he didn't.

"And did you tell him about our operation?"

I looked up, insulted by his lack of trust in me. "Certainly not. Whatever you may think of me, I'm not in the habit of betraying confidences."

He held up a hand. "I meant no offense. But a great many people are tempted to share secrets with . . . good friends." The insinuation was clear.

"I told you . . ."

"It doesn't matter," he said with a dismissive wave of his hand. "As long as you've kept this business to yourself, the rest is of no concern to me. How long is his leave?"

"He's home indefinitely. He lost a leg in France."

Major Ramsey looked annoyed. "You mean he's likely to be hanging about for the foreseeable future."

"He might," I said.

He let out a sigh. "This isn't at all convenient."

"Well, I'm sure he didn't lose a leg just to inconvenience you," I said tartly.

In that maddening way of his, he barely seemed to hear my retort and continued speaking as though I hadn't. "In any event, that wasn't why I called you here."

It wasn't? It seemed to me that confronting me about my personal business was exactly the reason he had hounded Nacy until I was found. But I waited for him to go on.

He settled those twilight-blue eyes of his on me. "We've decoded the message that was passed to Matthew Winthrop."

CHAPTER TWENTY

I was still annoyed with him, so I didn't want to show how interested I was in what he had to say. All the same, it had been quick work.

We looked at each other. He was waiting for me to ask what it said, but I was determined to wait him out.

After a good minute or so of silence, he let out the faintest sigh. "It was a message instructing him to meet his contact this afternoon at a certain tearoom. Apparently, the party was too crowded to pass the papers off and whoever had them decided to wait."

My brows went up. "Then the trail hasn't gone cold."

"No," he said. "Not entirely."

"So now what?"

"Will you sit down, Miss McDonnell?" he said, indicating the chair across from his desk. He was using his formal tone again, which probably boded ill.

I took a seat and he followed suit.

"This situation has taken a turn we had not anticipated," he said. "Your involvement was intended to be temporary, assuming we could retrieve something from either Sir Nigel's safe or from Mr. Turner-Hill's auction house. Alas, we failed to do either."

I tried to figure out what he was saying. Was I being dismissed? It rather sounded like it, and, though the man irritated me beyond

measure, I felt my chest clench with impending disappointment. I
didn't want to be dismissed. I wanted to go on helping. What was
more, I had felt, after last night's successful opening of the safe, that
he had seen my capabilities.

"What we're going to have to attempt now is beyond your pur-
view," he went on.

"In other words, I'm of no further use to you," I said. We might
as well cut to the chase.

"Miss McDonnell . . ."

"Just have out with it, Major."

There was a tapping on the door just then.

The major let out an irritated breath. "What is it?" he called.

The door opened and Oscar put his head in. "Kimble is here, sir."

"Tell him to wait."

"He says it's urgent."

"I don't care what he says. Tell him to wait."

"Yes, sir."

Oscar closed the door, and the major swore roundly before looking up at me. "I beg your pardon."

"I grew up in a house full of men," I said. "You needn't watch
your language around me."

"All the same . . ." he said, the words trailing off.

I had taken Major Ramsey's measure some time ago, and I knew
what he was feeling. He was a man who liked to be in control at all
times. Only sometimes his temper got the better of him. I knew what
that was like. I'd struggled with mine my whole life.

"You don't think of me like one of your society women anyway,
so there's no need for you to tiptoe around things as though a harsh
word will shatter me."

"I think it would take a great deal more than a harsh word to
shatter you, Miss McDonnell."

"I shall take that as a compliment."

"It was meant as one."

He threw me a bit off guard with that statement, for I hadn't expected him to so openly say something nice about me.

"Thank you," I said at last. "It's the way I was brought up, I suppose. There wasn't much of an opportunity to be dainty or fragile. Which means you can tell me if I'm getting the sack. You needn't find a diplomatic way to say it."

"What I'm trying to say, Miss McDonnell, is that I still need your help."

I stared at him. I hadn't been expecting this. Between the safecracking bit being over and, perhaps, with the help of Felix's overnight visit, I'd assumed they had decided that I could no longer be of use to them.

"You've proven that you have what is necessary to do this sort of work," he said when I failed to answer. "Your background may be in safecracking, but that's a job that requires more than skill . . . it takes nerve, especially under pressure. Anyone who can think like that, who has the patience and the resolve to accomplish a task under time constraints, can no doubt be an asset in other ways."

I felt a growing suspicion. It seemed to me that he was buttering me up, which was definitely a bit alarming.

"In what sort of other ways?" I asked.

He paused. "I need you to go on pretending to be my . . . sweetheart."

"Didn't get quite enough on the sofa last night, Major?" I asked, before I could think better of it. As soon as I said the words, I flushed. It was the sort of joking thing I would have said to Felix, but Major Ramsey was definitely not Felix.

All the same, he didn't appear to be offended. His eyes flickered ever so briefly to my lips, and I felt a flutter in the pit of my stomach.

"I trust there will be no further incidents where such a thing will be necessary," he said.

"What's the plan, then?"

There was another impatient tapping on the door. The major

rose from his chair, an irritated expression on his face, before the door swung open.

A man entered, Oscar Davies hot on his trail.

"Kimble, what are you doing?" Major Ramsey asked.

"I'm sorry, sir," Oscar cut in. "I tried to stop him, but . . ."

"It's an urgent matter, Ramsey. Or I wouldn't have interrupted."

The intruder and I turned to get a good look at each other then, and I realized at once he was the grim-faced inspector-like fellow who had interrogated me the night Uncle Mick and I had been caught housebreaking.

He gave me a slight nod. "Miss McDonnell."

I returned the nod with a cool one of my own. I had forgiven Major Ramsey for his behavior the night of my arrest, but this Kimble fellow was going to have to earn my approval on his own.

"You may go, Davies," Major Ramsey said coldly.

"Yes, sir," Oscar replied, closing the door behind him.

Without waiting for an invitation, Mr. Kimble came and took the other seat before the major's desk. "Something's come up, and I need a word with you. It's urgent."

"So you've mentioned," the major said, returning to his seat behind the desk.

"Shall I go?" I asked.

"No," said Major Ramsey at the same moment Mr. Kimble said, "Yes."

Major Ramsey looked at me. "Kimble here is another of our freelancers, though we acquired him from the opposite side of the law."

"A detective inspector," I said immediately.

"Yes," the major said. "Formerly of Scotland Yard. Dismissed from their ranks for 'unprofessional behavior,' which works nicely for us. How did you know?"

"He's got that copper air," I said, wondering, in spite of myself, what kind of behavior had gotten the man kicked out of the Yard.

"This is rather sensitive information, Ramsey," Kimble said, ignoring me completely. "Are you sure . . ."

"What is it?" Major Ramsey said impatiently.

"It's the bloke I've been watching," Kimble said. "He's gone."

I happened to be looking at the major as Kimble said these final words, and I had the interesting experience of watching his eyes go from twilight blue to cold steel gray in the space of a second.

"What do you mean he's gone?" he asked in a tone cold enough to freeze blood in the veins.

I had to give Kimble credit for not appearing much affected by the major's change of manner. "He left his house, bag in hand, and made for the station."

"Then you've lost him."

"Oh, as to that," Kimble said unconcernedly. "I had a man following him."

"You ought to have led with that part, Kimble." The major's tone was terse.

"But my man lost sight of him for a moment on the way to the station," Kimble continued. "Came around a corner a moment later and found him bleeding out in an alley. Throat slit."

Despite myself, I gasped. I hadn't expected such a violent turn in a story told in such a bland voice.

The major's eyes flickered momentarily to me before going back to Kimble. "Did your man get anything out of him before he died?"

Kimble shook his head. "Too far gone by that point. And he didn't see who might have done it either. It was quick work."

Major Ramsey sat back in his chair with a bitter curse, and this time he did not apologize.

"I thought you ought to know," Kimble said. "That lead's dead . . . so to speak."

The major appeared to think for a moment and then nodded. "Thank you, Kimble," he said. "I think that will do for now."

Kimble nodded and rose unhurriedly from his chair. "I'll drop by again this evening if I have any more news." He turned to me. "Good day, Miss McDonnell."

"Mr. Kimble," I said vaguely, still shaken by what I had heard.

He turned then and left without further remark. I looked at the major, my brows rising almost of their own volition.

"He's an interesting fellow," Major Ramsey said. "I've never met a person less inclined to emotion of any sort."

Coming from Major Ramsey, that was saying something.

"Who . . . who's died now?" I asked.

He sighed. "I had Kimble watching a different man, someone I suspect has been running messages between our key players. He was working as one of the waiters at the lecture last night. I suspect he was the one who slipped Winthrop that note."

"And now someone's killed that man to silence him."

"It would seem so."

I felt a little sick, but I fancy I managed to keep my composure.

"Is the meeting between Winthrop and the contact still going to happen?" I asked.

"Yes," he said. "That's what I was going to tell you before Kimble came barging in here. I would like you to accompany me to the tearoom to watch for their arrival. If we're together, I'm hoping Winthrop and the killer will merely think it a coincidence that we're there."

"And when Mr. Winthrop takes possession of the papers?"

"Then we can perhaps make one more attempt at stealing them."

If I hadn't realized how high the stakes were before, I certainly realized it now. Two men had been killed so far. This was a dangerous business.

"I could get Kimble or one of his men to do it, of course," he said, almost as though we were having the same thought. "But you've seen firsthand how his men operate."

"Are those the brutes that accosted me that first night?"

"Yes. They don't go in much for subtlety."

"I can see why you might not want them crashing around a tea-room."

He gave me one of those faint smiles. "Precisely. Additionally, since you're invested in this operation, I thought it was fitting for you to see it through."

"I'm glad," I said.

His eyes came up to mine. I had meant what I said, but it seemed I had surprised him a bit with my sincerity. I supposed sincerity wasn't something I often projected. It came from a lifetime of concealing my feelings, concealing myself. I had grown up learning to be guarded around people who weren't my family, and the fact that I had been comfortable enough with the major to let my guard slip for a moment was telling.

As it usually went with Major Ramsey, my good feelings were short-lived.

"You will, of course, have to stop seeing your friend until the job is done. Not the job tomorrow, but the whole thing."

"My . . . friend?"

"Mr. Lacey."

My reply was automatic. "I won't do that."

"This isn't a negotiation, Miss McDonnell." Something in his tone told me that it would do no good to argue, but that wasn't going to stop me.

"Why should I stop seeing him?"

"He's only going to complicate things, and we don't need that at the moment. If he is free to come and go at your flat at all hours of the day and night—" He held up a hand to ward off my protests and continued. "He may be difficult to work around."

Despite my strong desire to argue, I couldn't deny the logic of this. It would be rather hard to have Felix around while I was planning this very secret enterprise. For one thing, I had always been able to share the details of my jobs with him before. He had always had a willing ear and gave sound advice. I hadn't told him about my work for the government, but a part of me would likely be tempted to the longer we spent together.

"How am I supposed to ignore him when he's just returned home?"

"I suppose you'd better come up with something."

No doubt in the army he was used to people saluting smartly and obeying without question when he told them to do something, but he'd do well to remember that we weren't in the army now.

"He's been injured," I continued. "He needs friends who will support him."

"I'm sure that's so, but I need you more than he does at the moment."

From any other man, this might have been a flattering declaration. As it was, I knew a command when I heard one.

"He won't understand it."

His cool eyes met mine. "He's been to battle; I'm sure he'll hold up without your company for a fortnight."

I blinked. The words stung as they hit their mark. It was true enough, I supposed. I was overestimating my importance.

I thought of the way I had felt last night as we danced, of the way I had felt this morning. I didn't want to risk losing whatever it was that was growing between us. But perhaps the major was right. This mission must come first. The untangling of my personal feelings for Felix—and the discovery of whatever information he might be able to help me learn about my mother—would have to wait.

I let out a sigh to be sure the major knew I didn't like it.

"All right," I said at last, sounding unapologetically like a rebellious adolescent. "I'll do it. But under protest."

"Of course," Major Ramsey replied, with complete indifference. "Do you do things any other way?"

CHAPTER TWENTY-ONE

The thought of the conversation I would have to have with Felix left me melancholy, and I couldn't bring myself to ring him up before the major arrived that afternoon to escort me to the tearoom where the exchange of documents was supposed to take place.

He arrived a bit before I expected him, and I was still in my stocking feet, my hair flying free.

"Oh," I said, opening the door after his brisk tap. "I . . . will you give me just a moment, major? I just have a few things I need to do."

"Of course."

"Would you . . . like to come in?" I wasn't sure of the etiquette. Maybe he'd rather wait in the car.

But he seemed willing enough. "Thank you."

I stepped back and pulled the door open, allowing him to enter.

He took off his service cap, his fair hair still neatly in place beneath, and followed me into the sitting room.

He'd picked me up for our date to the party, of course, but he'd stayed outside. It was strange having him inside the house. For one thing, the room seemed smaller since he was so large. It was as though he absorbed a great deal of space.

For another, though we'd always been a family who'd enjoyed entertaining, I'd never imagined a government man in my flat. A great many of Uncle Mick's friends and associates had frequented the house over the years. I'd met thieves and swindlers, and even dangerous men. But Major Ramsey was a new breed altogether.

His eyes moved around my little room, taking the surroundings in with a practiced glance. He was an observant man, and I supposed he was making assumptions about me from this room. I tried to guess what he might infer from the tidy but brightly decorated living space.

Perhaps that I was a paradox of sorts. I had an orderly mind but was also capable of creativity.

I had never really thought how my private residence might reveal things about me to outsiders.

All of this passed through my mind in the space of a few seconds, and then his attention turned back to me. He must have noticed I was shorter than usual because his gaze dropped to my stockinged feet.

"If you'd like to have a seat, I'll be just a moment," I said.

I hurried back to my bedroom and slipped on a pair of shoes. Then, moving before the mirror, I ran my fingers through my curls, trying to intimidate them into behaving properly. They weren't intimidated.

Sighing, I let them have their own way and went back out into the sitting room.

Instead of taking a seat on the sofa, the major had wandered over to one of my bookshelves.

"I wouldn't have taken you for a reader of the Greek classics," he said, glancing at me over his shoulder. "But I suppose I should have guessed when you recognized Psyche in the mural in Sir Nigel's ballroom."

I didn't know how to interpret this, and my chin instinctively went up a bit. "What would you have taken me as a reader of?"

He turned to face me. I expected a flippant reply, but he seemed to consider it. "Tennyson, perhaps," he said at last. "A gentler sort of mythology: plenty of daring and adventure, yes, but justice and chivalry, too."

I said nothing for a moment, unsure of how to respond. He had thrown me off-balance.

"Ellie, that car is parked in front of the house again, and . . ." Nacy, as she was wont to do, came flying into the flat but stopped dead in the doorway at the sight of Major Ramsey.

She looked at him then over to me then back to him again. Major Ramsey made quite a handsome picture, his fine form adorned in spotless uniform, and Nacy seemed to be taking her time about appreciating it.

Clearly, she wasn't going anywhere, despite my hopes that she would just quietly see herself out, so I thought there was nothing to do but make introductions.

"Come in, Nacy. Major Ramsey, this is Nacy Dean. Nacy, Major Ramsey."

"How do you do?" he said, bowing his head ever so slightly. I had expected a dismissiveness, but there was something very courteous in his manner.

"I hope I'm not interrupting anything," Nacy said. She looked at me, her eyebrows rising.

I shot daggers at her with my eyes when Major Ramsey wasn't looking. She noticed, but she pretended not to.

"Not at all," Major Ramsey said.

"As a matter of fact, we're just getting ready to leave," I said.

He turned back to me. "I'll wait for you in the car, shall I, Miss McDonnell?"

I nodded, and he turned back to Nacy. "So nice to have met you, Miss Dean."

"And you, Major," she said, as pleasant as I had ever seen her.

He took his leave then, and as soon as the door closed, I turned to Nacy.

"You might have knocked before you came in."

"Since when have I knocked?"

"I was engaged in a private conversation."

Her eyes were uncharacteristically bright as she turned them on me, a bit of a sly smile forming at the corners of her mouth.

"I don't know what you're thinking, Nacy, but I'm sure you're quite wrong," I said primly.

She gave an undignified snort. "I've eyes, haven't I? I may be an old woman, but there's nothing wrong with my sight and that's as fine a specimen as I've ever seen. Those eyes of his! And so tall and broad! I've never been much of one for fair young men, but I'd make an exception for that one. Day or night."

"Nacy!"

She was unabashed. "If it were him sneaking out of your flat in the wee hours, I wouldn't blame you so much. But Felix . . ."

"Nacy, there's nothing going on between Felix and me. He slept on the sofa."

"Whatever the case, don't miss your chance with that man," she said, nodding her head in the direction the major had departed. "If I were thirty years younger . . ."

She left the rest unsaid, but I could very well guess what she was thinking.

I was only glad Major Ramsey had departed before she had begun to swoon over him.

We decided not to take the car directly to the tearoom that afternoon, as it was likely to call attention to ourselves. And so Jakub dropped us off several blocks away, not far from Piccadilly Circus, and Major Ramsey and I walked along together through the crowds of people, finally stopping across the street from the tearoom in question. There we stepped into the alcove of a building and pretended to be deep in conversation as we waited.

I watched the door of the tearoom. It was an elegant-looking place that catered to stylish—and a bit stuffy—clientele, if the people I saw entering and leaving were any indication. This definitely seemed to be the sort of place Major Ramsey would take a girl for tea, so that made our pretense of a coincidental meeting plausible, I supposed.

"No sign of him yet," I said, glancing out into the street.

"We've a good twenty minutes yet," he replied without looking at his watch.

I sneaked a glance at mine. He was right to the minute. Of course.

We said nothing for a few moments as we waited for sign of Matthew Winthrop and his contact, the person who presumably had killed Thomas Harden and taken the papers from him. After that, it would just be the matter of finding the chance to switch out the real documents for the false ones.

Something occurred to me then.

"Isn't this a bit of a public place for an exchange of highly sensitive documents?" I asked. "It seems as though they should've done it in a park or a deserted alleyway."

"This sort of thing is actually best done in a crowded place," he replied. "It makes it less noticeable."

I would have to take his word for it. All the illegal things I'd ever done had been best done under the cover of darkness.

"Stop looking out into the street every few seconds," he said when I again peeked around the corner of the alcove for a better view down the street.

I knew we were meant to look like young lovers having a private conversation in this little alcove, but I found, as I usually did with Major Ramsey, that I was having a devil of a time keeping a pleasant expression on my face.

"I don't want to miss him."

"We won't."

I had to admit I was a bit surprised Winthrop was our man. I'd have laid odds on Sir Nigel. There was something very fishy about the man. Granted, this didn't seem to be the sort of place he'd frequent for lunch. I thought he'd be more likely to dine at his club, where he wasn't likely to brush shoulders with the lower classes in the streets.

A poet, however, wouldn't mind mixing a bit with the bourgeoisie.

I didn't have time to make any more assumptions because I suddenly saw the major stiffen ever so slightly. It might not have been noticeable to most people, but I was perceptive about things like that. Something had taken him by surprise.

I had been looking down the street, but he was looking over my shoulder at the door of the tearoom.

I followed his gaze, expecting to see our quarry, Matthew Winthrop, who had come from the direction in which I hadn't been looking.

Instead, I saw Jocelyn Abbot.

CHAPTER TWENTY-TWO

I looked at the major. When I saw the grimness of his expression, I knew that things were serious. He so seldom looked anything but supremely confident, but now there was an expression on his face I couldn't quite interpret. I knew well enough, however, what he was thinking.

"It might not be her," I said. "Perhaps it's just a coincidence."

"You know as well as I do how unlikely that is," he replied.

He was right, of course. But one part of it didn't make sense.

"Surely she didn't . . . kill Harden and that other man herself?" I couldn't picture that elegant woman slitting people's throats, but I supposed anything was possible.

"I don't know," he said flatly. "Perhaps she has an accomplice."

The major didn't very often win my sympathy, but I could imagine how it felt, to discover definitively that someone you'd once cared about was involved in a plot against the country you were fighting for. She'd been on our suspect list, yes. But I assumed that he had secretly hoped the one person he truly thought he knew wasn't guilty of something like this. I almost felt like trying to say something comforting, but I knew I would make a muck of it, and he wouldn't want it anyway.

"There's a telephone up the street," he said after a moment. "I'll ring Kimble and tell him to come here. I told him to pick up your uncle and meet us back at my office to confer this afternoon. He may be there already."

"You think she won't exchange the papers if she sees you," I said.

"I very much doubt it," he replied. "If Kimble can get here in time, the two of you can go in together."

Apparently, he really hadn't believed Jocelyn Abbot was our quarry if he had not prepared for this eventuality. It was unlike him.

"I'll go alone," I said.

"No, you won't." He said this automatically. I think he was just used to contradicting me by this point, but his gaze was still not focused on me. He was weighing the options. There were few of those at this point.

I pressed on. "If we go in there together, she'll realize something is amiss. As you've said, it would be too much of a coincidence for both of us to arrive in the same place where she's meeting Matthew Winthrop. But if I go alone, she'll likely think very little of it."

"I can't ask you to do that," he said. "It may be dangerous."

"I think I could best Miss Abbot in a fight if it came to it." I was joking, but I'd grown up holding my own against Colm and Toby. If it came to it, I'd have her down in ten seconds flat.

For the briefest of moments, amusement flickered in his eyes, and then he was back to business. "It's out of the question."

"I've done things far more dangerous than this," I said. It was true. Even before I'd met him, I'd been breaking into houses in the dead of night. It wasn't exactly as though I was a shrinking violet. "Besides, all I have to do is observe the transfer of documents taking place, correct? Where's the danger in that?"

He seemed to consider it. That was all the space I needed to move ahead.

"We don't have time for anything else." Before he could reply, I began to move past him, stepping out of the alcove and onto the pavement. "I'm going."

I half expected him to grab my arm, but he surprised me.

"All right," he said.

I tried not to let him see how triumphant I felt, but he seemed to realize it because he added: "But you're not to approach her."

"It will look strange if I don't say hello when we've just met."

"Then just pretend you haven't noticed her."

I gave him a short nod and began walking away before he could issue any more commands.

I went into the tearoom and was greeted by the waitress, who began to show me to my table. As luck would have it, she led me right pass Miss Abbot.

Major Ramsey had told me to ignore her, but he ought to have known by this point how I felt about orders.

"Oh, hello, Miss Abbot," I said just as we were passing her table.

I'm a competent actress, if I say so myself. I suppose it comes with a profession where deception is a necessity. Whatever the case, I knew I looked mildly surprised to encounter Jocelyn Abbot in this place I had followed her to.

"Hello, Miss Donaldson," she said. She didn't seem particularly glad to see me, but I could tell that she thought it nothing more than a coincidence. It didn't occur to her to be suspicious of me.

"Lovely weather we're having, isn't it?"

"Yes." She didn't want to talk to me, which was fine because, under other circumstances, I wouldn't have wanted to talk to her either. And the major wouldn't approve, of course, but he wasn't here, was he?

I didn't know what my plan was, exactly, but I thought it would be good to get her talking. Perhaps she would reveal something without meaning to.

Looking at her, in a smart dark blue suit and a netted hat, her hair and makeup perfectly done, it was hard to imagine that she was involved in the murder of Thomas Harden and the unfortunate waiter. But it seemed there was no other explanation.

I decided to throw the first punch.

"I didn't make the connection, when we were talking at the party, that your fiancé is Barnaby Ellhurst."

I expected her features to close down at this invasion of her privacy, but I was good at reading faces and I didn't miss the sharpness that crossed her eyes before she shuttered them. A flash of something wary and canny.

"Yes," she said, her posture stiffening.

"I knew you looked familiar, but it didn't occur to me until later that I've seen your photos in the society columns," I went on. "I was so sorry to hear . . . that is, I hope that . . . I'm sure he will return safely." I didn't have to try hard to find awkward, inadequate words to reassure her that someone she supposedly loved would escape the death grip of war. I'd heard them often enough from all the people who found out Toby was missing.

She looked up at me and gave a tight smile. "Thank you." She was still guarded, but there was something strange that flashed in her eyes, something a bit vulnerable. It surprised me. There was something in it that was not at all in keeping with her role as a murderous spy.

"Well, nice to see you again," I said.

She didn't bother returning the lie but gave me a tight-lipped smile before the waiter led me to my nearby table and handed me a menu. I began to peruse it while keeping an eye on her table, waiting for Matthew Winthrop to arrive.

She glanced at me once, but I pretended to be absorbed in making my decision. That was all a show, too, because I didn't have much money on me. Enough for a cup of tea and a sandwich, perhaps. I should've asked the major to lend me a few bob.

When Miss Abbot was engaged with her own menu, I glanced at my wristwatch. It was past the appointed time. Matthew Winthrop was officially late.

She seemed to realize it, too, for she looked repeatedly at the clock on the wall.

The waitress came and took my order. She looked surprised that I wanted only tea and a slice of cake, but she was polite enough about it.

After that, there were then about five or ten minutes in which nothing occurred. Miss Abbot watched the clock, and I watched her. They were taking a long time about my tea.

I suppose spies and policemen and others concerned with the greater good usually have training that teaches them patience in situations like these. I, alas, had not had that training. With a safe set in front of me, a complex problem for my brain to solve, I could be patience personified, but sitting here waiting for something to happen was torture.

At last, they brought my tea and cake, and I lingered over them, waiting to see what would happen.

I had almost resolved to go back outside and confer with the major when I saw Matthew Winthrop walk in.

He glanced around the room, his eyes coming to light on Miss Abbot.

She wasn't glad to see him. That much would have been clear to anyone watching, for she didn't bother to hide it. But she'd been the one to arrange the meeting, hadn't she?

I wasn't near enough to hear what they were saying, but there was a smug expression on his face, and she was whispering something to him in hushed but urgent tones. It almost looked as though she was near tears and making an effort to hold them back.

Then I saw her reach for her handbag.

I stood up, tossing a few coins onto the table. She had just pulled a set of papers out of her handbag and slid them toward Mr. Winthrop as I approached their table. I made out a few sentences of hushed conversation before they noticed me. They weren't exceptionally competent at paying attention to their surroundings, but, in their defense, I'd always been stealthy.

"Wonderful to see you, Miss Abbot," I said brightly.

They both froze. It might have been comical under other circumstances.

"Oh, hello, Mr. Winthrop. Fancy seeing you again, too!" I said brightly. "I hope you both have a lovely afternoon."

Without waiting for a response, I walked unhurriedly away and left the tearoom.

Major Ramsey was waiting for me where I'd left him.

Wordlessly, he took my arm and we began walking down the street. It wasn't until we had rounded a corner that he stopped and turned to me.

"Did she give him the papers?" he asked.

"Yes."

I watched him closely, but whatever he was feeling, I couldn't tell.

He gave a short nod. "Then we'll make the switch at Winthrop's house. Kimble and his men are already keeping a watch. I'll put another man on Miss Abbot. Well done, Miss McDonnell."

There was more, however. He hadn't heard the worst of it, the sentences I'd caught when I approached their table. The information that turned the tables on everything.

"That isn't all," I said. "We've got a bit of a problem, I'm afraid."

"What is it?"

"She's written a note to accompany them, to verify their authenticity."

"What do you mean?" he demanded, a slight frown flickering across his handsome brow.

"The Germans have Barnaby Ellhurst. They're holding him hostage until she sends the documents. Your altered plans won't be enough. We need a note in her handwriting."

CHAPTER TWENTY-THREE

Jakub picked us up around the corner, and we drove back to the dungeon in a tense silence. I could feel the major stewing beside me. Not that I blamed him. This was certainly a spanner in the works.

He'd questioned me about it more than once on our walk to our agreed-upon meeting place with Jakub, and each time I'd assured him that I was quite certain of what I'd heard.

Matthew Winthrop had said quite clearly to Miss Abbot, "Ellhurst's life depends on you. You know that. Did you write the note?"

"Yes," she had replied. "I've replicated key passages by hand, as instructed. My handwriting will match my letters to Barnaby in their possession."

It didn't get much clearer than that. Barnaby Ellhurst had been shot down by the Germans and was being held hostage to ensure Miss Abbot's cooperation. She had secured the documents to save her fiancé's life, but it seemed the Germans had suspected that someone might try to make a switch. Her accompanying letter was insurance against that.

The pilot had apparently been carrying letters from Miss Abbot when he was captured. Now the Germans were using this to their advantage. Miss Abbot had been instructed to write a note replicating certain parts of the plans. Once they matched the handwriting in the note to the handwriting in her letters, they would know the plans were legitimate and would, presumably, release Lieutenant Ellhurst.

All of this meant we must substitute not only the plans but an artificial letter that corresponded to the artificial plans. Things had just become considerably more complicated.

The conversation Maudie Johnson had told me about between her and Thomas Harden about the comparison of handwriting samples now made sense.

I stared out the window as the car moved through the bustling streets. It was strange how, in so many ways, life was going on as usual. A week ago, I might have been walking along these streets myself, blissfully unaware that an enemy agent was preparing to turn weapons plans over to the Germans.

And the major had been unaware that the woman he had once cared about had involved herself with enemy spies.

"I don't think she killed Harden or that waiter," I said. "She's doing this against her will. Surely she wouldn't have committed murder."

The major didn't answer.

I knew he was still coming to terms with these newest revelations about Jocelyn Abbot. Now that I knew her motivations, I could understand—even sympathize—with her. What lengths would any of us go to to protect someone we loved? If the Germans had told me they had Toby and I must betray my country to save his life, what would my answer be? It wasn't an easy thing to consider.

But the major was very much a man who saw things in black and white, and I was sure that Miss Abbot's treachery was something he wouldn't be able to overlook.

We reached the dungeon at last and went inside. Oscar Davies, the major's aide, was already on his feet when we entered.

"Kimble and Mr. McDonnell are waiting for you, sir. I . . . I wasn't quite sure where to put them, but Kimble said your office would be all right, so . . ."

The major moved past him without answering and I followed, after shooting a sympathetic expression at Oscar. The major would no doubt berate the young man later for letting anyone into his office while he wasn't there.

Uncle Mick and Kimble were sitting in the leather chairs before the major's desk, and both of them rose as we came in. The air was heavy with cigar smoke.

"Hello, Ellie girl," Uncle Mick said. "How'd things go?"

I glanced at the major. "Not . . . quite as expected."

Kimble showed no reaction whatsoever, but Uncle Mick's brows rose in inquiry.

Since it was clear from the major's general demeanor that he wasn't in the mood to discuss the situation at the moment, I filled the other two in on what had happened and how our plans would have to change.

Uncle Mick let out a whistle when I had finished. "That is a bit of a problem, now, isn't it?" There was the slightest twinkle in his eyes as they met mine, however, and I realized he was thinking what I had been thinking on the drive from the tearoom. There was a way out of this.

It was a solid plan. The problem would be convincing the major.

As all of this was crossing my mind, it seemed that Kimble was making plans of his own.

"We'll have to deal with him, then, sir? Before he delivers the papers."

Despite the toneless, almost bored way Kimble said it, I knew well enough what that meant. They were going to kill Matthew Winthrop and take the documents. I was beginning to see why Kimble had not been a good fit for Scotland Yard.

My distaste for violence aside, killing Matthew Winthrop to retrieve the documents would rob us of the chance to give the Germans false information. I could understand it might be necessary to resort to such extremes if all else failed, but we hadn't failed just yet.

"Before we get to that," I said. "I have another idea."

The major and Kimble both turned to look at me. Neither of them looked particularly interested, but they didn't discourage me, so I ventured on.

I glanced at Uncle Mick, and he gave me a little nod, so I plunged ahead. "I . . . we happen to know a forger. Someone who could easily duplicate a letter."

There was a moment of silence.

"You do run with an interesting crowd, Miss McDonnell," Major Ramsey said at last.

I didn't bother to deny it. I knew most of my friends were not people of whom Major McDonnell would approve, but this was war and allowances must be made. They'd been made already, so why not go a bit further?

"Ellie's idea is a good one, Major," Uncle Mick put in. "It's the only way to see this thing through."

The major didn't answer. I couldn't tell what he was thinking, but at least he hadn't refused me outright yet. I assumed that he'd do that when he heard the rest of it.

"He's an excellent forger," I went on. "He could write something in my hand and make me believe I'd written it myself. I'm sure he would be able to replicate whatever is in Miss Abbot's note and convince the Germans that the false plans are legitimate. Like Uncle Mick said, it's our only hope of succeeding."

"Worth a try," Kimble said blandly, and I was glad for even this unenthusiastic show of support.

"You can contact this forger immediately?" Major Ramsey asked at last. "We don't have much time."

"Yes, I can contact him now." I drew in a breath and then plunged ahead. "You see, it's Felix Lacey."

CHAPTER TWENTY-FOUR

"Your gentleman friend is a forger, is he?" Major Ramsey said, his expression inscrutable.

"You've already thrown in your lot with criminals, so it's a bit late to be particular," Uncle Mick said, before I could respond. "And Felix Lacey is just the man for the job."

The major considered. "Ring him up," he said at last. "Ask to meet him as soon as you can."

I nodded. "What do I tell him about . . . all of this?"

"Ask him how he feels about doing a forgery job for the war effort. None of the particulars. If he's interested, you can bring him here to discuss it."

I nodded. Time was short, and we both knew things would have to fall into place quickly if we wanted to succeed.

I was glad the major was letting me introduce the topic to Felix. He wasn't the sort of man who would appreciate officiousness. It would be much better if I spoke to him before introducing him to Major Ramsey. I was also glad the major's previous command, that I stop seeing Felix, was being countermanded. He was a good man to have on our team.

I picked up the major's phone, feeling a bit self-conscious doing it there in his office with everyone watching. I rang the number, hoping Felix would answer. If he was out and about looking for work, I didn't know when I might be able to reach him.

To my relief, he answered after the second ring.

"Hello?" A rush of affection went through me at the sound of his voice. I felt, suddenly, that things were going to be all right.

"Hello, Felix," I said. "It's Ellie. I . . . I wonder if you would come around and speak with me."

"Of course. When?" It was just like him. No questions asked.

"Now, if it's convenient."

"Certainly. I'll be there in half an hour."

"No . . . not at my flat," I said. "Can you meet me at this address?" I gave him the address of a tearoom not far from the major's office.

"Is everything all right?" he asked. I looked up and saw the major's eyes on me.

"Yes. That is, I'll explain everything when I see you."

"All right. I'll be there in a jiff, love."

I rang off and turned to the men, who were all watching me.

"He's agreed to meet me."

"Naturally," the major said.

I didn't know exactly what he meant by that, so I thought it best to ignore him.

"What are the odds he'll do the job?" Kimble asked.

"He'll do it," Uncle Mick said. "For Ellie, if nothing else. He's a bit sweet on her. Always has been."

"He'll do it for his country," I countered, feeling a blush creeping up on my cheeks. "He cares about defeating the Nazis as much as any of us."

The major's cool blue eyes met mine. "Let's hope you're right, Miss McDonnell."

Half an hour later, Felix and I were sitting at a table in the corner of the quiet tearoom. It seemed I was to spend the majority of my day in tearooms, but at least this one was less stuffy than the last had been.

The waitress set our tea before us, and I found suddenly that I was nervous. I wasn't sure why, exactly. I supposed it was because I had never asked him for anything before, and I was suddenly going to ask him to put himself in the middle of a risky situation, one in which his life and the lives of many others might be at stake.

"What's the matter, sweet?" he asked, placing his hand over mine.

I looked up. I had wandered off in my head. I made a good show of appearing to be at ease while my mind wandered, but the truth was that I was uneasy. Few people would have recognized it but Felix.

"I have a favor to ask you," I said, deciding to charge ahead.

"I'd do anything for you. You know that."

"You'd better hear me out first," I said.

"I'm listening." He released my hand and took a cigarette from his pocket and put it to his lips.

I had debated the best way to go about telling him what I had to say, but I still hadn't quite come to a decision. After all, how did one go about recruiting a spy? That was, in essence, what I was doing.

"I'm afraid I've been keeping a secret from you," I said, as he struck a match and put it to his cigarette.

"Oh?" He was watching me carefully, but there was no sign of apprehension in him. Felix was always very calm, always certain that things would work out the way he intended them to.

"Yes, you see . . . I'm afraid I've been engaged in some rather clandestine work."

"With your uncle?" he asked.

"In a manner of speaking."

I realized that I was drawing things out unnecessarily. I might as well have out with it.

"Uncle Mick and I have been working with the government."

"You're working with the government?" he repeated. He didn't sound entirely surprised, but it was hard to surprise him. He always took everything as it came, with good humor and unruffled composure.

"Yes. I . . . well, it's a long story. We were . . . caught breaking into a house, and it came down to a choice between helping or going to prison."

His brows rose, concern flashing across his expression. "You should have told me."

"I wanted to . . . but I couldn't," I said.

"So you've been drafted into service. Doing what?"

"I . . . I can't say, exactly. Not until after I've told you the rest of it."

"Go on." He took a leisurely drag of his cigarette, as though I hadn't been telling him the most astounding things. It occurred to me that if anyone was born to do clandestine work, it was Felix. He was collected, resourceful, and unflappable. I suddenly wondered what the story was behind the loss of his leg. I wouldn't be at all surprised if it had happened when he was doing something heroic.

"There's been a bit of trouble, and we need your help."

He blew out a stream of smoke and then a smile tipped up the corner of his mouth. "It's all rather dramatic, isn't it?"

"Yes, I suppose it does sound that way."

"Well, why don't you tell me more about it."

He settled back in his chair, the picture of casual comfort.

"There is a certain set of documents that needs to be recovered. Well, not only recovered, but replaced with a different set entirely. There is a letter that must accompany them. We need an alternate letter written in a specific handwriting. You're the only person I know who could do something like that."

He said nothing, but took another long drag from his cigarette, staring out into the room as he blew out the smoke.

I didn't know whether I should remain silent and let him think it over or if I should press onward. When the silence lengthened, I decided to continue on.

"I know you've done your part," I said, my gaze flickering to his leg. "More than your part. But this is very important. If we don't get these documents back . . ."

"Who's in charge of this operation?" he asked.

"I . . . I don't know if I'm allowed to tell you, as of yet. Not until you've agreed to meet with him."

Felix seemed thoughtful as he put the cigarette to his lips again, breathing deeply and exhaling a cloud of smoke.

"You're under no obligation to do anything, of course," I went on. "But I hoped that you'd help us. You see, this cause is beginning to mean something to me. It's more than . . . more than something I've been obligated to do. I feel that it's my duty, just as Colm and Toby are doing theirs. As you've done yours."

There was a moment of silence, and I wondered, for the first time, if he was going to refuse me.

Then he looked up and gave me a smile, a genuine one this time. "How can a man say no to a woman of principle?"

CHAPTER TWENTY-FIVE

We left the tearoom and found that Jakub was outside, waiting for us with the car. It wasn't far to the office; Major Ramsey must have sent it in deference to Felix's leg.

"Rather luxurious, this," he said as we settled in the backseat. "Using rationed petrol to be toted about."

"Yes, I've taken the Tube to get to and fro before, but the major does send the car sometimes. It's just that he's usually in a hurry for me to arrive."

Felix glanced at me. "The major?"

"Yes, he's . . . he's in command of the operation."

He was looking at me closely now, and I found that, for some reason, I couldn't meet his gaze.

We reached the office a few minutes later and went inside. Oscar looked gloomier than ever, though I saw him shoot a curious glance at Felix. "He's expecting you," he told me, and there was a note of foreboding in his voice.

"Are my uncle and Kimble still here?"

He shook his head. "Major Ramsey sent them away."

I had rather hoped to have Uncle Mick and the bland Kimble as a buffer, but there was no help for it now. I only hoped the major would be pleasant when meeting Felix. After all, we needed Felix's help.

I led Felix down the long hall toward Major Ramsey's office, hoping that this meeting would go well.

My hopes were in vain.

I had known they wouldn't like each other. They weren't at all the same sort of men. But I hadn't really expected the aura of instant antagonism that seemed to exist when we stepped into the room. Major Ramsey stood as I closed the door behind us, and the two of them looked at each other for a long moment.

Then Major Ramsey came out from behind his desk. "Miss McDonnell. This is Mr. Lacey, I presume?"

"Yes, this is Felix Lacey. Felix, this is Major Ramsey."

Major Ramsey stepped forward and shook his hand. "How do you do, Lacey."

"How do you do?" Felix had a pleasant enough expression on his face, but I recognized it well enough. It was the one he used when he was going to try to fleece someone.

"Miss McDonnell tells me you're a man who can be counted on."

"I hope so," Felix said.

"She went over the details with you?"

"Such as they are. It's all a bit vague, isn't it?"

"At the moment. I'm afraid this is one of those games you have to decide whether you're in or out before the cards are dealt."

"I've always been fairly lucky at cards," Felix said lightly.

"Well, then. Let's hope your luck holds."

I could sense an undertone of something beneath this friendly conversation. They were, for some reason, both determined to dislike each other and doing only a haphazard job of trying to hide it.

I looked at the two of them. They were so different. Major Ramsey was tall and fair and rigid. His blond good looks and impressive build might have made him a fitting model for some Viking hero of days gone by. He had the air of a warrior, too, always on his guard, always watching, ready to take action.

In contrast, there was something very easy about Felix. He didn't slouch, but there was a kind of languidness about him at all times, even when he was standing. Dark-haired and suave with his trim mustache and easy smile, he had a cinema star quality. It was only in the sharp watchfulness of his eyes that one had the impression there was much more going on beneath the surface.

"Sit down, will you?" the major said.

I took one of the seats in front of Major Ramsey's desk, and Felix dropped into the other one, crossing one leg easily over the other.

"Do you mind if I smoke?" he asked.

"Not at all," the major replied.

Felix took his cigarettes from his coat pocket and offered one to Major Ramsey, who shook his head.

"I may as well be blunt with you," the major said. "We could use your services. As Miss McDonnell has no doubt told you, there is a set of documents we are hoping to substitute. The documents can be replicated, but we've discovered there is also a letter that must be altered in order to accompany them. It's handwritten."

"And if the letter can't be replicated?" Felix asked mildly.

"Then more drastic action will be taken," Major Ramsey said.

Felix knew what he meant as well as I did, but he didn't seem alarmed at the suggestion. "Wouldn't that just be the simpler way all around?"

I looked sharply at him. The suggestion that we resort to violence as an alternative measure was unlike him. Then again, I knew that the war had changed his perspective on a lot of things.

"It might be," Major Ramsey assented. "But it won't give the Germans the wrong information. That's our primary objective. If we can convince them they've recovered genuine information via this particular route, it may be an avenue we can continue to use for deception purposes."

"It's not a bad plan," Felix said, without any great conviction. "And I'm sure I can replicate the letter. There are a few things to be considered, however."

"Such as?"

"You can't keep making Ellie play spies with you, Major," Felix said. "It isn't fair to her. She doesn't know the game, and it's wrong of you to ask her to play for these stakes."

I was startled. This hadn't been part of the plan.

"Felix . . ." I began.

The major answered before I could finish. "Miss McDonnell is aware of the risks."

"That doesn't mean she should take them," Felix said.

"I think I'm the best one to speak for myself on that score," I cut in, before either of them could make another comment about me as though I wasn't there. I had never stood for that sort of thing from Colm and Toby, and I certainly wasn't going to take it from these two.

Felix glanced at me then, his expression softening ever so slightly. "I know you want to do this, Ellie, but that doesn't mean that you should. This isn't some harmless soft touch you're dealing with. The Nazis will kill to get what they want. Or to prevent you from getting in their way."

He turned back to Major Ramsey. "Asking me, or even Mick McDonnell, for help is one thing. But it's unconscionable to get an untrained woman to do your work for you."

Major Ramsey looked calm, but I saw that silver cast come over his eyes, and I knew well enough what that meant. When he spoke, his tone was quiet. "I understand your concerns, Lacey, but Miss McDonnell is working for us of her own free will. What's more, I'm perfectly capable of running this operation without your input."

"I'm not under your command, Major," Felix said. His tone was friendly enough, but I could see that his eyes were growing hard.

"You will be if you agree to this operation," Major Ramsey replied levelly. "This isn't going to be one of your little cons. The security of our nation is at risk, and I need to know you can do as you're told."

Things were spiraling out of control rapidly, and I wasn't sure how to fix it. I tried to decide which one of them it would be best to placate. I could manage Felix more easily, but the major was the one who was pulling all the strings.

I reached over and put a hand on Felix's arm. I could feel the tension in it.

He turned to look at me, and I gave him the barest hint of a smile. I appreciated that he wanted to protect me, but I hadn't brought him here to do that. I think my expression told him as much, for I felt his posture relax ever so slightly beneath my hand.

I looked back to Major Ramsey. He was watching the two of us closely. I remembered his insinuations about the night Felix had spent on my sofa. Well, let him think whatever he wanted. My relationship with Felix was not his concern.

"I think we're losing sight of the matter at hand," I said. I felt two sets of eyes on me, each telling me that this was none of my concern. I didn't take kindly to those looks.

"We're trying to help win a war, gentlemen. I don't suppose it's time for petty arguments. Besides, I'm a grown woman, and it's been a long time since I've let any man tell me what I can or cannot do."

Felix smiled. It wasn't his easy smile, but I could see that some of the tension had left him and he was beginning to appreciate the humor of the situation.

"She's right, of course," he said, looking at the major. "Ellie usually is."

"Then perhaps we can go ahead with the planning?" Major Ramsey asked.

Felix waved a hand. "I am at your disposal."

"Thank you."

I let out a breath. The rest of the meeting would go well enough now that they'd both had a chance to growl at each other a bit. I was certain that, though they didn't like each other, they would work well enough together when it came down to it.

"What, exactly, do you want in the forged letter?" Felix asked.

"We won't be entirely sure until we've seen the genuine letter," the major said.

I frowned. The other letter was in Matthew Winthrop's possession. "How are we to see the letter, to know what to write, before Felix writes its replacement?"

"We've had a man on Mr. Winthrop. He leaves his house in the predawn hours each morning for a walk in the park and then proceeds to his club for breakfast. We'll have to enter the house then. Mr. Lacey will accompany your uncle and Kimble when they make the switch. He'll have to write the letter then." He turned to Felix. "Can you do it quickly?"

"It's too dangerous for Felix to accompany them," I cut in. "I thought he was only to write the letter here. If . . ."

"Ellie . . ." Felix interrupted.

I turned to look at him, and though his words were gentle, I could sense something a bit firmer behind them. "You don't have to fight my battles for me, love."

I flushed. He was right, of course. I had been irritated when he'd tried to argue with the major on my behalf, and now I was doing the same thing to him.

Felix turned to the major. "I can do it, yes. Ideally, of course, I'll have some time to practice the handwriting in advance. Once I've done that, it should be a simple thing for me to write it when the exchange is made."

"You won't have any difficulties replicating a woman's hand?" Major Ramsey asked.

Felix shook his head. "None at all. Provided you have samples of the handwriting."

I had known somewhere in the back of my mind, of course, that it would be necessary, but I hadn't stopped to think much about it. If we had only the letter to go on, Felix would have to study her hand when they made the switch. That would lengthen the time they needed to be in the house and increase the possibility they might be caught.

Alternate possibilities fluttered through my mind. It would be possible, I supposed, to write a letter to Miss Abbot and hope for a reply, but any social note she sent was likely to be short and not enough for Felix to work with.

"We could get into her house, I suppose," I suggested. "I'm sure she has a diary or something lying about."

"Something like that is liable to be missed," Felix mused.

"Yes, I suppose you're right."

There was a moment of silence, and then Major Ramsey spoke, a strange note in his voice. "I have some samples you might use."

CHAPTER TWENTY-SIX

The major excused himself then, and Felix and I were alone in the office.

He cut to the chase right away. "Charming fellow, isn't he? Did I pass muster, do you think?"

"You did. He wouldn't have agreed to let you do it if you didn't."

"You know him well, it seems."

I shrugged. "He's not a difficult man to read. His intentions are generally clear."

"And what are his intentions toward you?"

I looked sharply at Felix. "What do you mean?"

The corner of his mouth tipped up just a bit. "You needn't do the innocent eyes and fluttering lashes with me, Ellie McDonnell. You know perfectly well what I mean."

I knew. But I didn't want to have this conversation with Felix. Things had been unsettled between the two of us the last few years, and I didn't know how to respond to his comments about other men. There was certainly nothing formal about our relationship, but nor had I ever really felt that I could move on from him.

Why must everything be so complicated?

"There's nothing going on between me and Major Ramsey," I said at last, making my tone as casual as possible.

"'Major Ramsey,'" he repeated. "Is that what you call him when you're alone?"

"Of course, it is." I think the words came out a bit more harshly than I had intended, for Felix's expression sobered.

"I'm sorry, Ellie. I shouldn't tease you."

"There's nothing to be sorry for. But there isn't anything between the major and me. We've been very professional." My irritation grabbed me again then, and I added, "Not that I suppose it's really any of your concern."

He smiled. "No, I suppose it's not. Except for that I care about you."

I sighed. "I know you do."

"You've never seemed to realize how beautiful you are," he said. "But men notice it. I can see the way he watches you when you're not looking."

I looked up at him. "I don't know what you mean."

"Perhaps you don't. You've never much cared for things like that, but there's an appreciative glint in his eye that any man would recognize."

"You're being silly, Felix."

"You're being purposefully obtuse," he countered.

I didn't reply to this. There was no good in our going back and forth on the subject.

"All I'm saying is that you should be careful," Felix went on. "He's a good-looking fellow. Don't let him turn your head."

"You would know about that, wouldn't you?" I said with a smile.

He laughed. "You flatter me, Ellie. But I'm serious. Be careful. He's not the type of fellow who . . ."

"I know," I said. I knew what he meant. Major Ramsey wasn't the type of man who was going to have a serious interest in me; the disparities between us were too great. Not that he had displayed any interest whatsoever.

There was, somewhere in the back of my mind, the memory of that kiss we had shared. I knew it meant nothing, was the same thing as a stage kiss between two actors. But if I hadn't been a smart, practical girl, I might have let my mind run away with me, thinking there had been more to it than that. Felix wasn't far off the mark when he said I should be careful.

"Thank you," I said at last, looking for a way to end the conversation. "It's sweet of you to worry about me, Felix, but you don't need to. I can handle myself."

"I know you can. But that doesn't stop me from wanting to look out for you."

The door opened then, and we dropped the conversation as Major Ramsey came back into the room.

"Got the samples already?" Felix said, rising. "Well, I'm ready to go to work." He took off his suit jacket and began rolling up his shirtsleeves.

The major came forward with a stack of letters, tied with twine, and tossed them onto the desk. From where I sat, I could see the bold, feminine handwriting scrawled across the envelopes in dark blue ink.

"Will those do as a sample?" he asked Felix. He didn't look at me.

Felix nodded. "This ought to be more than sufficient for my purposes."

Ramsey nodded. "There are paper and pens in the top drawer. Do you need anything else?"

"I wouldn't say no to a cup of coffee."

"I'll have Davies bring you some."

"Thanks."

The major turned then, and went out of the room.

"Where'd he get these letters?" Felix asked.

"I imagine she wrote to him while he was in North Africa," I said.

"The two of them were involved, then?"

"Yes," I said, glancing again at the thick stack of letters. "He told me they had 'seen each other socially' for a while, but I think it was actually quite serious."

"I'll say. I didn't get half so many letters from you while I was off fighting."

"I wrote you very often," I protested. "And you were dreadful about writing back." One would think a man with such a skilled hand with a pen might be a better correspondent.

He grinned, picking up the stack of letters. "Well, I suppose it's a lucky thing she wrote faithfully to the major. Let's see what she had to say, shall we?"

For some reason, I felt a twinge of unease. I was curious, I'll admit, but I also felt as though it was rather an invasion of privacy. After all, the things one said to a man who was away in the army were likely to be much more heartfelt than the flirtatious letters one sent to casual beaus.

"I . . . I suppose these are rather personal in nature," I said.

"Only one way to find out."

Felix had none of the reservations I did. He pulled the twine from the letters and picked up the first one in the stack, removing it from the envelope. He ran his eyes over the neat lines for a moment and then let out a whistle.

"Doesn't beat about the bush, our Miss Abbot. Rather hot stuff from page one."

I felt a bit irritated for some reason, though I wasn't sure if it was Felix or Jocelyn Abbot that was making me feel that way.

"Can you imitate her style?" I asked, though I already knew the answer.

"Oh, yes. That's easy enough. She's got a distinctive hand, but her lettering is inconsistent. It won't be difficult to mimic at all. But, Ellie, listen to this . . ."

I held up a hand. "I'd rather not hear it, Felix."

His eyes came up to me then. "Why not?"

"I . . . I don't know. It's just so personal."

"He knew we'd be reading them," he said.

"Yes, but . . . I don't know. I'd just rather not hear them."

He shrugged. "All right. I just thought they might amuse you."

I took my seat without comment. They might have amused me at another time, but not now.

The room settled into silence, except for the scratch of Felix's pen on paper. I knew he didn't require solitude to concentrate. He could jot off a letter in someone else's handwriting without thinking twice. But I was lost in thought.

Why had things ended between the major and Jocelyn Abbot? It seemed to me that there were still some lingering feelings, so what had caused their parting and her subsequent engagement to another man? Did the letters hold the answers? If so, I wasn't going to find out. Not that way.

I wondered where Major Ramsey had gone after he left us alone in the office. Had he been too embarrassed to stay while we looked over the love letters Jocelyn Abbot had sent him? I doubted it. He was not a man who was prone to embarrassment, and, looked at another way, such letters were only likely to improve him in Felix's eyes. Men liked to boast of their love affairs, didn't they?

Still, I couldn't help but wonder why he had avoided my gaze when he had brought the letters in.

Even more, I wondered why, if the relationship between the major and Miss Abbot had ended badly, he had kept all of her letters.

CHAPTER TWENTY-SEVEN

Oscar came in with the coffee perhaps ten minutes after the major had brought in the letters, and Felix drank three cups of the inky brew without ever putting down his pen.

It was fascinating to watch him work. In the same way that Uncle Mick was an artist where locks were concerned, Felix was a master of his craft.

He studied the letters before him and, on a blank sheet of paper, began to write various words, altering the slant and curves and spacing of the letters as he went until slowly the words began to look like the ones he was replicating.

He didn't rush to copy particular letters or words, but took his time, as though learning the style. It was quite a thing to behold.

At last, Felix nodded, looking down at the paper before him, where several lines of script flowed evenly across the page. "I think I've got it," he said, pushing it toward me.

I picked up the letter and scanned the writing, glad to see that he hadn't decided to mimic a love letter while practicing the style. Though I hadn't read any of Miss Abbot's letters, I could see that the writing on Felix's paper was an excellent match for the writing on the samples that lay strewn across the desk.

Not that I had doubted him. Felix had been brilliant at this sort of thing for as long as I had known him. As a boy he had written letters to teachers and other authority figures in parents' handwriting, excusing himself and his friends from events they didn't wish to attend.

"It's excellent," I said, smiling at him as I rose from my chair. "I'll go and find the major."

I went out of the office and back down the hallway to the foyer. Oscar was behind the desk in the sitting room, but he got quickly to his feet as I approached.

"No need to get up, Oscar," I said. "I'm just looking for Major Ramsey. Has he gone out?"

"No, I believe he's upstairs."

I had never given much thought to the upper rooms of the house, but I supposed that must be where the major lived. It was strange, in a way, to think of him living alone in this house, to suppose that he walked around in his stocking feet on the floor above after a long day in his office.

I don't know why the image of the major in stocking feet seemed endearing to me, but I pushed it away. Now was not the time for flights of fancy.

"Mr. Lacey is ready for the major whenever he's available," I said. Oscar nodded. "I'll tell him."

I went back to the major's office. Felix, to his credit, had returned all of Jocelyn Abbot's letters to their envelopes and tied the twine about them once more. I felt better, somehow, knowing the love letters were no longer out in the open.

The major came in a moment later, glancing at the clock on the wall. "Less than an hour," he said. "Are you sure you have it perfected?"

"Judge for yourself," Felix said, pushing a sheet along the desk.

The major stepped forward and picked it up. His eyes scanned it briefly and then he looked up at Felix. There was a long moment of silence before he said, "You could have fooled me with this letter."

Felix grinned. "I shall take that as a compliment, Major."

Major Ramsey didn't answer. I supposed he hadn't exactly meant to compliment Felix on the quality of his forgery, but, under the circumstances, I thought it fitting. The way I looked at it, good work was good work. Credit where credit is due.

Felix rose then, rolling down his sleeves and pulling on his jacket. "If that's all, then, Major?"

Major Ramsey nodded. "You'll come back early in the morning, say around four o'clock? We'd like to make the switch before sunrise, if at all possible."

Felix nodded. "I'll be here."

I also made a move to rise, to accompany Felix out, but the major's voice stopped me. "You'll stay for a bit longer, Miss McDonnell?" he asked, still looking at the documents on the desk.

He wanted to have a word privately with me, then. I turned to look at Felix. He, too, had understood the request, and gave me a short nod.

"I'll be on my way, then," he said.

"Our car will drop you anywhere you want to go," Major Ramsey said.

"I can walk."

"Felix . . ." I began, but then I stopped. He knew his limitations better than I did, and it would only embarrass him for me to mention his leg.

His gaze flickered over to me. "I'll see you later, Ellie?"

"Yes, I'll ring you up."

He nodded and turned back to Major Ramsey. "Good afternoon, Major."

"Good afternoon."

He left then, and we were alone.

Major Ramsey was silent for a moment as though thinking something over. It was something I had learned in my short acquaintance with him, that sometimes you just had to sit and let him think.

The silences weren't uncomfortable. I don't know if he meant them to be, but I found there was something reassuring, almost soothing, about them, as though answers were coming together in the quiet.

"Do you trust him?" he asked at last.

It wasn't exactly what I had expected, but it was easy enough to answer.

"I wouldn't have recommended him if I didn't." Under other circumstances, I might have been affronted, but I knew how seriously Major Ramsey took his job. I knew how serious all of this was.

"I trust him, too," he said.

I looked up at him, surprised. I hadn't expected such an admission, especially not when he had not particularly cared for Felix. I ought to have known, however, that it wasn't a compliment without restrictions.

"He's exactly the sort of chap I wouldn't trust in regular life, which is what makes him perfect for this job."

There was a gibe in there somewhere, but I smiled nonetheless. "He's a very good sort of person when he makes up his mind to be. And he's very good at what he does."

The major nodded, looking down at the letter again. "That's apparent."

A silence fell over the room then, as we both looked at the stack of letters on the desk. I didn't know what he was thinking, but I felt suddenly like I ought to let him know that Felix and I hadn't been sitting here together sifting through the pieces of his broken relationship.

"I . . . I didn't read her letters," I said.

He looked up at me. "You could have. There's nothing in them I wish to hide."

"Yes, but . . ."

He waited, but I didn't know what I wanted to say.

"I . . . I'm sorry," I said at last. "That she was involved, I mean. I know it must be unpleasant for you."

"Things were over between Jocelyn and me long before this."

"Yes, but . . ." I sighed, the weight of all of it hitting me suddenly. "It's all so awful, isn't it? All the secrecy and deception, not knowing who can be trusted. All these solid British citizens that could conceivably be working with the enemy."

"We like to think that people become better during wars," he said. "That they band together and help one another and do what's right. But it isn't always that way. For every neighbor helping neighbor and stranger doing acts of kindness, there are people taking advantage of the weak and defenseless. That's just the way life is."

I knew he was right, of course. I'd already seen the way some people were behaving, the way people were using the war to their advantage. Hadn't we been doing something similar ourselves, robbing the homes of people who were gone, perhaps who were even away fighting for our country? It gave me a sick feeling in the pit of my stomach. The only consolation was that we were doing something now to make it right. "It's all such a complicated muddle," I said.

"Not so very complicated."

I looked up at him. "No?"

"It boils down to a fairly simple formula." His eyes, when they met mine, were that stormy twilight shade again. "One thing I've discovered about war, Miss McDonnell: either it brings out the best in people or it brings out the worst in them."

I accompanied Felix and Uncle Mick to the dungeon well before dawn the next morning. As we had arranged the previous evening, Felix and I met up with Uncle Mick at the house, where Nacy had prepared a hot breakfast the men ate quickly and with little conversation. I only ate a bit of toast and jam, but I had two strong cups of tea.

I wasn't usually so anxious about a job, but this was bigger than the things we normally did. This was bigger than all of us.

Nacy didn't ask for the particulars as the men ate the food Uncle Mick had asked her to prepare in practically the dead of night, but her face was grim as I kissed her cheek before we left the house, and I heard her mutter under her breath, "You'd better all come back alive. I've a big dinner planned."

It was still dark as we made our way to the Tube station, but the city was already coming to life, the pavements peppered with people on their way to do the jobs that kept our city up and running. Life goes on, as they say. Even in wartime.

Major Ramsey hadn't exactly invited me to come along this morning, but he hadn't told me not to either. At the very least, I could wait at the office until Felix and Uncle Mick returned and would know all the sooner that they were safe and that everything had gone off all right.

Besides, it was not as though the major had to entertain me. I just didn't want to be alone at my flat, waiting. And anyway, I was just as much a part of this as any of them were.

We reached the major's office and Oscar let us in. He looked sleepy this morning as well as gloomy.

"You look as though you could use a cup of tea," I told him.

"I've already had three," he said. "The major's waiting for you . . . ah, that is, he's waiting for Mr. McDonnell and Mr. Lacey."

"It's all right," I said. "He won't be surprised I'm here."

I led the way to Major Ramsey's office and tapped on the door.

"Enter."

I pushed it open. "Good morning," I said brightly.

He rose from his chair. He was in shirtsleeves again this morning, with no tie and his collar unbuttoned.

"Good morning," he said, though I could tell what I had told Oscar wasn't entirely true. He hadn't been expecting me. Perhaps he had thought either Uncle Mick or Felix would've made me stay at home; well, he ought to have known better by now.

"And a lovely morning it is, Major," Uncle Mick said cheerily. He was the sort of person who was up long before the sun and was always unreasonably happy about it.

Felix nodded his greeting. He'd had two cups of coffee at breakfast, but I thought they probably hadn't quite worked their way into
his system.

Major Ramsey had every hair in place, of course. He was freshly
shaven and, though he was a bit more informal than usual, his uniform shirt was crisply pressed. It was a bit annoying, really, to see
him looking so well at such an hour.

There were footsteps behind us in the hallway, as I hadn't yet
closed the door, and Kimble came into the room. He looked exactly as
he always did, completely void of any emotion. There was generally so
little expression on the man's face that I was uncertain if he actually
felt anything at all.

"All ready?" he asked without a greeting.

The major looked at Uncle Mick and Felix, the other two members of the operation. "Are you gentlemen ready to proceed?"

Uncle Mick smiled. "I'm always ready."

"Ready and able," Felix said.

The major glanced at his watch. "Go ahead, then. When it's
done, come directly back here."

Kimble turned without a word and started out of the room.
Uncle Mick followed, but I stopped him with a hand on his arm.
"You'll be careful, won't you?"

"I'm always careful, Ellie girl," Uncle Mick said with a wink. He
patted my head. "Don't you worry your pretty little head." It was a
little joke of ours, something he'd always said to rile me when I was
arguing with him about whether or not I ought to be included in
something the boys got to do.

Felix reached out to squeeze my hand on his way out the door,
and I smiled at him, knowing he understood my silent good luck
wishes.

Their footsteps receded, and then the front door opened and
they were gone.

I turned back to look at the major.

"I couldn't stay at home," I said.

"No," he replied. "I don't suppose you could."

We looked at each other for a moment.

"I'd ask you to sit and wait here," he said, "but I'm afraid I have some business to tend to."

"Oh. Of course." I hadn't particularly expected him to keep me company while we waited, but his manner stung a bit nonetheless. I made sure, however, not to let him see it.

Without another word, I turned and left the room, closing the door behind me.

I found Oscar at his desk, just ringing off a phone call, and waved him back into his seat before he could get up. "The major's busy," I said. "Do you mind if I sit out here with you?"

"Not at all," he said. "I could do with a bit of company. Sit down, won't you?"

He motioned to an arrangement of furniture in one corner of the room. There was a beautiful sofa, upholstered in yellow silk, and two blue chairs, left over from the days when Major Ramsey had entertained in this room, no doubt.

I took a seat on the sofa. It was much more comfortable than I had expected.

"Would you like some tea?" Oscar asked.

I shook my head. "Thank you, no."

"It will come out all right," he said.

I looked up at him.

"Whatever they've gone to do. It will come out all right."

"Does he tell you? The things that go on, I mean?" I asked.

"Some of them. A lot of it's need-to-know, of course. But I'm a good judge of character, and your uncle and the others know what they're about."

I nodded. "They're all very capable. I think you're right, that it's all going to come out fine."

He smiled. It was one of the first smiles I'd seen from him. I was surprised to see he had dimples. He was a good-looking young man when he wasn't looking so glum.

"I've good instincts about these things," he said. "I know I'm not much more than a secretary, but I . . . well, I'm capable in my own way."

"Certainly, you are," I said. "I'm sure the major wouldn't have asked you to work for him if he didn't have faith in your capabilities."

His expression darkened ever so slightly. "It's not how I wished to spend the war."

"No?"

"No. I'd much rather have fought. But I'm blind in my left eye."

"Oh," I said. I had never noticed that anything was amiss. "I'm sorry."

He shrugged. "I have been since an accident when I was a child. It never bothered me much until this war. People can't tell, you see, that there's anything wrong. And they think I don't fight because I'm afraid."

"It doesn't matter what people think," I said, but we both knew that, in some ways, it did. "Besides, Major Ramsey thinks highly of you."

He gave a bitter laugh. "He dislikes me more than anyone."

"I'm sure he doesn't."

"He resents me because when they called him back from North Africa to this job . . . I . . . well, I got my father to put in a word for me. Ramsey is my cousin, you see."

It suddenly fell into place. "You're the earl's son!"

He flushed scarlet. "I . . . no, I . . . that is . . ."

"It's all right," I said quickly. "I won't tell anyone."

"We don't like to mention that around here," he said. "I go by my mother's name or there'd be a fuss, at least in certain circles. But I wanted to do something. Anything other than sit at Overton Hall and feel useless. And so, when Ramsey came back from North Africa and began working here, my father got a place for me. But

Ramsey seems to think he's got to mind me rather than viewing me as helpful. The military has been his life since he was young, Sandhurst and all that. He takes it very seriously. And now I've come in as a sort of burden to him."

I supposed that explained that antagonism I'd noticed the major seemed to have for the young man. And perhaps it explained why Oscar always looked so miserable. He was stuck in a job that was, in many ways, probably beneath him, capable of more but not given a chance to do it.

"But you are helpful, Oscar . . ." I paused, wondering if I ought to call him something else now that I knew who he really was. "May I still call you Oscar?"

"Of course! I should hate for you to call me anything else."

"But aren't you a . . . viscount or something?"

He shook his head. "I'm not the heir, in any case. It's my older brother. And we've two little brothers besides. Plenty of spares to go around."

I laughed.

"But don't tell him that I told you, not if you can help it."

"I won't," I said. "It'll be our little secret."

I let Oscar go back to his work and settled against the cushions of the sofa, trying to plot out in my mind how long it would be. Uncle Mick would get them into the house. He and Kimble would go over the place until they found the documents and the letter. Felix would read the letter and rewrite it as needed. Then they could exchange the documents and be on their way.

How long would it take? It would depend on where the documents were and how long it took to find them. Longer, of course, if they were in a safe or well hidden. But perhaps Winthrop would be sloppy. We could only hope.

The early morning must have caught up with me because, without intending to, I dozed off, leaning against the sofa cushions.

I was awakened some time later by the sound of voices. It took me a moment to gain my bearings and to realize it was Kimble, Uncle Mick, and Felix talking amongst themselves.

They were back! Had it been a success? I was still too groggy to fully take note of what they were saying.

I rose sleepily from the sofa, moved past Oscar, and followed them down the hall.

The men had just reached the door to the major's office and opened it. I approached just in time to hear Kimble's words.

"We've a bit of a problem," he said in that flat tone of his. I felt a surge of dread, knowing how given the man was to understatement.

I was right to have worried, unfortunately. "Winthrop's gone, and he seems to have taken the papers with him," he said.

Major Ramsey shot up from his chair, uttering a curse. "What do you mean he's gone?"

"We did the job just as planned," Kimble said. "But when we got inside the house, his office was in disarray, as though he'd been going through things in a hurry. The documents you're looking for were nowhere to be found. I think he took them with him."

I gave a little gasp, and Felix turned to see me standing behind the group. He reached over and clasped my hand in his.

"I thought your men were watching the house," Major Ramsey was saying, his gaze fastened on Kimble.

"They were. One of my men said he saw Winthrop leaving the house as usual. It didn't strike him as odd. But I sent a man to the park where he usually walks and then to his club to ask for him. He isn't there."

Major Ramsey swore again, viciously.

"That means he's on his way to meet the German contact now, with the plans," I said.

"Yes. He'll be meeting the German agent to pass off the documents to him," Major Ramsey said grimly.

We're too late.

That's what most people would have said when faced with this sort of news. After all, we didn't have any way to know where he was going. Common sense said the South Coast, but where, in all those miles, would Matthew Winthrop have planned to meet a German agent?

I think most people would have given up at that point. After all, what could we do?

But the people in that room were made of stronger stuff than that. The major, Uncle Mick, Felix, Kimble, and I were a motley group, but we all had one thing in common: dogged determination. We weren't going to go down without a fight.

"There's got to be some way," I said.

No one answered.

My mind was whirling, a thousand thoughts coming all at once. There was something, something important, nagging in a corner of my brain. I tried to recall what Matthew Winthrop had said to me that night at the party. There was something he had said, some little thing that had lodged itself in the back of my mind, something that had seemed familiar.

And then suddenly I realized what it was. I looked up, triumphant. "He's going to Torquay."

CHAPTER TWENTY-EIGHT

Major Ramsey looked at me sharply. "Why Torquay?" he asked. There was no doubt in his tone, just that professional voice he used when he was being a commanding officer. I imagined he probably gave that same look to whomever had done reconnaissance in the desert or whatever sort of stuff he had done in North Africa.

"Sir Nigel has a beach house there, called Larksong," I explained, putting the pieces together. "I saw it in a newspaper once. Then, at the party, Matthew Winthrop was telling me about a poem he had written. 'Lark's Song in the Evening,' I thought he said. But it wasn't about a bird. It was about a place. He's been to Larksong and probably plans to go again."

"It makes sense," the major said. "I've thought from the beginning that there was someone bigger than Winthrop behind this, someone more powerful."

I nodded. "Sir Nigel is the obvious option. And his nephew was killed in a car crash coming back from a stay in Torquay. Now I think the nephew must have discovered something he wasn't meant to and was killed."

How horribly callous to have killed his own nephew. I supposed, though, that he had got Jerome Curtis to do the dirty work.

The major was looking at me, wondering, I imagined, just how I had come by all this information.

"I did some research at the Newspaper Library," I said.

"Did the papers say where the beach house is located, Ellie?" Uncle Mick asked, pulling my attention away from the major's searching gaze.

I shook my head.

"It's actually on a cliff just past Torquay," Kimble said. "A secluded spot on the coast." Apparently, he was up on the details of Sir Nigel's life as well.

"Just the sort of place for a drop, I should think," Felix said.

The major paused for just a moment, as though running the options through his head. Then he nodded. "All right. We'll go to Torquay."

He opened a drawer and pulled out his service revolver. I blinked. The gun was necessary, I supposed, but it was startling to see the easy way he handled the weapon. It was a reminder that there was an experienced military man, toughened by desert service, that lay behind the major's polished exterior.

I wasn't the only one who had an eye on the weapon.

"Are you still going to try to switch out the papers, lad?" Uncle Mick asked, wondering if violence was now our only option. "Or is it too late for that?"

"I don't know," Major Ramsey said. "It depends on whether we get there in time."

"He can't have much of a head start on us," Felix said. "If we beat him there, we may be able to find a way."

"He's likely to have taken the train," Kimble added. "If we take the car, we might be able to get to Torquay before he does."

"I don't think there need be a rush," Uncle Mick said easily, and we all turned to look at him. "If he's bringing handwritten papers as proof, he's going to have to pass them off directly to a German agent, am I right? And in a seaside town, that's most likely to be by boat. And no German agent's going to row to shore in broad daylight."

"Yes," Ramsey said. "You're right. We should have until night-fall."

Silence fell for just a moment as we waited for the major to issue his orders. It didn't take long.

"Kimble, you'll come with me," he said. "Lacey, I'll need you to come along to write the letter if we can somehow manage to get our hands on it. McDonnell, I think you should come, too. We may need to get into the beach house."

"What shall I do?" I asked.

"You'll wait here," he said.

I stared at him. "You're not serious."

"Miss McDonnell . . ."

"Don't 'Miss McDonnell' me, Major Ramsey," I said sharply. "I've been with you on this thing from the beginning. You can't mean to leave me out now."

I realized that the room had gone quiet as the major and I faced each other. Well, he might be the one with the military experience, but I was ready for battle. There was no way I was going to back down.

"There's no reason for you to come along," he said.

"With all due respect, Major," Uncle Mick cut in. "If you need someone to get you into the beach house, Ellie will do a fine job of it. I'm afraid I've been wounded."

He held up his hand. For the first time I noticed that it was wrapped in a thick white bandage. Blood was seeping through.

"Uncle Mick!" I cried, taking his hand in mine. "What happened? Are you all right?"

"It's just a scratch," he said easily. "I caught it on a fence when we were leaving Winthrop's property. I'm afraid we were in a hurry."

"Sliced nearly to the bone," Kimble said unemotionally.

I gasped. "You need to see a doctor at once!"

"Nacy will fix me up, but I don't think I'll be much use in

Torquay." He looked at the major. "I need both hands for lock picking, or at least my good hand."

"Then you'll have to take me," I added, glaring at Major Ramsey.

The major hesitated. He didn't want to give in, but I was fair enough to realize it wasn't just as a matter of principle. There was some part of him that thought a woman should be protected from this sort of thing. That ingrained chivalry nonsense was difficult to overcome.

He was going to refuse me; I could sense it.

"Please," I said softly. I had never said that to him before. "This means something to me. I . . . I know, in the beginning, it was something that we didn't have a choice in. But then we did, and we kept making that choice, kept choosing to believe that we could do something good for our country."

"You have," he said. "We couldn't have done this without you. But you've done enough."

I was so frustrated and angry that I felt tears spring to my eyes. I would not cry. Not in front of him. I would not.

He seemed to sense my distress, and, though I knew he was a man who was impatient with emotion, he seemed to soften ever so slightly. "I understand your position," he said in a voice that was less stern than usual. "And I appreciate it. But you must understand that this is for your own safety."

"There's no such thing as safety," I said. "Not with Nazis in England."

He looked at me for a long moment. His eyes had gone silvery gray, the way I had noticed they did when he was conflicted over something.

"We'll need someone to get us into the beach house," Kimble said. "I'm no good with locks, unless it's breaking them, and we can't do that if we want to stay undetected." I glanced at him, surprised but grateful he was taking my part.

Felix said nothing. He knew that an argument from him was not likely to carry weight with the major. I could sense him behind me, though, lending me his silent support.

Finally, the major let out an irritated breath. "Fine. But you will do exactly as I say at all times."

I nodded. "All right." I could take commands when it was necessary. I wasn't a complete renegade.

He turned away from me. "Kimble, you and Lacey take the train. See if you can learn anything along the way. Miss McDonnell and I will go in the car. We'll rendezvous at seventeen hundred hours. Get me a map so we can find a suitable place."

Things happened quickly after that. The major began moving swiftly about the room, barking out orders to Kimble and Oscar, looking at maps, and jotting down telegrams to be sent and such.

Felix came over to me in the midst of all the chaos. "Are you sure about this?"

"Of course, I am."

"You know I've always been on your side, urging the boys to let you join in. But this is different than climbing trees or playing British Bulldog."

I started to speak, but he held up a hand. "I know you're capable, love. It isn't that. But I . . . I don't want to see you hurt, Ellie."

I looked up at him, feeling a wave of affection, and maybe something more. "I feel the same way," I said. "So let's both be careful, shall we?"

He smiled and squeezed my hand.

Uncle Mick came up to us then. I suspected it had been purposeful, to disrupt the tender scene. Uncle Mick liked Felix a great deal, but he had always discouraged any sort of romantic relationship between us.

"You're ready for this, Ellie girl?" he asked, though he knew as well as I did what the answer was.

"I'm ready."

"Take this," he said. "You'll be needing it." He reached into his pocket and pulled out a small leather pouch, not much bigger than a wallet. It was his tool kit. He pressed it into my hand and his eyes met mine. Something unspoken passed between us.

"Are you sure your hand is going to be all right?" I asked after a moment, reaching down to touch the bandage gently.

"Yes, yes. It's fine, love. Don't worry about me. You need to focus."

"I will."

Uncle Mick fastened me in his gaze then. It was serious, his normal joviality dimmed by concern. "You'll be careful?"

"Yes," I said. "Don't worry. Everything is going to work out. I can feel it."

In truth, I knew there might be danger ahead of us, but that didn't matter. All that mattered now was that we succeed. And that was something we McDonnells had always been good at.

A short time later, we were on our way out of London. The major had dispensed with Jakub's services and was driving himself. I sat beside him in the front seat.

He had changed into civilian clothes to keep from being conspicuous, but even in the gray suit he now wore, he looked grim and severe.

We started out on Cromwell Road, eventually crossing back over the Thames and making our way in a southwesterly direction, passing through Twickenham and Sunbury-on-Thames.

He had said little since we'd left the office, and I wondered if he was miffed with me. He hadn't been happy to bring me along, I knew that. But surely he could see that I was going to be of use.

I also suspected the only reason he had allowed me to accompany him in the car instead of taking the train with Kimble and Felix was that he didn't think me trustworthy. Well, whatever the reason, I was just glad to be going along.

We were on the outskirts of London when the quiet began to

wear on me. I came from a family of talkers, and it felt strange not to have a conversation when there was nothing better to do.

"Are we just going to drive along in silence?" I asked him.

He didn't look at me. "That was my intention."

That set me back for a minute or two. I looked out the window for a bit, not really noticing the scenery, then looked back at the major.

I studied his profile. The strong line of his jaw, the straight nose, the sunlight through the window turning his eyes the color of lilacs. I noticed that the bronzed shade of his skin was beginning to fade ever so slightly. In a few more weeks, that remnant of his time in the desert would be gone.

"Did your uncle really have you brought back from North Africa?" I asked. I'm not sure why I decided to voice that question, the one he was probably the most sensitive about, but it came out almost before I realized I was going to ask it.

There was a long silence in which I thought he would either not answer or tell me to go to the devil.

At last, however, he spoke. "I was working with military intelligence there. When they began to put things together for this operation in London, they needed officers here. My commanding officers thought I would be suited to the job. My uncle had nothing to do with it. At least as far as I know."

"But you didn't want to be sent back from North Africa," I said.

"No," he replied, his eyes still on the road. "I didn't."

"You'd rather fight than work behind the scenes?"

"Yes," he said. "I wanted to do my duty."

"You're doing your duty now."

He looked over at me for the first time, and, for just a moment, his guard was down and I saw the frustration in his eyes.

"It's a difficult thing to explain," he said, "the feeling a man has when he knows that there are other men fighting and dying, and he should be among them."

"One might argue that you can do more good by stopping spies here in England than you could dying in the desert."

He said nothing to that, and we drove along in silence for a while longer. The city was behind us now, and we were driving through the countryside. It was beautiful in the summer afternoon sunlight, everything so green. Flowers bloomed, sheep grazed in the distant fields, and birds darted to and fro about the hedgerows. Everything was just as it should be, it seemed.

It was sometimes hard to remember that we were fighting a war. Sometimes, in quiet moments like these, I could forget that the world as we knew it was at risk, and my heart would flutter happily upward like one of those birds.

But then, when the heaviness of that realization came settling back on my shoulders, it made me even more resolute in my determination to do all I could to protect this place I loved so much.

The major's voice called my attention back to the present. "You got to ask me a question," he said. "Now let me ask you one."

"All right," I said. There was something in his tone that made me wary.

"Why do you steal?"

The question was not what I had expected. "What do you mean?"

"Your life of crime. Why did you choose it?" he asked.

I didn't answer for a moment. I supposed it was fair enough. I had asked him about the issue that was most sensitive to him, and so he was pushing back with searching questions of his own. But I didn't know quite how to answer.

"In theory, I suppose it's for the money," he went on when I didn't reply. "But there's more to it than that, isn't there? You might say because of the way you were raised, with your uncle, but you might have chosen to do something else. You followed him into the lifestyle instead. Why?"

"I enjoy it," I said brusquely.

"That isn't the reason. You're being flippant."

People didn't often call me out on that, and I wasn't sure I liked it. I could feel my temper beginning to rise, but I knew that it was defensiveness. I was used to hiding that part of me, of keeping it deeply buried, and he was doing his best to bring it to light.

"You've got a file on me," I said at last. "Why don't you tell me?"

The words came out sounding less sharp than I had intended them to. I suddenly felt tired, like I had been running for a very long time. In a way, I supposed I had.

"You have a resentment for the law. Is it because of your background? Because you were born in prison?"

I flinched a little, clenched my teeth against a welling up of feelings I always worked so hard to suppress.

"Or is it because of the circumstances . . . ?"

He was doing it. He was pushing me to the edge, and there was no choice but to go over. Well, why hide it? If he wanted to know why, then I would tell him.

"No," I said, my voice thick with bitterness. "It's because my mother didn't kill my father and she was sentenced to hang for it anyway."

CHAPTER TWENTY-NINE

And there it was. The darkest of my secrets.

My father was murdered in December of 1915, stabbed in the heart with a butcher knife in his own home. It was Uncle Mick, his brother, who found him dead after returning from a locksmithing job. Two months later my mother, despite protesting her innocence, was convicted and sentenced to death.

But they'd discovered by then that she was pregnant with me, and she was granted a stay of execution. I was born in Holloway prison, six months after my father's murder, and Uncle Mick took me to raise. Aunt Mary was dead by then, and he had hired Nacy, a distant relation, to look after me and the boys.

Then Spanish flu had ravaged its way across the world, and my mother had been spared the indignity of walking to the gallows. She had died, still protesting her innocence, and was buried in the prison cemetery. I had never seen her grave.

It wasn't a secret within the family. Uncle Mick was never one for keeping things quiet, and he had never tried to hide the truth. But it wasn't a topic we dwelt on. It was just a fact: my father murdered, my mother convicted. Simple mathematics.

I knew my father's death must have been hard on Uncle Mick, for it was clear they had been close. I saw it in his eyes sometimes when he watched Colm and Toby laughing with each other. I could see that memories were passing through his mind, memories of the times he had spent with his own brother. If they had been half as close as Colm and Toby, I knew it must have been very hard indeed.

I have one photograph of the pair of them, my mother and father, aside from those that appeared in the newspapers at the time of the trial. It's their wedding photo, in a silver frame. My mother is dressed in satin and lace. It wasn't the fashion to smile, but there is a hint of one on her lips, and there was no disguising the joy in her gaze. My father looked a lot like Uncle Mick, only younger and with a handsome mustache. His eyes sparkled.

Looking at the two of them, it doesn't seem possible that their union would end in bloodshed.

I'd learned more details about my father's murder and my mother's trial as a young teenager. I'd read every newspaper article and sordid, gossipy piece I could get my hands on, trying to understand what had happened. Once I'd had my fill, learned everything I possibly could, I filed it all away and left it there.

I didn't talk about it now. I tried my best not even to think about it. But it was always there, in the back of my mind, hovering like a dark shadow.

And it was that dark shadow that had urged me on. For every safe we opened, for every time we broke the law, I felt like it was a tiny bit of revenge for my mother. It wasn't exactly rational, but I supposed the buried emotions that urge us forward seldom are.

Things were quiet for a long moment after I'd spoken. I was so lost in my own thoughts that I'd almost forgotten where I was.

"I've read the trial transcripts," Major Ramsey said at last.

This surprised me. I had not expected him to delve so deeply into my background. Then again, I had seen, time and again, how thorough he was, how much effort he put into each small aspect of what he did. It shouldn't be entirely surprising that he had looked into my mother's case.

"And?" I said.

There was the slightest pause. "And I don't see how the jury could have come to any other conclusion."

It was what I had expected him to say, but still, somehow, it felt a bit like a punch to the stomach. "Juries have been wrong before," I said at last.

"Yes," he assented. I could feel the "but" hovering at the end of his sentence. He didn't say it, but he also didn't believe that my mother was innocent.

"She loved Greek mythology, too," I said. "And she named me Electra. The avenger of her father's death."

"Agamemnon was murdered by his wife." There was nothing cruel in his tone—his voice was almost gentle, in fact—but the factual way he said the words hurt nonetheless.

"I think she meant something else."

"And so you steal to avenge her in some way?" He wasn't mocking me, merely trying to understand. But I realized there was no way I could explain it, not to him. I couldn't fully explain it to myself. I only knew that, until I had met Major Ramsey, there was a void in my life I had tried to fill with the thrill of theft. And I had justified it by telling myself I was flouting the laws that had taken my mother unjustly.

"I steal because it's the only life I know," I said. "And as for my mother, there's nothing that can be done about it now, so there's no use in discussing it. It doesn't matter."

But that wasn't true, of course. It did matter. Because if, as I believed, as Felix's shipmate had hinted, my mother was innocent, then my father's killer had gotten away free.

Torquay was beautiful in the bright golden light of the late afternoon sun, the pale buildings arranged neatly around the harbor and an array of boats bobbing on the calm surface of the water. I had never been there before, though of course I'd seen postcards and the like.

"The English Riviera" wasn't a place my sort of people would generally spend much time.

The water looked a bright blue beneath the cloudless sky, tranquil and serene. Hard to believe that not a hundred miles away, the Nazis were occupying the Channel Islands. Harder, still, to believe that a German spy might be making his way across those waters under the cover of darkness this very night to retrieve the documents we had been working so hard to get our hands on.

My glimpse of Torquay was brief, alas. We didn't spend time in the city proper. The major drove on, through the streets, the cheeriness of the shops and cafés dimmed only slightly by the sandbags piled high to protect them, and along a road that wound its way up toward the bigger houses and hotels along the cliffs.

The buildings were spaced farther apart here, separated by green lawns and flower gardens and little copses of trees. It was all rather idyllic.

At last, the major pulled the car into a shallow ditch and behind a hedgerow, well concealed from the road.

"The beach house should be a mile or so up the road," he said, consulting a map that lay on the seat between us. "We'll walk the rest of the way."

"All right."

He opened his car door and got out, and I did the same.

"We'll stay off the road as much as possible," he told me, indicating the ditch behind the hedgerow. It was thick with weeds, and up ahead, there was a denser section of foliage.

I looked down at my new silk stockings. I'd been wearing them since the night of the party, carefully laundering them by hand and hanging them up to dry each night. Would I sacrifice them to the cause?

The answer was clear enough. Not if I didn't have to.

"Turn around," I said.

He frowned. "What?"

"Turn around. I need to take my stockings off."

"Miss McDonnell . . ."

"There's no reason for me to ruin a perfectly good pair of stockings."

With an ill-concealed sigh of irritation, he turned his back to me.

I kicked off my shoes and pushed up my skirt, unfastened my garters, and quickly peeled the stockings off. It would have been much better to wear trousers, but I hadn't known when I dressed this morning that I would be tracking down spies in the woods. Such was life.

Opening the car door, I put the stockings inside. They'd be safe enough there. Then I slipped my shoes back on.

"All right," I said, smoothing down my skirt. "I'm ready."

Without turning back to me, he started walking.

We trekked the mile in silence. Or, more accurately, to the sound of birdsong and the distant crash of the waves. We were moving parallel to the sea, and gusts of salty air made their way even through the trees.

The major walked a few paces ahead, his steady stride creating a path for me of sorts through the undergrowth, but it was still rough going some of the way, and I was scratched several times by twigs and brambles. I was immeasurably glad I'd had the foresight to remove my stockings; they would have been shredded to bits. At least it was only my flesh taking the brunt of it. New skin was easier to come by these days than silk stockings.

We finally stepped out onto the road. We had reached the end of a long drive, a gate stretched across its entrance, and the major motioned for me to stop.

"This should be it," he said.

I took the opportunity to remove my jumper and unbutton the top two buttons of my blouse. Despite the shady trees and the sea breezes, I'd grown quite warm from walking. I tied the jumper around my waist as I made my way to the major's side.

"The house is just up ahead. We'll go through the trees here," he said, motioning to the wooded area along the drive. "We'll need to watch it for a while to make sure that Winthrop hasn't beat us here. It will be important to keep absolutely still and quiet. Can you do that?"

"I'm not a child, Major," I said irritably.

"I'm quite aware of that," he replied. It seemed to me that his eyes dipped, almost indiscernibly, to where the unbuttoned part of my blouse had flapped open to reveal more than I'd intended. Of course, I probably imagined it.

"Come along, then," he said, and started forward into the trees. I followed him, trying to make as little noise as possible.

We stopped a moment later in a thicket at the edge of a small lawn leading to the house.

I looked out at the building before us. Sir Nigel's Torquay beach house was not entirely what I'd expected. Having seen the opulence of his house in town, I wasn't prepared for the sight of the quaint cottage that sat not too distant from the edge of the cliff. The property was covered with shady trees, like the ones in which we were concealed, and overgrown flower gardens.

All told, it was unassuming, cozy even, not the sort of place that would call much attention. Which, I supposed, made it the perfect place to meet a German spy if one was so inclined.

We were well concealed in our hiding place and stood for a long time watching the house. I had to believe that we had beat our quarry here. If not, everything would have been in vain.

We watched and waited. There was no sign that Matthew Winthrop had arrived. Everything was still and quiet. It was also hot. A bead of sweat trickled down the back of my neck, and I wondered how Major Ramsey was faring in his suit jacket. Of course, he'd no doubt faced much worse wearing a uniform in North Africa.

I glanced at him. He didn't seem to be sweating. As a light breeze passed, however, I could smell the faint scent of his shaving soap, and I hoped I smelled half as good when warm.

Despite my discomfort, I was very good at sussing out a target. Uncle Mick and I had done it dozens of times. I knew how to let my mind wander while my eyes watched and my body remained perfectly still. I was sure not even Major Ramsey could find fault with my technique.

It must have been an hour before he turned to me and spoke in a low voice, barely audible above the rustle of leaves in the breeze. "I'm going to move closer. Wait here until I signal you."

I nodded.

He moved out of the trees and across the lawn with that catlike grace of his that was so uncommon in such a tall and well-built man. I appreciated it in a professional sort of way as he approached the house and then disappeared around the side.

I was fairly certain the house was empty, but I was a bit tense as I waited nonetheless. After all, if Major Ramsey were to get shot or something, it would leave me in quite a bind.

At last, however, he appeared around the opposite corner and motioned me forward.

I moved out from among the trees, brushing away a few stray leaves that clung to my skirt. My legs were scratched and bleeding in a few places, but it was nothing too severe. And, after all, growing up roughhousing with the boys I'd gotten much worse.

"All clear?" I asked, as I reached the major's side.

He reached up and plucked a leaf from my hair, tossing it to the ground. "It seems so. Can you get us inside?"

"Of course."

I took the small tool kit Uncle Mick had given me from my pocket and moved toward the back of the house, the side facing the sea. Here there was a small, poorly tended flower garden and an arrangement of wooden chairs. A sandy path ran toward the cliff and then over the edge, presumably leading down to the beach.

But it was the house we were interested in at the moment. Removing a slim pick from the kit, I moved to the door. It was a simple enough thing to open a standard door, much easier than getting into a safe. I inserted the pin and moved it at varying angles while my other hand gently twisted the knob. It was a matter of a few moments before the lock gave, and I pushed the door open.

"Well done," the major said, as he stepped in front of me. He stood in the doorway for a moment, listening. When it seemed all was clear, he stepped inside, motioning me to follow. I did so, closing the door behind me.

The house, though simple on the outside, had clearly been outfitted to Sir Nigel's exacting standards. The kitchen gleamed with modern appliances and sleek table and chairs, none of your standard old-fashioned beach cottage décor.

Major Ramsey moved on to the next room, and I followed. This was the living room area. It, too, was decorated in the modern style. There were white sofas and pale blue rugs and a lot of art on the walls. There were also several shelves displaying a good deal of pottery. I didn't consider myself an expert on the subject by any means. After all, I'd spent the majority of the lecture sneaking about Sir Nigel's house and necking with the major. Nevertheless, I had an eye for these things, and it didn't look authentic. Probably best not to keep the good stuff in an unguarded beach house in wartime, I supposed.

"What are we looking for?" I asked the major.

"Incriminating evidence against Sir Nigel, for a start."

"Isn't the fact that his house is being used enough?"

He shook his head. "Anyone in his social circle is likely to know about this house; it would be an easy enough thing for them to gain access, just as we've done."

We passed through the living area and into the front hall. The major moved into another room, which was probably the study, and I decided to go upstairs.

The stairs led to a long hallway that ran the length of the house, with several doors on either side. I opened the first door and found a sparse bedroom. Likely a spare used for guests. Several more doors revealed more of the same, as well as a bathroom with a tub large enough to host a swimming party.

There was very little to see here. At last, I entered the bedroom at the very end of the hallway. It seemed someone had been staying in this room, and recently, for the bed was unmade and I spied, across the room, some clothing hung in the open wardrobe.

I was just about to go and report this to the major when I heard the unmistakable sound of a car pulling up the drive.

CHAPTER THIRTY

I darted from the room, ran down the hall, and started down the stairs. The major was halfway up, and, when I came around the landing, I propelled myself directly into him. It was rather like hitting a wall. He caught me with one arm, steadying us both with a hand on the railing.

"Go back up," he whispered into my hair. "We don't have time to get out the back."

Turning out of his semi-embrace, I began going back the way I had come with him directly behind me.

"Here," I whispered, opening the door of the first bedroom. I had noticed during my exploration that the room seemed untouched. Hopefully, whoever had arrived wouldn't think to look here.

The major followed me and closed the door behind me.

"Who is it?" I asked.

He shook his head. "I didn't see."

Well, this was a fine mess. I wasn't sure how we were going to work our way out of this one. Unless, of course, the major shot our way out, and I wasn't too keen on that outcome.

"What now?" I asked.

"Now we wait," he said.

I wasn't too keen on more waiting either, but I supposed it wasn't to be helped.

"Stay away from the windows," the major commanded. But I had already edged closer. I couldn't help it. Some part of me had to know what we might be dealing with.

It was then my eyes fell on a steamer trunk near the window. It was a relic of an older time, heavy wood with weathered leather straps and studded strap tabs. But it was the lock that caught my attention. There were several large scratches on it that looked to be fresh.

"Someone's tried to pick this lock," I said, running my fingers over the grooves in the metal. "And did a poor job of it."

The major moved to my side. "Can you open it?"

"Yes." This was a simple lock, as locks went. I took the tool kit again from my pocket and withdrew a flat-tipped file. Inserting it carefully into the trunk's lock, I pushed it at an angle and began to slowly turn the pick in a clockwise direction. I felt the pins release and held the file tight to pull the lock out. And just like that, the lock gave way. Whoever had tried to open this trunk clearly had no experience with locks.

Unlatching the two burnished brass latches, I pushed open the lid of the trunk.

The major and I looked inside. The contents proved disappointing. A few items of men's clothing, carefully folded. A hat. A pair of worn but carefully cleaned leather boots. A stack of well-read novels. A wool coat. I searched the coat's pockets, just in case, but they were empty.

My attention was drawn away from the trunk by the sound of a car door closing. Whoever had been driving up had arrived. Throwing caution to the wind, I rose from the trunk's side and moved to the window. I hazarded a peek out of the window and blinked. There was a figure I recognized. Not Matthew Winthrop. Someone more familiar.

He turned then, and the name shot out of my mouth much louder than I'd intended. "Colm!"

I turned and rushed from the room and hurried back down the stairs, the major behind me. "Miss McDonnell . . ." he called to me as I sped ahead of him, but I paid him no mind.

Opening the front door of the house, I stepped outside to see Felix and Kimble standing near a car, alongside Colm.

"What the devil are you thinking?" I heard the major hiss at Kimble as I moved toward my cousin.

"Colm!" I cried again.

"Ah, Ellie, darlin'!" He swept me up into his arms, and I felt perilously close to tears. For a moment, I just enjoyed the feeling of his strong, safe embrace.

Then I stepped back. "What are you doing here?" I demanded.

"Felix found me," he said, glancing at Felix, who stood smiling beside us. "Said you might be able to use some help."

"You told me he was stationed in Torquay," Felix said with a smile.

"But how . . ."

"Kimble's a resourceful fellow," Felix answered. "Had Colm located, recruited, and had commandeered a car within the space of an hour."

I looked up at my cousin, trying to see if he looked any different than he had when last he'd been home on leave. I supposed I couldn't expect to see much change in a month, and there wasn't any that I could tell. He looked the same as always: solid and hearty and strong.

Nonetheless, I had a thousand questions I wanted to ask him. "How have you been, Colm? Is everything all right? Are you going to . . ."

My stream of inquiries was interrupted as the major strode up to us, his expression hard. He was wearing his commanding officer face again. Not the best of signs.

"Major, it's my cousin, Colm McDonnell," I said, unable to keep the cheeriness from my voice, despite his obvious displeasure. "Colm, this is Major Ramsey. He's in charge of this operation."

"Supposedly," the major said, with a dark glance at Kimble.

Kimble shrugged. "You said to gather resources. As Lacey pointed out, he's got a game leg, and I'm not as young as I once was. We figured we could use the big fellow. Never hurts to have a bit of extra brawn."

I saw the major look Colm over. Colm was a big fellow, all right. They were about the same height, but, despite the major's well-built frame, Colm was broader and bulkier. "A right bruiser," he'd been called often enough. Indeed, I'd yet to see him lose a fight, and more than one man had backed down from one at the sight of him.

"Major," he said, stretching out a hand.

The major shook it. "McDonnell."

I wondered what Felix had told Colm about the major, for there was the same look in my cousin's eyes that there had always been when I'd gone out for ice cream with a Hendon boy. The look that said he'd be keeping an eye on things.

"Did you think driving a car up here might call attention?" the major asked, turning his anger back onto Kimble.

Kimble, as ever, was unmoved.

"I sent a wire ahead and one of my men was waiting for Winthrop at the train station. They've followed him to a hotel, and he hasn't left his room since he arrived. I didn't suppose he'd arrive here before nightfall."

It was logical enough, but I could tell that Major Ramsey wasn't exactly pleased.

I remembered then what I'd discovered in the bedroom at the end of the hall. "Someone's been staying here," I said. "There's an unmade bed and clothes in the wardrobe in the last bedroom upstairs."

"Then whoever's been staying here may return soon," the major said. He paused for a moment and seemed to consider. Then, as usual, he began with the orders.

"Kimble, you and Lacey go back to the hotel and keep an eye on Winthrop. When he leaves, follow him back, but from a distance. Don't let him see you. Mr. McDonnell and I should be able to detain him before he makes contact with the agent and make the replacement of the documents. When you and Lacey get to the cottage, he can complete the forgery."

"I thought you wanted to make the switch undetected," I said. "You won't be able to do that if you capture Winthrop."

The major shook his head. "There's little chance of doing it surreptitiously now. But, if we can apprehend Winthrop once he arrives, we can still make the switch and deliver the documents to the German agent. With any luck, they won't know that I'm not Winthrop when I hand off the papers and won't question what happened to him after the drop is made."

I didn't ask what Major Ramsey intended to happen to him.

"And what about me?" I asked.

He looked at me. If he so much as suggested that I go back to Torquay and wait this out, I was going to kick him in the shin.

"You can stay," he said at last. "But you're to keep out of the way. Understood?"

"Understood," I replied ungraciously.

He ignored me and turned to Colm. "You'll keep a watch from inside. I'll watch from the woods. When he enters the house, I'll follow and subdue him. You can back me up. Miss McDonnell will wait outside with me, where she'll be clear if we have to resort to the use of weapons."

"He wants you alone in the dark woods," Felix whispered to me with a smirk as he moved close to my side.

"You're talking nonsense," I said.

"I know what I'm talking about." His grin widened. "Because that's exactly where I'd like to be with you."

"Stop it, Felix. It's no good your flirting with me on the cusp of a dangerous escapade."

His face softened. "When would be a good time, Ellie?"

I was surprised by something in his expression. It was more earnest than it usually was, and that caught me off guard. "Perhaps when all this is over," I said as lightly as I could manage.

"All clear?" the major asked, his voice breaking into our conversation. I couldn't help but feel he was directing this at Felix and me, as we had been whispering at the edge of the group.

I met his gaze. "All clear, Major," I said.

Colm nodded. "It sounds like a fine plan, Major. There's just one thing I'd like to know."

"Yes?"

"How in the dickens have you managed to get Ellie so well trained? For the life of us, my brother and I can never get her to listen to a single thing we say."

In the end, it was Colm who received the kick to the shin.

And so we all assumed our places and waited for darkness to fall. Waited to see what sort of mark we would leave on history.

It was very dark. I could barely see my hand in front of my face within the shade of the trees, especially when the moon went behind the clouds. But there was the wind and the sound of the waves, and I found it soothing somehow.

No matter that there was a German spy making his way toward these grounds or that a traitor was preparing to meet him; the sound of the water was a reminder that although the world might be falling apart, some things were as they had always been, and would go on being that way no matter what the future held.

The major and I stood close in the wooded darkness. I could feel the warmth coming off him, but I was still chilled by the evening breeze.

"Are you cold?" he asked me suddenly.

I had put my jumper back on and pulled it tightly around my-self to fight off the chill, but I wasn't going to admit that. "No," I whispered back.

After a moment I heard his voice, closer to my ear this time. "Stay here. Don't leave. I'll be back in a few moments."

Then before I could even reply, he had slipped off into the dark-ness.

I was a bit annoyed he had left me alone. I didn't expect, as Felix had insinuated, that the major would try to take advantage of our being alone in the darkness, but I hadn't exactly expected him to wander off either.

There was a small sound somewhere to my left, in the direction of the road and the opposite direction from where the major had gone. I stilled, listening. It could be anything: a mouse, a rabbit per-haps, or an owl. Or it might be a Nazi spy who would think nothing of knifing me and leaving me to die in the dark woods all alone. That was a cheery thought.

I forced myself to stand still and listen. Whatever the noise was, it didn't repeat itself. I didn't know whether to be relieved or alarmed. After all, it was so intensely dark that someone might very well be standing in the shadows nearby and I wouldn't know it.

How very silly all of this was. I took a few careful steps forward, and then a few more. I thought I heard a sound again in the dark-ness behind me, and I stilled, listening. I was searching for Major Ramsey, Major Ramsey was searching for the killer, and perhaps the killer was searching for me. What a tidy little circle!

There was no sound at all for the next several minutes, and I thought it would be safe to move again. I felt that I needed to get my bearings and make sure that, if the moon should emerge again from behind the clouds, I wouldn't find myself vulnerable.

I moved a bit farther in the direction of the house.

Suddenly, a hand clamped over my mouth as an arm encircled my waist.

"Don't scream," Major Ramsey said in my ear.

I jerked my mouth from under his hand. "Stop telling me that," I hissed at him.

In truth, I might have been tempted to scream when he'd grabbed me, but I had known almost immediately that it was probably him. For one thing, the spy would have been more likely to slit my throat than pull me against him.

"What do you mean by crashing around in the woods?" he hissed back, his arm still around me.

"I heard something," I whispered. I hadn't been crashing about; I was perfectly quiet. I didn't argue the point with him, though, because I was a bit distracted by the solid warmth of his chest against my back.

We were both still for a moment, listening. I could feel his chest rising and falling, and my own breath seemed to come a bit faster.

"I don't hear anything," he said at last. "You should've waited for me."

"I didn't imagine it," I told him.

He let out an irritated breath. "I didn't say you did. But you do appear to be completely incapable of following orders."

I'm afraid this provoked my temper. I struggled free of his grasp and turned to face him. The moon had emerged now, and I could just make him out in the light shining through the branches above. "I'm not one of your soldiers, Major," I said.

"Even more reason for you to do as I say. You must learn to do as you're told so you don't get hurt."

"You need to learn that we can't all be like you," I shot back. "The great Major Ramsey. The perfect soldier. Sometimes I really do think you're made of stone."

I felt more than saw him step closer to me, closing the distance I had just put between us, felt the heat and the tension coming off him. My skin prickled with warmth—and something else.

"I am definitely not made of stone, Electra," he said in a low voice.

Electra. It was the first time he had said my given name, and there was something in the low, rough way he said it that set all my senses to tingling.

I looked up at him, realizing how very close he was. A few inches of air, that's all that stood between his mouth and mine. I wondered if—no, I thought—he was going to kiss me again. It seemed as though time stood still.

But whatever either of us might be hoping would happen next, our attention was pulled away by the sound of a car coming up the drive.

I think he swore, but it was too quiet for me to be sure. Then he stepped away from me, the cool evening air swallowing me up again.

"Wait here," he said. "I mean it."

He was gone before I could formulate a retort.

From where I stood, I could just make out the front door of the house. I saw the car pull up and then I saw Matthew Winthrop get out.

He stood still for a moment and looked around him. Even though I knew there was no way he could possibly see me within the dark copse of trees, I froze.

There was nothing to hear but the sea and the wind, and so he went to the front door, brought out a key, and, unlocking the door, went inside.

A moment later, I saw the figure of Major Ramsey cross the lawn, pistol drawn, and charge into the house.

CHAPTER THIRTY-ONE

I had been ordered to stay in the shade of the woods, and, given my tense confrontation with the major about my inability to obey orders, I perhaps ought to have done it. But the longer I waited, the more I worried that something had gone wrong. Was it possible that Winthrop had somehow harmed Major Ramsey? No, I had seen how quickly and silently the major moved. And he was much bigger than Winthrop. Even if Winthrop was much stronger than he looked, he'd have had no chance against both the major and Colm.

If there had been a gun battle, I would have heard it.

No, I was quite sure, just as the men inside the house were, that they had caught the traitor and secured the documents.

Nevertheless, after ten minutes of waiting in silence, I could take it no longer and made my way stealthily toward the house. I had just reached the front door, which faced away from the sea, when I heard the sound of a second car approaching. I pressed myself against the house, deep in the shadows.

The car pulled to a stop a moment later, and I let out a relieved breath as Felix and Kimble emerged. They had followed Winthrop from the hotel as Ramsey had instructed them to do. Now Felix could make the forgery of Jocelyn Abbot's letter, and they would be ready to meet the German agent.

"It's me," I whispered, stepping forward.

"Everything all right, Ellie?" Felix asked, coming to my side.

"I think so. Matthew Winthrop arrived and the major followed him into the house. I didn't hear anything after that."

Felix grinned. "Well, I'm sure if Winthrop had any thoughts of putting up a fight, he gave them up when he saw Colm."

I nodded.

"Let's go in," Kimble said. He led the way, slowly and quietly opening the front door. Felix and I followed.

Inside the house, we found Matthew Winthrop tied to a chair in the living room, the major and Colm standing over him. The stolen plans lay on a desk, along with a smaller envelope containing the letter from Miss Abbot to Barnaby Ellhurst.

The major looked up as we entered, and his eyes landed on me. I expected him to glower at me, but he seemed indifferent to my presence. I realized I was not his particular focus at the moment.

"Now, Winthrop," he said, turning to face the young man. "Why don't you tell me all about it?"

"I'm not going to tell you anything," Matthew Winthrop said, his gaze fastened to the wall before him.

"It's Sir Nigel running your scheme, isn't it?" the major said. "This is his beach house, obviously, and you've been working for him, using your collector's club as cover for your activities."

Winthrop looked at him for a moment, then averted his eyes and said nothing.

"What time is the drop to take place tonight?"

He still didn't answer.

"Is the German contact to meet you on the beach?"

This went on for what seemed a long time, the major asking questions and Winthrop silently refusing to answer them.

Then Kimble stepped forward. "Let me have a crack at him, will you?"

"You're wasting your time," Winthrop said. "Do what you like to me, but I'm never going to talk."

"I could have you singing like a bird in two minutes," Kimble said flatly.

Winthrop's eyes darted nervously to the cold, expressionless face of the man who had threatened him.

That first night, when Uncle Mick and I had been captured, Kimble had questioned me. I had had the impression he'd seemed uninterested, almost bored, with the whole thing. I'd since come to realize I had been seeing Kimble's polite side that evening.

"Shall I, Major?" Kimble asked.

My heart picked up the pace a bit. They weren't going to do him harm, were they? But one look at the hard faces of all the men present, and I knew that they would do whatever they needed to. Perhaps this eventuality was the reason Major Ramsey had wanted me to wait outside.

"You're not going to let him near me," Matthew Winthrop said, but there was a quaver in his voice. He was a university student and poet, not a hardened spy, and he was in over his head.

The major shrugged. "I'd wager it would only take him a minute and a half, even."

"I'll take that wager, to keep things sporting," Felix said. "Shall we say a pound?"

"Make it two," Major Ramsey said.

"Done."

"I'll keep time." This came from Colm, who pushed up his sleeve to look at the watch on his wrist.

Matthew Winthrop had begun to sweat by this point, and he looked at Major Ramsey again. "You can't let him hurt me," he said.

The major sighed regretfully. "I'm afraid there aren't very many things I won't allow under situations like this."

Matthew Winthrop's jaw clenched, and I pressed my lips together to fight the instinct to intervene on his behalf. They were empty threats to make the young man talk, surely.

"Ellie, you oughtn't see this," Colm said suddenly. "Go upstairs."

I felt I was frozen in place.

The major didn't look at me but at Felix. He jerked his head toward the doorway, and Felix, in answer to the silent command, came to me, took my arm, and began leading me from the room.

"Time starting . . . now," Colm said.

I couldn't help but look over my shoulder. Kimble took a step toward Matthew Winthrop.

I like to believe they wouldn't really have harmed him, that it was all a bluff, but I decided not to think too much about it. Major Ramsey had warned me that a lot of cold things are done in wartime, and Kimble was the sort of man who didn't seem to mind at all doing them.

In any event, it wasn't a chance Matthew Winthrop was willing to take. "I'm to pass off the papers to the German agent at two a.m.," he said quickly, his expression dark.

"Two seconds," Colm said.

"Where?" the major demanded.

"Here at the house. He . . . he's coming up from the beach."

"That path that leads to the back door?" the major asked.

Winthrop shook his head. "No. That was too obvious. We planned for him to take another beach path down the road a bit and then come up the drive."

"Just one man?"

"Yes, just one."

Matthew Winthrop continued to babble on about the meeting he was to have with the German agent while keeping an eye on Kimble.

I was feeling a bit shaken by the whole experience myself, and decided I needed a breath of air.

"I'm going to go outside for a moment," I told Felix in a low voice.

"I'll come with you."

"No, they'll need you to do the forgery," I said. "I'll be fine."

So I left him and slipped back out into the cool night air, which was how I happened to miss the next bit of extremely pertinent information. According to the account I had later, it went something like this:

Colm wandered over to the desk and glanced down at the documents there. Then he frowned. Picking up the papers, he glanced over them.

"What are these?" he asked after a long moment.

"Sensitive weapons plans," the major said, glancing away from Winthrop. "Put them down, if you please. They're classified."

"These aren't weapons plans," Colm said.

There was a brief pause. Everyone went still at once, as though Colm had set off some sort of explosive in the room.

"What do you mean?" Ramsey asked, his voice tight.

Colm held up the papers. "This is a bunch of nonsense. Gibberish. These plans would never work."

"What do . . ." Felix began, but the major interrupted him, stepping toward my cousin.

"How do you know?"

"I'm a mechanic, mate. I may not be an engineer, but I know how plans work, and these plans don't make anything. Looks like someone was either blotto when they drew them up or made them up off the top of their head."

Colm had inherited Uncle Mick's head for figures. He hadn't had any advanced schooling, but he might easily have been an engineer or a chemist. If he said the plans were wrong, then they were wrong.

The major didn't know him as well as Felix and I did, of course, but there had been something in his tone that was convincing. Perhaps the major recognized that aura of absolute confidence that comes from knowing one is right.

Whatever it was, he stared at him for a moment and then strode to the desk, picking up the envelope. Ripping it open, he pulled the letter from inside. It was not in Jocelyn Abbot's handwriting.

"They've already done the switch," Major Ramsey said, turning to the men. "Winthrop is a decoy. Someone else is meeting the German agent on the beach."

I, meanwhile, believing that our culprit had been caught, had wandered out toward a copse of trees not far from the cliffside. From that vantage point, I was concealed from anyone who might be watching from a boat out on the water. The sea was beautiful in the moonlight, the crash of the waves soothing after the excitement we'd just had in the cottage. I felt a great sense of relief, knowing that we had succeeded.

Which was why, when I once again heard rustling in the woods behind me, I thought it must surely be an animal.

I went right on thinking that until I heard the snap of the twig too close for comfort and then, before I could turn around, felt the cold blade of the knife pressed against my throat.

"Don't make a sound," a voice hissed in my ear.

It was a vaguely familiar voice, but there was something about it that was so off-kilter from the way I had heard it before that I couldn't place it.

"Start walking toward the sea," he commanded. "If you try to run or scream, I'll have to kill you."

There was something in his tone that made me believe him. So I started walking.

We moved through the forested area, him pushing me ahead of him, heedless of branches or the thick undergrowth. I stumbled more than once on roots or fallen branches but hurried to catch my footing, afraid that the knife would accidentally slice my neck.

My heart was pounding, but I did my best to keep a cool head.

Who is it? I thought. I didn't think it was the German agent because the accent was British. Surely there were German agents who could mimic a British accent or who might even have been raised here, of course, but I still had the feeling I had met him before.

We reached a clearing, and before us there was a stretch of green that led toward the cliff.

"Keep going." He took my arm and pushed me ahead of him in the darkness. There was barely enough light to see by, but I did my best to make my way in a straight line toward the cliff. I knew there was a path that led down to the beach. I had seen it in the daylight.

We reached the edge of the cliff, and I could barely make out a steep trail of sorts in the sandy red earth.

"Go," he said roughly, and so I kept moving. It was difficult to make my way down the steep path with the sand crumbling beneath my feet and a dark figure with a knife at my back. If I made it out of this alive, I'd be qualified for a circus act, I thought darkly.

We reached the beach at last and the man, with one arm across my chest, holding the knife to my throat, reached into his pocket for something. A torch, I realized.

He turned it on and flashed it out onto the water.

A moment later there was a responding signal from far out across the water. The German spy was coming.

What should I do?

One thing was painfully obvious. There was no good reason for this man to keep me alive. They'd killed Harden and the waiter-messenger when he was of no further use to them, and I was sure they'd have no qualms about doing the same to me.

If I was going to survive this, I had to do something. And quickly.

Once I'd decided that, it didn't take long for me to act.

Grabbing his arm to steady the knife, I slipped quickly from beneath his grasp and began to run. I didn't know if I could make it back up the cliff without his catching me, but I had to try. Major Ramsey had a gun, and that was the only thing that would trump the killer's knife.

I scrambled up the embankment, the sand giving way beneath

my feet with each step. I lost a shoe, but continued my climb, clutching at the sand and stray weeds that had managed to find purchase in the grainy soil. There were no thoughts in my head but escape. Every part of my being was focused on my flight, my body moving almost of its own accord.

I'd made it nearly halfway up when I felt the blow from behind. He tackled me, grabbing me around the waist as I struggled and pulling me back with him. He slipped on the sand then, and we both tumbled down the embankment in a tangle of limbs.

We hit the ground hard, me on my stomach and the man atop me, and the air was knocked out of me. I felt the grit of sand in my eyes and mouth, and I struggled to catch a breath. I expected at any moment to feel the hot slice of his knife, but he must have dropped it in the fall because I could feel both his hands on me now, holding me down.

I managed to turn in his grasp onto my back and dragged in a ragged breath. The burst of oxygen cleared my head a bit, and for the first time I got a good look at my assailant, who was still pressing me down into the sand. The shock of it stilled me for a moment.

It was Oscar Davies.

CHAPTER THIRTY-TWO

I stared up at him, trying to make sense of it. I had never seen him outside the office, and I couldn't seem to wrap my mind around the fact that he was here. Trying to kill me.

"I'm sorry, Ellie," he said, a bit winded from our skirmish. "I didn't want you to get hurt. You should have stayed out of it."

"I . . . I don't understand."

"It's simple enough. I'm giving the documents to the Germans."

"You can't do this, Oscar," I said softly.

"You're wrong. I can, and I'm going to."

He grabbed me roughly by one arm and pulled me to my feet. I saw the gleam of something in the sand. The knife. Could I reach it?

But no. Oscar saw it, too, and pulled me along as he went to pick it up, wiping the sandy blade on his trousers.

"Oscar, it's not too late to stop this," I said. I was trying to keep the panic from my voice. I had always been steady under pressure, but I had never faced anything like this before.

I was still trying to figure out how he had come to be involved in all of this, but, to be honest, that part was of secondary importance to me at the moment. I was more interested in finding a way to get out of this alive.

Could he be reasoned with? Something told me there was very

little chance of that, not when he had already come this far. That meant I was going to have to find another way to stop him from killing me.

"You're wrong about that, too," he said, answering my comment from what already seemed like a hundred years ago. "It's much too late to stop any of this. I realized it a long time ago. That's why I've got to do my duty."

"Your duty is to your country," I said, indignation overtaking my fear for just a moment.

"This country won't exist as it is in another year," he said. "Germany subdued France in a matter of weeks. How long do you think England can hold out?"

"As long as we need to," I said defiantly.

He gave me one of his sad smiles. "You've been listening to too many of Churchill's pretty speeches, Ellie. The Germans have a saying—a lucky thing I was schooled in the German language, don't you think?—*Ein Volk, ein Reich, ein Führer.* It means 'One People, One Nation, One Leader.' That's how this is all going to end. Germany's going to rule the world, and I'd rather be a part of it than fighting a losing battle from the outside."

"But how . . . how did you even get involved in any of this?" I asked. I didn't really care, to be honest. I had no interest at all in Oscar Davies or whatever sad story had led him to betray his family, his country, and his principles. But I needed to keep him talking, while I figured a way out of this mess.

"I met Matthew Winthrop at university," he said. "We became friends and stayed in touch."

"You were part of his underground group of fascists." I didn't bother to keep the disdain out of my voice.

He shook his head. "No. I don't care much about philosophies. But to the victor goes the spoils, as they say, and it's clear who the victor is going to be."

So it was a matter of money, not ideology. That was just as despicable. Maybe even more so.

"Are you really Major Ramsey's cousin?" I asked.

"Oh, yes. But not the earl's son. I threw that in for a bit of fun. I'm his nephew. My mother is the earl's youngest sister. But the old man does have a soft spot for me and agreed readily enough to get me a position working for Gabriel."

"You knew what kind of work he was doing then?"

"I knew he was in military intelligence. The family's always been rather keen on lauding him for his military career. When he came back to London I figured it was to do some sort of clandestine work, and I thought there might be something in it for me. I ran into Matthew Winthrop a short time after I got the job, and I could tell he was sounding me out about the German cause. When it became obvious he was involved in some sort of scheme that might prove profitable, I decided to throw my lot in with him, and everything fell into place rather nicely. Even when the government found out that Thomas Harden had taken the documents from the factory and they began watching him, I was ideally placed to keep an eye on things and promote the German interests from the inside."

"And Major Ramsey never suspected you."

"No," he scoffed. "I was his little cousin Oscar, practically beneath his notice. That part of what I told you was true. He was always striding about, issuing orders to the younger cousins ever since we were children. He's the golden boy, the earl's favorite. The way the family fawns over him! The accident—where I lost the sight in my eye—is just one example. My brother's horse bolted when we were out riding. Gabriel and I took off after him, but my horse threw me, and I hit my head. Gabriel stopped the horse and saved the day. And so I was the one who lost sight in one eye, and he earned yet another feather in his cap. I've hated him ever since."

He had had my sympathy once, but not now. Nevertheless, it would be foolish to antagonize him.

"Oscar, please . . ." I said calmly. "If you'll just think this through . . ."

"I have," he said. "I'm sorry, Ellie, but this is the way it has to be."

I recognized the look on his face. It was the one my own cousins would have when they weren't going to hear reason. It was the look of stubborn assurance in their own sense of rightness. I knew then that I wasn't going to change his mind.

We looked at each other then, both of us knowing that our causes could not be reconciled. There was a German agent coming toward us at this very moment, and only one of us could succeed in our goal.

With a sudden movement, he pulled me into his arms, so my back was against his chest. Ironically, I thought of how Major Ramsey had done the same thing not long ago.

The knife gleamed as he brought it up.

"I'm sorry," he said.

He was going to slit my throat. Or try anyway. I wasn't going to be cut up without a fight. My body tensed in readiness. Before I could act, however, there was the sound of a voice from behind us.

"Oscar!"

Oscar whirled, turning us both, and I looked up to see a figure at the top of the cliff. It was Major Ramsey.

I felt a flicker of hope, and then I felt the sting of the knife's blade pressing into my throat.

"Let her go, Oscar," the major called. His voice was raised to be heard above the wind and the sea, but it was perfectly calm.

Oscar's game was up. He knew that as well as I did. There was no way he could get the papers to the Germans now, no way that he could escape arrest for what he'd done.

But that didn't mean he couldn't still kill me out of spite.

"I think he's sweet on you," Oscar said in my ear. "It's going to hurt him to watch you die. Such a waste of a pretty girl."

It was the "pretty girl" bit that did it. My temper had been building up over the last few minutes as Oscar revealed his treachery, simmering like a volcano about to erupt, and that final crack was what pushed it over the edge. I felt the anger surge through me in a hot wave, and I let it have its way.

The movement was instinctual, coming back to me from years spent playing with the boys, learning to best them at their own games. Bracing my feet, I shifted the weight of my lower body backward while clutching Oscar's arm and pulling him forward with all my strength. In one smooth motion, I flipped him hard onto the sand.

Young, hotheaded Ellie would have given him a few blows while he was down for good measure, but I still had some common sense in me. I turned toward the cliff and started running in the major's direction.

Oscar recovered more quickly than I expected, and, in a moment, he had sprung up, knife in hand.

A shot rang out, and I heard a thud as Oscar hit the ground behind me.

I walked unsteadily a few paces closer to cliff and then, my head spinning, collapsed to my knees in the sand.

"Miss McDonnell. Electra. Look at me, Electra."

Major Ramsey was crouching beside me. I hadn't seen him come down the cliff or approach me on the beach. I was too busy clutching my head in my hands and clenching my teeth to keep from being sick.

The major gently pulled my hands away from my face and held them so that I was forced to look at him. His eyes looked silver in the darkness, and I focused on them for a moment, trying to clear my head. I was still breathing very hard, a mixture of exertion, fear, and having had the wind knocked out of me only moments ago.

"It's all right," he said, his voice the softest I had ever heard it. "Everything's all right."

I looked over my shoulder to see Oscar lying very still in the sand.

"He's dead," Major Ramsey said.

I nodded, my gaze still on the lifeless body. The knife was still gripped in his hand. He had been so very close to killing me.

"Electra, look at me." I turned my gaze back to him, and he squeezed my hands. "You don't have to worry about him. Focus on me. Take a deep breath. That's right. Now another."

I did as he said, taking comfort in the warm calmness of his presence beside me, though I wasn't really in as much of a state as he seemed to think I was. I was dizzy, a bit breathless from having the wind knocked out of me, and shaking hard from an excess of adrenaline, but my mind was clear enough.

A moment later, there was the sound of voices, and I turned to see Colm and Kimble making their way down the cliff path. Felix stood at the top, looking down. He couldn't manage the terrain.

I removed one of my hands from the major's and waved to Felix, to let him know I was all right.

The major followed the direction of my wave and then turned back to me. Rising, he helped me up with the hand that was still in his. I found my legs were a bit shaky, but I was none the worse for wear. Not physically anyway.

"Are you all right, love?" Colm asked as he reached me.

"Yes. I'm fine."

He grasped my upper arms and held me firm, studying me. "Are you sure?"

"Yes. Quite sure. There's no need for you to wring your hands over me like Nacy."

He grinned at the others. "She's well enough if she can scold me," he said, but he couldn't hide the relief on his face.

I smiled at him before I turned to the major. It wasn't over yet. "Oscar was signaling and I saw a return signal. The German agent is coming. What do we do now?"

The major considered for just a moment.

"Kimble. McDonnell. Take the body and hide it somewhere, farther down the beach if necessary. And quickly."

"But the shot . . ." I said.

"If they're far enough out that we can't see them, it's likely that they didn't hear it over the noise of the waves. If they ask, I'll make up a convincing story about it."

I glanced at him. He was so very calm. He didn't seem at all affected by the fact that he had just taken a man's life, his own cousin's life at that.

I couldn't know, of course, what was happening in his mind. Perhaps he would mourn his cousin later, in his own way. At the moment, however, he had a job to do, and emotion could not be a part of it.

"He'll have the papers in his pocket, I assume," Major Ramsey said, moving to the body. He didn't waste any time in retrospection, instead patting down Oscar's pockets. The packet of papers was there, and he pulled it out.

"With luck," he said, "Lacey can create our forgery before the agent arrives."

I glanced out at the sea. There was still no sign of the boat. Perhaps, just perhaps, we might still be able to pull this off.

"But . . ." I said, suddenly worried. "The Germans are expecting Oscar."

"I doubt the agent has ever seen the contact; if I have the papers and the letter from Jocelyn, it should be enough."

"He told me he speaks . . . spoke German," I said, my head still spinning a bit. "They're likely expecting a German speaker."

He gave me a little smile. "Then it's a good thing I speak German, too. Come along. We haven't time to spare."

He took my arm and led me back toward the cliff. I knew he was purposefully turning me away from the sight of Kimble and Colm moving Oscar's limp body down the beach, but that was all right. I had already seen more than enough.

The major escorted me up the path, his steadying hand on my arm the entire way. At the top, Felix took my hand and pulled me to him in a tight embrace. For just a moment, I sagged against him, feeling the relief of being safe again finally hit me.

"Are you all right, Ellie?" he whispered into my hair.

I nodded against his shoulder.

"You're sure?"

"Yes, Felix."

"I do hate to interrupt," Major Ramsey said, his tone just bordering on terse, "but we don't have much time. You'll have to act quickly, Lacey, to get the forgery done."

"Yes, sir," Felix said jauntily. With his arm still around me, we walked quickly back to the cottage.

I sat on the sofa, wiping at the bleeding scrapes and scratches on my arms and legs with a wet cloth, while the major and Felix went over the documents. They switched out the real plans for the false ones, and Felix made a copy of the letter in Jocelyn Abbot's hand, replicating certain passages of the false document to verify them as Jocelyn had done with the original.

At last, he pushed the letter toward the major. Major Ramsey glanced at it and then nodded. He folded it and put it with the false documents and put them in his pocket. He put the gun in the other.

"Good luck, old boy," Felix said.

"Be careful," I told him, suddenly afraid.

He nodded. His eyes met and held mine for just a moment.

Then he turned and left the cottage to meet the German agent on the beach.

CHAPTER THIRTY-THREE

It was a long, tense wait.

Felix sat smoking, and I sat looking down at my bruised and scratched limbs, neither of us saying much.

My body ached from the tumble down the cliff, the struggle on the beach, and the tension of this whole day. My head was pounding, too. All told, I felt rather like I'd been run over by a truck.

I pride myself on being made of strong stuff, but the events of this evening might have put a good dent in a cruiser tank.

A short while after the major had gone, there was a sound at the front door. We looked up to see Kimble and Colm had returned.

Colm gave Felix a nod that I interpreted as meaning they'd managed to stash Oscar's body somewhere. I tried not to think about it. He had been a traitor and a killer, but I still didn't like the idea of his body lying out on the sand like something washing up on the beach. His mother, Major Ramsey's aunt, would want to bury her son.

But that was something to think about when all of this was over.

There was still danger to be faced, after all. Still enemies to be met head-on.

I heard a slight thump from the other room as Colm took a seat beside me on the sofa. Matthew Winthrop. Felix told me the men had locked him in one of the other rooms after they'd finished their questioning.

"I'll go check on the prisoner," Kimble said, leaving the room.

This gave me a thought. Whose clothes had been in the bedroom upstairs when I was first searching the house this afternoon? Matthew Winthrop had been staying at the hotel, not here, so I didn't think they belonged to him. And Oscar had been in London every day. Who, then, had been staying in Sir Nigel's beach house? Someone had clearly been here, and recently. Was there another accomplice yet to emerge?

I was about to phrase the question when we heard the unmistakable sound of the back door opening.

I stood, and Colm did, too. We all looked toward the kitchen.

And then the major appeared in the doorway. We stared at him. It felt as though we were all holding our breath, waiting to see what he would say.

And then he smiled.

Before I could think about what I was doing, I ran to him, throwing myself at him in an exultant embrace. He tensed for the briefest of moments, and then his arms came around me.

"You've done it," I said, a feeling of pride swelling up in me.

"We've done it," he replied, looking down at me. Our eyes met for just a moment, and there was a warmth I hadn't seen in them before.

"Well done," I heard Felix say behind me.

It was his voice that called me back to my senses, and I stepped back from the major's arms, flushing a bit, but still thrilled to my very bones at what we had achieved.

"The German agent didn't suspect anything?" I asked.

"No. He barely said a word, in fact. He just took the documents and disappeared back into the sea."

"Then it's all a go," Felix said.

"So long as your letter verifying the contents of the plans can fool the Germans into believing that Miss Abbot wrote it."

Felix smiled. "My forgery could fool Jocelyn Abbot herself."

There were still a few things about all of this that weren't making sense to me, parts of this story that were still a jumble in my head.

"But I don't understand," I said softly. "What . . . How . . . How did Winthrop, and Oscar, and Jocelyn Abbot fit together?"

It was the major who spoke. "Winthrop and Jocelyn are both members of Sir Nigel's collector's club. When Barnaby Ellhurst was shot down in France and captured by the Germans, they began sending messages to Jocelyn Abbot that they wanted information in exchange for Ellhurst's life. She knew Harden from the collector's club, knew that he might be in a position to get the information for her. He agreed to it, and Matthew Winthrop agreed to help facilitate the exchange with the Germans. She knew, I'm sure, about his political leanings. Everyone did."

"And that's how Oscar came into it," I said. "He told me he was able to get a job working for you because of your uncle, and when he got reacquainted with Winthrop he thought he could make a profit."

He nodded. "Davies was always clever at arranging things. I think he was the one who began to pull the scheme together. It was something of a double cross, really. He didn't care what happened to Ellhurst. He expected the Germans to pay for the information."

"But then Harden began to have second thoughts," I said, thinking of the poor dead man we had found at the beginning of all of this. It seemed like a very long time ago.

The major nodded. "I think he was either going to refuse to give them the documents or had even decided that he was going to go to the authorities. He had to be stopped."

I asked the next question, even though I wasn't sure I really wanted to know. "Was it Oscar, then, that killed him?"

The major nodded. There was a flicker of some emotion in his eyes for just a moment, but it was gone so quickly that I couldn't quite interpret it.

"He killed Harden and took the papers. But the Germans were still demanding a letter in Jocelyn Abbot's hand verifying certain portions of the documents. They didn't believe that she would lie when her fiancé's life was at stake. So Davies passed them off to her and sent a message to Winthrop at the party that he should collect the documents—and the letter authenticating them—from Jocelyn at the tearoom that day. He then killed the waiter who he sent to deliver the message to Winthrop at the party so that there would be no loose ends."

Oscar. That glum-faced, apparently meek young man had had a violent streak that none of us had seen. I thought of the cold blade of the knife against my throat and clenched my teeth to keep from shuddering.

"But how did he come to be here tonight?" I asked. "Why didn't he leave Winthrop to do it?"

"Because he had gleaned, from our actions at the office, that we were onto Winthrop. So he sent him as a decoy to distract us and planned to meet the German contact on the beach himself. It might have worked, too, had your cousin not been so sharp-eyed."

"Do you think they'll release Ellhurst?" Felix asked.

"I doubt it," the major said. "But I'd not lay odds against him. A man like that knows how to survive."

"Miss Abbot had no choice but to do what she did," I reflected. "She just wanted to save her fiancé."

"She had a choice," the major said grimly.

As much as I didn't care for the woman, a part of me felt the need to defend her. After all, she had been blackmailed. To my mind, she hadn't been a willing participant. I had seen for myself the angry looks she had been giving Matthew Winthrop. She had been acting to save a man's life. Didn't that count for something?

I was distracted by these thoughts and was startled when every man in the room suddenly got to their feet.

I looked up to see that the front door had opened and Jerome Curtis, Sir Nigel Randolf's hired brute, stood in the doorway.

Major Ramsey's hand reached for his gun even as a surprised expression crossed Jerome Curtis's face. "What the . . ."

"Stay where you are, Curtis," the major said levelly, his gun pointing in that direction.

"What's going on?" Jerome Curtis demanded. "What are all you people doing here?"

"Have a seat, will you?" the major said politely, even as he motioned with the gun toward the sofa.

Curtis looked angry enough to spit, but he did as he was directed. What else could he do? He glanced at me as he sat, and I offered him a vague smile.

"Now," the major said. "Why don't you tell us what you're doing here."

"This is Sir Nigel's house," Curtis said. "Sir Nigel Randolf. I work for him."

"Yes, we know," the major said. "The question is, why have you come tonight?"

"I've been staying here for two nights," he said. "I've just come from dinner and a few drinks at a nightclub."

If the scent of alcohol drifting off him was any indication, that part of his story was true.

"Are those your things upstairs?" I asked. "In the far bedroom?"

"Yes," he said. "Sir Nigel sent me down here to keep an eye on things. He said he had the feeling that someone had been in his property."

I recalled the bit of conversation I had overheard while the major and I were in Sir Nigel's office. It seemed to confirm at least a portion of Jerome Curtis's story.

"Who did he think had been here?" I asked.

Major Ramsey looked at me, and I had the sneaking suspicion

he didn't care for me butting into his interrogation. I ignored him, though, and focused on the sinister giant in front of me.

"Matthew Winthrop," Curtis said. "Sir Nigel told me Winthrop made a joke to him at the party about having an inferior pottery collection. The only place Sir Nigel keeps his cheap goods is here."

He nodded at the pottery that lined the walls, the pieces I had noticed earlier in the day.

"Sir Nigel had the feeling Winthrop might have been in the house, so he sent me down to take a look. Sir Nigel hasn't been down here since his nephew was killed. Everyone knew that he was leaving the house empty, and there's a spare key on the head of the front door."

That would've been a handy thing to know, I thought.

"Someone had been here, all right," Jerome Curtis went on. "I had a look around the place, and there were things missing. Silver and the like. Someone's been stripping the valuables. Tried to pick the lock on a few of the cabinets, too, but couldn't get in."

I remembered the scratches on the steamer trunk lock in the first bedroom. And the neatly preserved items inside. Had Matthew Winthrop simply been looking for more valuables to steal, or was he involved in John Myron's death?

"Did Winthrop kill Sir Nigel's nephew?" I asked.

Curtis frowned. "No. Mr. Myron was in an accident in his car. Took a curve too fast on his way to London in the dark. Sir Nigel took it hard, had his nephew's things packed up and hasn't come back."

I thought of the items in the trunk, not valuable but carefully preserved. It did not seem to me the work of a guilty man but rather a sentimental one. Was it possible that Sir Nigel's nephew's death had nothing to do with what we had discovered?

I glanced at Major Ramsey. Did he believe this story? For some reason, I was inclined to. I knew that several members of the collector's club had been caught up in the scheme, and Sir Nigel had seemed like an obvious leader.

But Jerome Curtis, whatever else he might be, was no actor. I didn't think he could have been faking the genuine surprise and confusion on his face when he had walked in to see us in the house. Besides, he reeked of cigarette smoke and cheap drink; he clearly hadn't gotten that stench hovering in the woods nearby or waiting on the beach for spies.

"All right," Major Ramsey said at last. He put his gun aside, and I supposed he'd come to the same conclusion that I had.

"You chaps haven't answered my question," Curtis said then, crossing his meaty arms over his chest. "What are you doing here?"

There was a moment of silence. I looked at the major, wondering what he would end up telling the man. I was a bit surprised when he came out with the truth.

"Catching traitors," Major Ramsey said at last. "Matthew Winthrop came to make a drop to a German spy on the beach. He was using the beach house as a headquarters."

Jerome Curtis scowled with anger, his already misshapen face contorting. "A filthy spy, was he? Giving our secrets to the Germans?"

He then let out a stream of language, the likes of which I've seldom heard and which Nacy would never allow me to repeat. In a way, though, it summed up a lot of what I felt about the entire evening.

Then he turned to me. "They're just lucky me and your Uncle Laddy wasn't here to get our hands on 'em."

CHAPTER THIRTY-FOUR

It was two days before Jakub knocked on my door again, asking if he could escort me to the major's office.

Things had been quiet since our return from Torquay. I had crawled into my bed upon our return, scratched, bruised, and exhausted, and had slept for nearly a day straight.

Then I had risen and consumed the banquet Nacy had prepared for me. She always cooked too much when she was nervous, and I ate more food than I would've thought could fit in a girl my size.

"I'm so glad you're all right, Ellie," she said. "I knew, of course, that you've got a good head on your shoulders, but glad I am to see you home, safe and sound."

"I'm glad to be home," I told her. And I had never meant it more.

My only regret was that I'd had to leave Colm behind in Torquay. I'd fought the tears in vain as I hugged him outside the cottage.

"Don't cry, Ellie," he said, patting my back. "I'll be home on leave again before long. Chin up. And it was an exciting night we had, eh? Memories to last until next time."

I nodded, brushing back the tears, and managed a smile.

The constant goodbyes were the one part of war I knew I could never get used to.

Feeling a bit melancholy after my meal, I went in search of Uncle

Mick. He was right where I knew he'd be: in his workshop. I stepped inside and saw him at his worktable, busily tinkering with something.

He'd had the whole of the story immediately upon my return, before I'd collapsed in my bed, and I was glad that now we could just sit in a comfortable silence, pretending for a few moments that our lives hadn't turned into a whirlwind.

Wordlessly, I slipped into the desk chair and sat watching him as his nimble fingers moved over the tools spread out before him. There was something soothing about watching him work, about seeing the way that everything came together—or apart—with such ease beneath his skilled hands.

It was a moment before I realized something was off. I frowned, trying to figure out what it was. And then I knew.

"Where's your bandage?" I asked.

He looked up at me, a hint of a twinkle in his eye. "Bandage?"

"Yes. From the cut on your hand."

He held up his hand, the one that he had supposedly cut so deeply the day before our escape to Torquay. "It's all healed up," he said. "Right as rain."

I gave a shout of laughter. "You faked it, Uncle Mick. You old fraud!"

"I knew the lay of the land, Ellie girl," he said. "When we found out Winthrop was gone, it was clear enough he'd have to be followed. The major would've made you stay in London if I was able to help him with the locks, and this was your fight. I knew you wanted it."

"I did, Uncle Mick," I said softly. "Thank you."

I knew what it had cost him to let me go, he who had always been so very protective of the niece who was more like a daughter to him.

I rose from my chair and moved to his side. "You're a dear," I said, dropping a kiss on his cheek.

And Kimble had vouched for him. So, in a way, he had vouched for me. I didn't think Kimble would ever be a dear, but he was a sporting fellow, and I appreciated it.

Jakub drove me to the major's office in the big black car, and I wondered if it would be the last time that I rode in it. I made sure to bid him a cheerful farewell, just in case.

At the office, I went slowly up the stairs to the front door. I was expecting to have to ring the bell and wait for Major Ramsey, to walk past the silent desk in the front office, a sad reminder of Oscar.

But the door was opened as I reached the top step by a fresh-faced young woman with blond hair and bright blue eyes.

"Hello," she said.

"Hello," I replied. "Ellie McDonnell to see Major Ramsey."

"Oh, yes, miss. Come right in, please. The major's expecting you."

"You're . . . new here," I said when we were inside.

"Yes, miss. My name's Constance. I'm the major's new secretary."

"I see." Major Ramsey had wasted no time. Efficient as always.

"Shall I show you to his office?"

"No, thank you," I said. "I know the way."

I went down the hall to the major's door and knocked.

"Enter," he called.

I opened the door to his office. He wasn't sitting behind his desk as usual. Instead, he stood near one of his well-stocked bookshelves, a book in his hand.

He had turned as I came in. "Hello," he said.

"Hello."

We looked at each other for a minute. We had been through a lot together, had a shared history now. It had changed the dynamic that existed between us, but I don't think either of us knew quite how it had changed or how to address it.

His ingrained manners took over at the end, though, and he motioned toward one of the chairs. "Will you sit down?"

I took a seat, and he came to sit at his desk, bringing the book with him.

"I'm sorry about Oscar," I said softly. I hadn't had the chance to tell him before, had never found a moment alone. It was the thing that had been most on my mind, and I wanted to say it before I somehow lost my nerve.

"Thank you," he said. "So am I."

For a minute I thought he would leave it at that, but then he looked up at me, and, for the briefest of moments, I saw a hint of sadness in those twilight eyes of his. "We were never close," he said at last. "But it's been a blow to my family. I couldn't tell them the truth, of course."

"No," I said softly. It was a secret he was going to have to keep, one that would weigh him down at times, but one he would, like the rest of us, do his best to push to the back of his mind and bury deep.

"I did what had to be done," he said, his eyes meeting mine. "That's what it comes down to in the business of war. We all do what needs to be done."

"Yes," I said softly.

"Jocelyn Abbot has been turned over to the appropriate authorities," he said. He was purposefully changing the subject, but I could see why his mind had gone in that direction. No doubt she had also felt she was simply doing what had to be done.

"Will she . . . go to prison?" I asked.

"That has yet to be worked out, but I believe not. The Germans don't know she's been compromised, and we may still be able to use her."

I didn't miss the "we." I wondered if they would be working together. If so, she would have to work hard to earn back the major's trust.

Something occurred to me then, something I ought to have thought of before. "Even if the two of you . . . parted ways, why didn't she come to you with her troubles? I would have." I don't know why I added that last part, and I tried to pretend that I hadn't said it.

"She told me she wanted to," the major answered. "But she didn't know if she could trust me because Davies worked for me."

He had spoken to her, then. I wondered how that conversation had gone, how painful it had been for both of them.

Whatever the case, her excuse for not coming to him for help wasn't a good one. Anyone who knew Major Ramsey would know they could trust him.

"Have the Germans released Barnaby Ellhurst?" I asked.

"Not yet. I believe they'll want to keep using Jocelyn to get information. If that's the case, we'll be able to feed them a good deal of misinformation."

"That will be unpleasant for her," I said. "And for you."

He looked up at me. "Things were over for Jocelyn and me long before this. We . . . wanted different things from life."

I didn't know how to respond to that because I understood what he wasn't saying. They had wanted different things from life, but that didn't mean they had stopped wanting each other.

"And what of the others?" I asked. This time it was me who was shifting the conversation away from an uncomfortable topic.

"There is no evidence that either Sir Nigel or Leslie Turner-Hill were involved," he said. "No one has implicated them directly in the plot. It may just be that their slanted loyalties put them in with the wrong crowd."

"Hopefully they'll realize the error of their ways," I said.

"That remains to be seen."

Silence fell for a moment.

"And that was why I called you here," he said. "To tell you how it's all worked out. To wrap things up, as neatly as possible in situations such as these."

There was something like finality in his tone.

"And so this is it?" I asked.

"You've fulfilled your side of the bargain," he said. That familiar half smile touched his lips. "More than that, in fact. I asked you to open a safe; I think you've gone above and beyond the call of duty."

I didn't know why I suddenly felt so dreadfully sad. I had been annoyed to be roped into this, after all. I hadn't wanted to work with Major Ramsey. I'd been forced to participate against my will.

But that was before we had been able to stop a traitor and a German spy, done our part to save the country. That was a bit dramatic, I supposed, but there was the feeling that we had done something that really mattered, that we had been a small part of history. A part that would never be told, perhaps, but an important part nonetheless.

And now it was over.

"You've acquitted yourself admirably," he said. His choice of words was not lost on me.

"You had to blackmail us into it," I reminded him.

"In the end, though, it was your choice. And the end is really all that matters."

The end.

I looked up at him with a smile I didn't feel. "It's all been most enlightening, Major. I've enjoyed it. Truly."

There was a moment of silence, and then he put the book he was holding on the desk and pushed it toward me. "I thought you might like this."

It was a thick, leather tome with gold embossing. I picked it up and looked at the title. *Gods and Heroes: Tales of Courage and Cunning in Greek Mythology.*

Suddenly, I could think of nothing to say. Even if I'd wanted to, there was a lump in my throat.

"I hope, when you read it, you'll remember that the warriors in that book are myths, not men," he said, his voice low and warm. "Achilles and Ajax and Hector, those heroes have nothing on ordinary people who step up to do the impossible when they're called upon. People like you, Electra McDonnell."

The tears did spring to my eyes then, but I couldn't brush them away because his gaze caught mine and held.

"Thank you," I whispered.

"Thank you."

I nodded, my throat too tight to say more, then stood and turned toward the door. I had just reached it when his voice stopped me. "Miss McDonnell."

I turned.

"You're still on the payroll," he said, his commanding officer tone restored. "You and your uncle are to stay out of trouble and be ready if I need you."

I smiled, a strange sensation of happiness flooding through me. "You know where to find us, Major Ramsey."

Then I left his office and closed the door behind me.

Bidding farewell to the cheerful Constance, I stepped out of the office into the fresh, damp air. There had been a brief rain shower while I was inside, it seemed, but now the sky had cleared and the sun was shining.

I closed my eyes and breathed deeply. Everything was bright and clean, and I felt a new sense of appreciation for the homeland I had secretly helped to defend from the enemy. Then I turned and started down the street, an ordinary citizen of London on her way home.

"Going my way?" a voice asked.

I turned. "Felix!" I said, surprised. "What are you doing here?"

He came toward me, looking dapper and handsome in a pinstripe suit.

"I stopped by the house to see you, and your uncle was quite evasive about where you'd gone. I figured you'd come here."

I smiled. "Just wrapping things up with the major."

"All's well then?"

I nodded.

"And may I escort you home?"

"I'd like that very much."

We walked along together in companionable silence for a few moments.

"I've written to that shipmate of mine," he said. "I suppose it shouldn't be too long before I hear something back."

"Thank you, Felix," I said. I couldn't think too much about it now, about the possibility I might learn something about my mother's innocence. I would wait until we received a reply. Today had brought too much contentment to consider the past.

"I had supposed, after our adventure, that life would go back to normal," Felix said after a few moments. "But it occurred to me that normal no longer looks the same as it used to."

He was right, of course.

Would life ever go back to normal, the way it had once been? I supposed that it wouldn't. It couldn't. Nothing could ever be the same after this war. Despite the idea that we would endure until the end, despite our unwavering confidence that we would win, it was going to change us. None of us could be what we had once been.

And perhaps that was a good thing.

I took Felix's arm, holding Major Ramsey's book in the other, and walked toward the Tube station feeling quite on top of the world.

ACKNOWLEDGMENTS

Writing may seem a solitary task, but any writer will tell you that there are so many people who are instrumental in the creation of a book. I feel an overwhelming sense of gratitude to everyone who has had a part in the process.

I would like to thank Ann Collette for being not only a terrific agent but a good friend, for her excellent advice, and for her belief in my stories from the beginning.

I am extremely grateful to my wonderful editor, Catherine Richards, whose skill, insight, and keen eye for detail helped to shape this story and bring Ellie and company fully to life.

Many thanks to Nettie Finn for her valuable input and unfailingly cheerful assistance. And to everyone at Minotaur who worked to turn my manuscript into a beautiful book.

To the many wonderful friends who have offered encouragement, companionship, and commiseration throughout the writing process, I am also indebted. Thanks to Angela Larson, Stephanie Shultz, Sabrina Street, and Becky Farmer for writing buddy sessions and late-night pep talks. And to Chalanda Wilson, Amanda Phillips, Courtney LeBoeuf, and Ty Cedars for both daily laughs and deep conversations.

And, finally, many, many thanks to my wonderful family—Dai Weaver, DeAnn Weaver, Amelia Lea, Caleb Lea, Larson Lea, and Shauna Weaver—for all the love, support, and good times.

My most heartfelt appreciation goes out to you all!